D0990697

PETER ALSON

The Only Way To Play It

For Peter + Cusi,

The West Village misses
you. We miss you. But the
upside of the pandemic is that
rents are going down!
So come on back!

♡ Pete

ARBITRARY PRESS
New York

To Alice and Eden

"You never know what worse luck your bad luck has saved you from."

CORMAC MCCARTHY

I

2005

1

Two Years from Now You're Gonna Bump into Her

Three-thirty in the morning and the game was down to me, Freckles, Rugs, Drunk Mike, and Danny the Jeweler.

Fifty-Cent Bill pivoted mechanically in his chair, flicking out cards. The break dealer, a stringy-haired dude named Jingles, slumped on a threadbare brown couch in the corner, reading yesterday's *Daily News*. The boss man, Iggy, a burly former pro wrestler with cauliflowered ears, sat by himself at another table, sullenly nursing his sixth or seventh Molson's, staring glassy-eyed at a muted TV tuned to a porn channel. Iggy didn't just run the Siena, he was a featured attraction, generously redistributing the house profits to us whenever he sat in the game. But even Iggy had his limits, and he'd quit in disgust hours ago, after dropping multiple thousands, most of them to me.

Named after an Italian soccer team, the Siena consisted of one room and an alcove, just big enough for three tables. Dingy white walls were bare except for a signed picture of Tony Bennett and an old *Playboy* pinup, Miss June 1992, a bronzed brunette with flecks of what looked like coffee spatter across her swollen breasts. There was a small grease-stained kitchen, where Umberto, the moody chef, whipped up the best pasta with red sauce you'd ever tasted. Except Umberto had slammed off in a huff a while ago, back to whatever lonely world he inhabited outside this place, far from the small green-felt dramas that seemed so important in here.

It had been a weird night. Hand after hand the chips kept getting pushed my way to the point where it was almost embarrassing. I went from three thousand to five to ten. And I began to think there had to be some dark reason for my rush. Not that I was superstitious or prone to such thinking, but a hot run like this had to have a price. *Lucky at cards, unlucky in love?* Except I hadn't really been unlucky in love. Unless being unlucky meant being terrible at it.

"Two of you now," said Fifty-Cent Bill, dealing the turn card.

I bet again and to my surprise, Freckles check-raised me. Six black hundred-dollar chips. "Why don't you fold this one, Nate? Let somebody else win a pot."

I sat there deliberating, leveling him with a stare. I liked Freckles, with his wiry reddish hair and cheerful latte-brown freckled face. He was cocky as hell, always talking, always selling.

"You want me to paint you a mental picture of my hand, Nate?" he asked. "Or maybe you should do it, since you're the painter."

This was typical Freckles bullshit, designed to confuse and disorient, though more often his chatter consisted of out-of-school stories about his music-biz fellas and the crazy shit they got into, "shit like you can't believe, Nate. *Freaky* shit. Taking-no-prisoners shit!" It actually made me wonder if he talked about *me* that way when he was with *them*, like

4

"Lemme tell you about this artist guy I play with who runs like God and crushes souls!"

It wasn't just one night either. I'd been on a heater for the last month, steamrolling anyone in my path, running so good they *all* wanted to kill me. Fifteen hundred one night. Two thousand the next. A thousand the night after that. Seventeen straight winning sessions, a $25,000 upswing. Thirty-six dimes, if you counted tonight's sick rush. Hell, I'd probably have wanted to kill me too.

"I got you beat this time, brother," Freckles purred in his chocolatey voice. "I'll show you either way. But if I were you, I'd fold this one....Or call if you don't like money."

I almost felt bad for him. Well, not *bad* exactly, because I knew if the tables were turned, he wouldn't shed any tears for me. But this wasn't about feelings or the fact that we liked each other. It was about making the correct decision, whatever it was, so that at the end of the night, regardless of what the cards decided to do, I'd know I played it right.

"Ah for Chrissakes, Nate," Drunk Mike said, losing his patience. "You're up a million dollars. Call. Fold. Do *something*." Mike liked to drink at the table and he sometimes got a little sloppy and loud, but nobody minded, because the drunker he was, the more he sucked at poker.

"You calling a clock on me, Mike?"

"I'm calling a fucking clock," said Rugs, a machete-faced older guy in a light zip jacket, who was testy even when he wasn't losing, maybe because somebody had once sold him his cheap beige-colored toupée.

"Clock has been called," said Fifty-Cent Bill matter of factly. "You've got sixty seconds, Nate."

Freckles looked down at the table, avoiding my gaze, fingers on his cards, uncharacteristically quiet, not moving a muscle but breathing unevenly. To me, it felt like acting.

"Ten…nine…eight…" Bill counted down.

I flicked my cards toward the muck.

Freckles looked up, meeting my eyes, shaking his head. "You're too good, man," he whispered. "Too fucking disciplined."

"Bullshit," said Drunk Mike. "You're just telling him that, Freckles. You bluffed his ass." He turned to me. "He bluffed your ass."

"Show the bluff," Jeweler implored. "Put the motherfucker on tilt."

Freckles pushed his cards facedown into the muck, then dragged the pot.

"He can't." I rose to my feet and stretched my legs, stiff from the hours of sitting. "If he could he would have shown it."

"So that's it? You lose one pot and leave?" said Mike. "Pick up your ball and go home?"

"I need permission from you monkeys to take a piss?"

The bathroom at the Siena was a decidedly unhappy place, especially at this time of night: lit by a naked hanging bulb, stray pubic hairs glued to the porcelain rim of the toilet by a brownish-yellow glaze, empty cardboard toilet paper tube still in the holder, half-used roll on top of the tank. I unzipped, closed my eyes, let out a gush, thinking, even after that little speed bump, up eleven grand, holy shit.

When I looked at myself in the mirror over the sink, I realized how tired I was. Eyes bloodshot, pupils the size of pennies, forehead sporting a visible sheen of greasy sweat. I splashed some hot water on my face and blotted it dry with a paper towel. It again crossed my mind that I should leave. Cash out and go.

What if I just showed up at her door? Took her out someplace nice, waved my roll around like an asshole and told her I was sorry? I tried to picture myself through her eyes. The 33-year-old man-boy who'd never held a real job or worked in an office or had to wear a suit. I was just an artist who made money however he could and figured out his life one day at a time. What the fuck did she even see in me? Except for a confidence I seemingly had no right to, an ability to notice things that other people didn't, like the sadness behind her smile and the way, when the morning sun tricked her eyes open, she looked almost as if she were taking in the world for the first time?

Our first three months I hadn't been able to get enough of her, nor she of me, but then, as Fantasy Laura became Real Laura, I found myself pulling back. Unexpectedly really, because Real Laura was actually better, kinder, less troubled than the figment I had dreamed up. Maybe that was the problem. I didn't trust the real Laura. Or—more likely— myself. Either way, it was my standard operating procedure and Laura—Real Laura—saw through it. She called me on my bullshit. Which was refreshing but didn't seem to matter. I still kept her at arm's length.

It had now been six weeks since the night she'd stalked through my apartment, her patience with me finally exhausted, and collected the few belongings she'd left during our various sleepovers—a red-and-white striped toothbrush, her Wesleyan track-team sweatshirt, the 14-karat turtle-shaped earrings I'd picked up for her in the airport gift shop after a long weekend in Vegas. "The saddest part," she'd said stuffing her things into a flimsy plastic bag, "is that you're not going to do a damn thing to stop me, are you?" I wanted to tell her that she had me all wrong, that I wasn't who she thought I was. I wanted to say, "I know what you want, and I'm the guy who can give it to you." But I didn't say anything. I just sat there and watched her leave.

Making my way back from the bathroom now, I checked my phone as if it wasn't absurd to think she might be awake and missing me too. Who was I kidding? Why would she be? She wasn't the kind of girl to settle for less than she deserved. The only real mystery was why I hadn't been able to shrug off the loss and move on the way I always had in the past. Why was that proving to be so hard this time?

"You don't need an excuse," said Drunk Mike. "If you want to leave,

leave."

"I'm tired is all." It was impossible to know the hour in here without a watch. The two windows at the far end were blacked out. The outside world didn't exist.

"A session like this comes along once every five years," Mike said. "But fuck it. Go home."

"I said I'm tired. I didn't say I was leaving."

That she was cool about poker was also no small thing. I'm not saying she loved that I played, but she knew I was never gonna stop and she hadn't seen that as a deal-breaker or some kind of major character flaw.

In fact, on the recent night I'd brought my painter pal Charlie Bascombe to the Siena so he could get a first-hand glimpse of how I was making my monthly rent, he said, "You mean Laura actually saw this joint and didn't leave skid marks? You're even dumber than I thought."

Jingles the dealer rifled cards around the table. Danny the Jeweler said, apropos of nothing, "Hey, how's that nice girl of yours? The redhead?"

I looked at him wonderingly. Had he somehow crawled inside my head? Or was he fishing, probing for weakness, a way to tilt me?

"You and her still a thing?"

Sensing my discomfort, Rugs said, "Apparently not."

"What happened?" Jeweler asked. "She have a problem with your gambling?"

"This isn't gambling for him, fishcake," Rugs said. "He's a pro-*feshional*."

"So it's not the fact you stay out all night playing cards or that you don't have a job?" Jeweler said.

"This *is* his job, Jeweler. Don't you get it?"

"I thought you were an artist," Jeweler said to me.

"A con artist…" Freckles said, the needle extra sharp because he'd actually bought a painting from me, speculating it might one day increase in value.

All this noise and bullshit, but the hand was still going. I hadn't lost focus. When an ace came on the river, I flung a handful of chips at the pot.

Freckles made a face like he'd taken a sip of sour milk. "You hit the ace? You bet two streets with nothing and hit a fucking ace? Or are you trying to bluff me again?" He muttered a bit more then said, "Call."

I flipped up ace-eight.

"Ridiculous." Angrily, he flung his hand, which had been good until the last card, into the muck. "You fucking river rat. I can see why your girlfriend got tired of your bullshit."

"Whaddaya talking about? Women love guys who treat 'em like shit," Jeweler said.

"Hey, if you guys all know so much about women," I said, speaking up at last, "how come you're sitting here, like, in a poker club at four-thirty in the morning, completely alone, no women anywhere?'"

There was a pause, then Drunk Mike said, "By choice, man," and everyone laughed, including me.

Five a.m. Six. Freckles' breath smelled like he'd eaten a dead rat. Drunk Mike was so drunk he couldn't form words anymore, his face as lifeless as a cinderblock. The game finally broke at eight when I busted Danny the Jeweler, who basically donated his last buy-in to me. I walked him to the door, patting him on the back. But he took it well. He said, "Listen, bubbellah, if you ever patch things up with your girl, I can give you a deal on a ring." He slipped me his card. "You never know, right?"

"Yeah, sure," I said.

Iggy was asleep, all 250 pounds of him, laid out across three side-by-side chairs, snoring up a symphony. Jingles let me out, saying, "Nice win, dude."

* * *

Outside the Siena, I was momentarily blinded, shielding my eyes against the raw morning glare along Houston Street. The air was cool for June, clouds overhead, people heading swiftly this way and that, armed with cell phones, paper coffee cups and thermoses. I wondered how many of them had been up all night or had fifteen thousand dollars in cash stuffed in their pockets.

It was always strange and a bit jarring to re-enter the outside world. Like coming out of a dream. Or leaving the bed of a girl you just met and fucked all night long. There was that dazed, tired sense of well-being accompanied by the desire to share your story of conquest with somebody, anybody, a guy on the street, the driver of the taxi you hadn't yet hailed.

At the Starbucks across from the club, paying for a Grande Mocha Latte with the twenty-dollar bill I'd stuck in my back pocket so I wouldn't have to pull out a fat loaf of cash in public, my thoughts again turned to Laura. Here I was, up thirty-six large the past month. I should have been feeling like a superhero. Instead, all I could think about was how much I missed her, how there was this hole in my heart a mile wide.

Something else Charlie Bascombe said had been haunting me. "Two years from now you're gonna bump into her. She'll be with the guy she married instead of you and the two of them will be pushing a stroller down the street. I know because that exact thing happened to me. I regret it to this day."

Fucking Charlie. I flagged down a cab and directed the driver across town and down to the familiar beat-up green door on Rivington Street. Outside on the sidewalk, I hesitated for a moment, thinking about what to say, wondering if I was going through with this. Finally, I worked up the nerve and rang her bell, and when her crackly voice asked who it was, I said, "It's me."

2

I'll Be the One

She was standing in the open door when I got to the top of the stairs, still in the T-shirt and panties she'd obviously slept in. Her dark red hair was sticking out in different directions, falling across her face.

"Well look who showed up," she whispered.

"Were you asleep?"

"Uh huh." She squinted and rubbed at the corner of one eye. "What time is it?"

"Early. Sorry. I was up playing."

She laughed, short and dismissive. But instead of shutting the door in my face, she said, "Well, come in since you're already here."

She turned. I followed. The door swung shut behind me with a thump and a click. Her compact studio apartment was neat and orderly, the piles of magazines and books on her desk stacked at right angles. On the queen bed in a small nook, the sheets and covers were pulled back, one pillow dented.

"Coffee?"

"Um..."

"I'm making some for myself anyway."

"In that case, sure."

In the kitchenette, she filled a teakettle, turned on the burner and took a French press out of a cabinet. "Why don't you sit down?" She bent back the paper-wire clasps on a plain brown bag of coffee. "You're making me nervous."

I took a seat on one of the two folding wood chairs at the small round café table.

She spooned ground coffee into the French press. "I wasn't sure I was ever going to hear from you again."

"I was under the distinct impression you didn't want to."

"Why? Because I said it?" She turned back to the whistling kettle, poured the steaming water into the French press. Still with her back to me, she said, "God, men can be fucking stupid sometimes."

I got to my feet and came up behind her. As soon as I touched her, she stiffened, but before I could back off, she turned, said, "Damn you," and started kissing me.

* * *

Naked on her bed. Sticky. Breathing hard. My finger traced the contours of her body, the firm flesh of her thigh, the little downy goosebumps on her ass, the lovely ravine along her back.

Her familiar scent was warm and sweet, but she looked different. Sex had softened the hard edges of her face. Her wide-set pale blue eyes seemed a shade softer, less piercing.

I reached gently between her legs where it was still slippery, the graze of my finger setting off little tremors, aftershocks, a sharp intake of breath.

She took my hand, stopped me.

"What's wrong?"

Her lips tightened.

"What? What is it?"

"I can't do this, Nathan."

A bit late for that. But I played along and asked, "Do what?"

"Be, like, your post-game booty call."

"Is that what you think?"

"Isn't that what this is?"

"C'mon, Laur, I'm not that guy."

"Really?" Her voice broke. "Are you sure? Because there's the potential here for me to get really fucking pissed."

I felt a rising panic. It was quite possible I was fucking up again.

I looked off to one side and tried to wrap my head around what she wanted from me, what I was supposed to know about myself that in some way I hadn't already made clear. "Okay, so the thing is, I've been having a really good run…"

She looked at me, her eyes a blank.

"In poker. This whole past month. And then last night—I had this crazy night where no matter what I did, I couldn't seem to lose."

She continued to stare in a way that unnerved me.

"I'm trying to tell you something."

"I'm listening."

"Because while it was going on, what I was thinking—really the only thing I was thinking—was that I wouldn't be able to tell you about it and how that made it all kind of empty…"

"Oh, come on, Nate."

"I know how that sounds, but it's true."

She laughed. "I gotta give you credit, waltzing over here as if the past two months never happened and telling me about this moment you had in a poker game and how it had to do with me…I mean, wow. It almost makes me think it's real."

"It is real."

She suddenly hit my chest with the base of her closed fist, hard enough that it hurt.

"Jesus, what the fuck was that for?"

"For just assuming I would let you back in."

"I wasn't making assumptions, Laur—"

"Then what?"

It was tough without telling her how big this actually was. How scary. I thought again about Charlie's story.

I wanted to tell her what I was thinking. Instead, I looked in her eyes and kissed her fingers and mumbled, "This isn't easy for me."

And then my voice went even lower and quieter, and I said, "I want to be with you, Laura. I want us to be together."

Which is when she began to cry.

II

2010

3

The Best Part of the Trip

"Daddy read." Hannah jabbed me in the ribs with her sharp little-girl elbow.

"Hey," I snapped at her, "where's the 'please?'" I glanced at the green plastic art-deco clock over the stove. It was nearly six o'clock and still no Laura. If I didn't leave soon, the game would fill up. I'd be shut out again. Two days earlier, I'd waited three hours for a seat. By the time my name was called I was so aggravated that I tilted off two grand.

Hannah dropped her plastic-handle Hello Kitty fork and burst into tears.

"Honey, I'm sorry. I didn't mean to yell at you, but that's not the way to ask for something."

"Sorry, Daddy. I'm sorry," she whimpered.

She waited a few seconds, still snuffling, then patted the page. I picked up the battered falling-apart-at-the-seams copy of Curious

George, but put it back down, thinking maybe I heard the sound of footsteps on the hall stairs.

"Daddy! You're not reading."

She'd barely touched her cut-up turkey burger or her Dr. Prager's spinach pancake. I kissed her sweet-smelling brown hair and said, "Eat."

She poked at the book again.

"If you want me to read," I said, "you have to eat."

She sulked, moving the spinach pancake around with her fork.

At a quarter past six, I finally heard footsteps on the stairs. The apartment door swung open and in she came, slim as an unfinished thought, putting down her backpack and yoga mat and mustering a joyless smile. Her wavy dark red hair was lank, in need of washing. I could see weariness etched in her face.

Lately, in these moments, one of us arriving, the other departing, it was like we were characters in a play, briefly united on a stage but with real lives that took place elsewhere. Yet when I watched my daughter spring from her chair, skitter across the room and hurl herself into my wife's arms, I was oddly reassured. I stood up and joined the embrace, sneaking in a kiss, grateful for this tiny moment of connection even as I said, "I gotta get going," and disengaged to find my subway reading material, *The Moviegoer*, at the other end of our railroad-style apartment.

"Can you at least give me two minutes to go pee?"

"Sure, sure." I snuck another glance at the clock while Hannah tugged me back to the dining table, saying "Daddy, read." Sitting down again, bouncing my leg, unconnected to the words coming out of my mouth, I heard the toilet flush, though the bathroom door stayed shut.

I knew that Laura had been bending and pretzeling for the past hour and a half after a morning of writing and an afternoon composing ad copy for Groupon offers. I knew that yoga was her outlet, a reward for her diligence. But that wasn't going to help if there were no seats in the game. I stood up, ready to bolt the moment she reappeared. Hannah grabbed and pulled at my shirt.

Laura came back, saying, "I realize you're in a hurry, but can you spare me a couple of minutes before you're gone for the night?"

I was already leaning hard toward the door. "Is it important?"

"In the bedroom?"

"You can't say it here?"

"Forget it."

I tried to stay calm. "Just tell me."

"It's okay. Go."

Fuck. "You're sure?"

"It's fine. Just go."

The moment I stepped out the door, regret set in. But I couldn't afford to get shut out again. Whatever it was she wanted.

* * *

Above ground, at 34th Street, I picked my way quickly through the thronged midtown streets, heading down Sixth Avenue. Herald Square's deafening thrum of trucks and buses and cars, police sirens, car horns, and construction machinery hit me like an assault after the tree-shaded tranquility of Brooklyn.

On 28th Street, I turned west, dodging pedestrians in a sidewalk lane narrowed by a sweet-smelling thicket of fresh-cut tulip bulbs, geraniums, and potted palm trees. Halfway down the block, I came to a nondescript doorway between Jade West Florists and Super Fine Foliage.

Jabbing the bell labeled Zicon Industries, I blew an air kiss at the security camera. Someone buzzed me in and I rode a squeaking elevator to the fourth floor where I was greeted by an extra-large man wearing a pinstriped suit that encased him like the wrapping on a sausage.

"S'up, Nathan?"

"Jimmy." I gave him a fist pound.

He motioned for me to lift my arms. "Sorry, my man, no one's exempt tonight."

"Come on, Jimmy, you actually think I might be packing?"

"Didn't you get the memo? The Clover got stuck up."

I whistled. "For real?"

"That's right. Some bad people out there."

I flinched slightly as Jimmy's hand grazed my crotch, but a moment later the frisk was done and he gave the high sign to whoever was watching. The sturdy metal door clicked open.

The first thing that hit me was the noise: riffling chips and the din of a hundred voices. I looked across an open loft space at ten nearly fully occupied green-felt-covered oval-shaped tables.

Overhead, fluorescent bulbs turned already unhealthy-looking faces cadaverous. Television screens suspended along the walls were tuned to baseball and football games and sports highlight shows. Looking at this room of degenerates, it was easy to pass judgment, but unless you'd experienced what it felt like to pull off a well-executed bluff or make a hero call after picking up a tell or squeeze the last ounce of value out of a marginal hand, I'll admit it might be hard to understand the attraction. For me, at the root of it was the competition, the idea that a bus driver could outsmart an investment banker and that anyone could claim a place at the table—bookies, lawyers, secretaries, music moguls, mob guys, writers, cops, anyone—the only qualification needed being money for a buy-in.

Sure, some of my opponents turned out to be sick gamblers who actually wanted to lose. But since my addiction was to winning, it worked out pretty well for all of us. Was that immoral? Too glib?

Maybe. I wasn't blind to the darker side of what went on here. But from the first time I sat on my dad's lap at the age of eight and he allowed me to rake in the chips after winning a hand of five-card draw against one of his drinking buddies, there was never any doubt in my mind that I was poker player.

By the time I enrolled in art school at Pratt, I was winning enough in the dorm-room games to keep me stocked in Heinekens and tubes of acrylic. Later, sharing a crappy Williamsburg loft with Lenny and Polly (one now dead, the other ascendant), I found out about the Siena from Nick, the muralist who'd painted Veselka's storefront. The first time he took me, I won fifteen hundred bucks in under four hours. I couldn't believe that was even possible. Before long, I was going nearly every night, making enough to quit the construction work I'd been doing to pay the bills.

Here, in the fall of 2010, the Fish Tank along with the Lucky Seven and the Clover were the big rooms in town. Except for the Siena, most of the old places had been shut down in a round of raids over the years. The Fish Tank was my current venue of choice on account of the location and because it got players stepping up from the smaller games who were basically just taking a shot and didn't stand a chance.

In the wake of the financial meltdown in 2008, some of the loose Wall Street money dried up, but not for long, and in a way not at all, because ordinary taxpayers—schoolteachers, factory workers, garbage men, police—had been forced to foot the losses faster than you could say, "Rebuy." At first, I felt a little sorry for the Bear, Stearns and Lehman Brothers guys who lost their jobs, but not that sorry because they thought poker was their next logical move, and I was more than happy to show them otherwise. And fuck them, anyway.

A lot of the TARP beneficiaries came to the Fish Tank because it was clean and well run. I mainly came because of them. Oh sure, if I heard about a particularly juicy lineup somewhere else, I might venture out of my comfort zone. But that was rare. I'd become a creature of habit. At 38, discovering something I liked, I tended to stick with it. In Laura's view that was a weakness, not a strength. She thought that I'd gotten accustomed to settling for the comfortable instead of stretching myself or taking risks. Which was funny, considering at least a couple of the choices I'd made, like playing poker for a living and marrying her. The truth is, marrying Laura had been impulsive, like one of those what-should-I-do moments in a hand where you suddenly pushed at your stacks while blurting "All in!" or "Call!" without even really knowing what the fuck had just happened.

Five years later, I was still trying to figure out the answer to that one. And so, I suspected, was she.

* * *

At a chest-high counter across from the entrance sat Caitlin, the cashier, a tangle of dark-rooted blond hair falling in front of her face, nose buried in a book. She was so deeply absorbed that she didn't see me at first. I stepped closer, waving my own book, trying to get her attention.

She raised her eyes from a trade paperback of Celine's *Journey to the End of the Night*, noted the book in my hand, and said, "I see your angst and raise you some alienation."

"In that case I fold," I said. "Celine makes Walker Percy look like a beach read."

"Sure, if you like to lie on the beach and contemplate the meaninglessness of life."

She was beautiful in a Kate Mara grad-student-with-glasses, I-don't-work-at-it-but-I-don't-have-to kind of way. In fact, she *was* a grad student, going for her masters in philosophy at NYU, earning tuition money here instead of at some bar. It took effort on my part not to get sucked in by her intelligent and playful gaze or wonder if our flirtations could actually lead somewhere. I was probably one of the few guys in the place who hadn't actively tried to fuck her.

"Everybody's a little on edge tonight," she said in a low voice.

"Jimmy just told me."

"Nate, they had guns! And ski masks."

I felt a prickle along the back of my neck. "I guess we ought to be scared."

"We ought to be. But..." She flipped her palms, nodding toward the tables. "Degeneracy apparently trumps fear."

"I'm not quite sure how to respond to that—given that I'm here too."

We both laughed, as I dug my roll out of my pocket and started peeling off hundreds.

"Twenty-five?" Caitlin asked.

"Twenty-five."

"Rack of green okay?"

"Perfect."

She took my money and counted it. Her strong youthful fingers had the practiced dexterity of a bank teller. She slid a Lucite tray of green chips across the counter. Twenty-five hundred dollars.

"Do some damage," she said.

"Hopefully not to myself."

I headed toward the back, past the lower-limit tables, nodding at players I knew, mumbling hellos. In the far corner, in front of an enormous illuminated fish tank built into a dividing wall, a few of the $5-$10 no-limit regulars looked up, acknowledging my arrival. I was gratified to see Jojo Pizza, a notorious untanked fish, who had somehow managed to finish 28th out of 6,844 in the World Series of Poker Main Event the previous year, good for $193,000 (a nice chunk of which he later parted with in our game). I'd played the Main twice, myself, coming home empty-handed each time—empty-handed being a euphemism for twenty grand in the hole. It was bad enough trying to explain tournament variance to your spouse under normal circumstances, but when you factored in her being home caring for your child while you were off in the land of lap dances and bottle service, you grudgingly concluded that WSOP bracelet dreams were probably best left deferred.

I'm not saying it didn't sting a little to watch my buddies head off to Vegas each summer looking for the end of the rainbow, but I wasn't in this for ego and glory. My bread and butter was grinding New York City and had been for the past half-dozen years. Clock in, clock out, book more wins than losses.

Before Hannah I'd considered myself the best cash-game player in the city. I had a focus and clarity then that seemed to insulate me from the leveling factors of bad luck and variance. I was able to smell weakness as if it had an actual scent. I knew when to get away from second-best hands and when I could push out the best hand with nothing, betting just the right amount to bet to get a guy to do exactly what I wanted him to do—fold, call, sometimes even raise. I expected good things to happen and more often than not they did. I took chances, played with aggression, was fearless in the best way.

Though still a winning player, I didn't have that feeling of invincibility anymore. Maybe it was just variance, the normal ups and downs of the game. I desperately wanted to believe that was true even though my gut was telling me another story. I'd read studies about fatherhood lowering testosterone and discouraging risky behavior. There were other things, too. Right before Hannah was born I'd sold three big paintings in a solo show, one to Larry Gagosian. That not insignificant breakthrough had given my gallerist, Richard, optimism about my future. Sure, I knew that going forward I needed to sell more to maintain the momentum. I actually thought I did a pretty good job of blocking out the pressure of that just like I ignored outside noise when I was sitting in a poker game. But the lead up to my last show hadn't gone smoothly. Richard left town unexpectedly, the gallery intern fucked up the mailings, then eight inches of snow fell on the night of the opening, and none of the nine people who showed up spent a dime. In the aftermath, Richard and I got into a terrible fight. I called him a dilettante. He told me marriage had turned me timid.

Three weeks after the show came down, I dragged myself back to my studio in Gowanus, greeted by the familiar smell of oil paint, turpentine and must, along with the familiar sights: a worn beanbag chair on the floor near the arched window, a hot plate on a counter, old empty white spackle buckets placed strategically under the leaks in the ceiling. My unsold paintings were where I unpacked them, leaning against the walls. The intentionally dull, oppressive colors I'd used to portray a city seen only through windows now looked insipid to me. I'd talked myself into believing the paintings worked, convinced Richard too despite his uncertainty.

Standing there in my studio, I decided he was right, the things he said. What felt like a balloon of frustrated energy expanded in my upper chest and throat, bringing with it a suffocating sense of claustrophobia. I hadn't listened. I'd been stubborn and obstinate. I got up close to one of the paintings and, wielding my rage like a bludgeon, lashed out with a fist, punching the canvas so hard I tore a rent in it. If I didn't leave, I knew I'd destroy everything. So I fled.

For weeks, I stayed away from Gowanus, spending my days at D'Amico Coffee, Bam Rose matinees, the Chelsea galleries, MoMa, telling myself that I was regrouping, trying to find a way back. Poker filled the hole left behind, became the one thing that grounded me and gave me purpose. My days turned into a kind of waiting for the moment each night when I would walk through the door of the club. Results mattered more than they ever had. A winning session and all was right with my world. A losing session and I wanted to kill myself.

Sometimes, while playing, I found myself thinking wistfully about the days before Laura, before Hannah, when my life didn't seem so weighed down, when I was poised for takeoff and everything I did was just because I felt like it. Weekend road trip to Vegas or Atlantic City? Damn straight. Stay up all night painting or drinking Johnny Walker or chasing after a girl who smiled at me in a bookstore? Why not? I didn't need to run plans by anyone then or get permission or feel guilty for basically doing whatever the fuck I wanted.

It was easy to forget what it was like always coming home to an empty apartment, turning on the lights knowing that I would see the same round wooden thrift shop table and Ikea blue-and-white-striped couch, that I'd hear the low hum of the refrigerator and know that no one had missed me, no one had thought about me while I was gone. All the same, when I did forget, when I thought only about the things lost and given up, it became possible to imagine that I might actually destroy the life I'd built in place of that one, not willfully, but unconsciously, because deep down I wanted to.

* * *

There was an open seat between Lawyer Dan, a buzz-cut late thirties lawyer who tended to squint quizzically when facing a raise or a bet, and Asian John, a young guy in sunglasses who shuffled chips so effortlessly they looked like water running through his fingers.

As I settled down into one of the flimsy Aeron knockoffs, I nodded at Benny the Dwarf, who wasn't actually a dwarf but was extremely short, at Too Tight Tim, whose pinched, narrow face matched his personality, at Drunk Mike, who was swilling whiskey from an ice-filled plastic cup, and Jojo Pizza, picking his nose with vigor. Lastly, I reached behind Asian John's back to bump fists with D.J., who was probably my closest friend in the poker underground.

"Don't take it the wrong way, brother," D.J. apologized, "but this is

28

my last hand."

I looked at his chip stack, counting five stacks of green, three of red. If he'd bought in for his usual $1,500, then he was up almost $1,300. "You're really leaving?"

"Yeah, the fucking hit-and-run artist," grumbled Too Tight Tim.

"I'm having dinner with my grandmother."

"Awwww, that's sweet," said Benny the Dwarf, grinning around the table. "His grandma. Isn't that sweet?"

"You know what's sweet, Benny?" D.J. said, patting his chips. "That you mopes are picking up the tab for the meal."

"Bullshit. A hundred percent you're gonna let her pay, you cheap bastard."

"You coming back after?" I asked.

"Maybe. I'm thinking of driving down to A.C., getting a room. Wanna go?"

When Laura and I were first married, she was jealous of D.J., treating him almost like a rival. She complained that whenever I was around him I turned into a fanboy. "You have him on this pedestal," she said. "It's weird."

There was no question I could sometimes be led astray, like the night he dragged me out of bed for a midnight run to Foxwoods in a hired Town Car with his Scores girlfriend and a vial full of X. Still, Laura needed to butt out. My friends were my friends.

"I think you just have a boner for him because he's you ten years ago," she said.

In truth, he wasn't me ten years ago, he was the guy I wanted to be. The good-looking bad boy that girls wanted to fuck, with his thick swept-back hair, movie-star square jaw and I-don't-give-a-goddamn assurance. I guess I hoped that his charisma would rub off on me, though it never had. As long as it wasn't over girls, I enjoyed competing with him. Poker, pool, tennis—anything you could gamble on. D.J.

was always up for a bet. We arm-wrestled, shot free throws, once put a hundred bucks on which one of us had a longer tongue. Even walking down the street became a competitive sport with him. You had to race just to keep up. Funny part was, the motherfucker had absolutely no place to go.

"Come to A.C.," he said. "We'll win some money, have a few laughs."

"You know I can't."

"Why not?"

"Because he's old," said Benny the Dwarf, "and married, and boring as fuck."

I extended my middle finger in Benny's direction, which elicited peals of laughter it was such a lame comeback.

"Hey, Nathan, ya hear the news?" Dan asked me in a cheery voice as I unracked my chips.

"Yeah, I heard."

"Didn't know you were gambling with your life here, did ya?"

"I'm actually trying not to think about it."

But of course, I was thinking about it, thinking about how Laura would react if she found out about masks and guns and vanished bankrolls. Not that I'd be dumb enough to tell her. Still, there were all the what-ifs. Like everything that happened here, the specter of bullets and blood was just another version of risk and reward, probability and expectation.

"If I had a wife and kids," Lawyer Dan said, reading me perfectly, "I'd probably just stay home and play online."

"If you had a wife and kids," I shot back, "you'd probably be here twenty-four-seven."

Except for Benny, who had an ex-wife he hated, most of the other regulars in this game weren't married or even close to it; the major relationship in their lives was with poker. They were addicts and sickos. For them, the time between games was spent waiting for and thinking about the next game. It had been that way for me once, when my only thought was how soon I could make my getaway from wherever else I happened to be.

"You can joke about it," Lawyer Dan said, "but the truth is, I wish I were fucking married. Seriously. You married guys look at a forty-year-old single guy like me and think, I shoulda waited, had more fun first. But these young girls, they're brutal. I was seeing this one in her twenties, she found out I still had an AOL account, she was like, 'Dude, what are you doing? Now you're unfuckable. I can't fuck you anymore.' I'm telling you, I'd rather run kings into aces than see the look on the face of some chick when I tell her I was born the year the Beatles broke up."

* * *

Around ten o'clock, a kid named Max showed up and planted himself behind my right shoulder, waiting for a seat to come open. He was the kind of kid who got on everyone's nerves—obnoxious and full of himself and oblivious to how he came off. There was always a kid like this. In many ways, a poker game was like a family get-together. Everyone had their assigned role and felt obligated to play it. In this case, Max had been on a sick heater, a lucky winning streak that exaggerated his youngest-son sense of entitlement.

"Hey," Benny the Dwarf said, peering up at Max over his shoulder. "I can feel your hot breath on my neck."

"What? I'm not looking at your cards, Benny," Max said.

"Do I need to call the floor?"

"All right, I'll move. Hey, Nathan, you got a minute?"

"Why?"

"I want to ask you something."

"Feel free."

"I mean in private."

I sighed, got to my feet, and walked him back behind the fish tank, shrugging at the others as I went.

"So?" I said when we were out of earshot.

"I see you here every day," Max said. "I know you know what you're doing."

"Really? You been watching lately?"

"I've seen you win a lot."

I studied him, trying to figure out what he was after. It was no secret I'd been getting crushed the past month. He was clean-cut, with dark thick curly hair, hopeful eyes, a kind of dewy flush to his shaven cheeks. He'd been to law school, worked doing something in real estate, didn't love it, didn't know what else he wanted to do. I actually knew much more about Max than I wanted to because he was such a nonstop motor mouth. In fact, Jojo Pizza had recently won a hundred bucks betting him that he couldn't shut up for half an hour. Max barely lasted ten minutes.

"The thing is," Max said, "I'm considering quitting my job. Going pro. I want to know what advice you can give me."

"Keep the job," I said.

"Why? You don't think I'm good enough?"

"You might be."

"So?"

I took a deep breath, wondering if it was worth the trouble. Guy like Max didn't want my advice, he was just looking for permission. But I launched into my little sermon anyway, out of some misplaced sense of responsibility. I told him how most guys, even the ones with talent, couldn't take the swings. Truth was, after all this time, I might be one of them.

"You've been running good," I told him. "That doesn't mean it'll keep going. Plenty of guys run hot for a while, build up a nice little bankroll, strut around like they're bulletproof—until it turns."

"You think I've been strutting around?"

"I'm just saying that what you're feeling is an illusion. You think it's always going to be like this. It's not. A couple of bad sessions, things start breaking the other way, and suddenly you'll be losing the same way you're winning, feeling like it's never going to end. That goes on long enough, well…"

"I don't know," Max said. "It doesn't feel like that's what's going to happen."

"It never does."

"What about you? You seem to be managing it okay. Your little bad streak."

"Trust me on this," I told him. "Keep the paycheck. I know it's nice rolling out of bed whenever, pockets always full of cash, not having to suck up to some dick of a boss or cram into a crowded morning rush-hour subway car or have to powwow with Eric in marketing or check a tracking number on that Fed Ex package that was supposed to arrive yesterday. I know that's nice. But trust me, if you can't fade the downside, and I'm telling you it's coming, if you can't ignore the kick-in-the-gut one-outers, the fact that today is Sunday, the rent is due Monday, and if you lose this hand you don't know how you're going to pay it, if you can't deal with the feeling that you must be the unluckiest motherfucker on the planet, then going pro is probably not for you."

Max looked like he was trying to absorb what I was saying, but it was clear to me that it wasn't penetrating, that he was going to have to learn things the hard way.

* * *

Near midnight, I found myself in what would normally have been a good spot though lately had offered nothing but pain. I'd flopped a set against Asian John's flush draw in a three-thousand-dollar pot. In real math that made me a 75% favorite, meaning three out of four times I'd win the hand.

But that wasn't what happened, and knowing that I was a mathematical favorite was no consolation when John rivered his flush.

"Again? Really?" I slammed my fist on the rail.

None of the other players said anything but their silent glee was palpable.

It was weak, showing emotion this way. I knew better. Or should have. Four years I'd been on the tight rope, four years supporting my family by performing this high-wire act, the last six months with the added pressure that followed the failure of my show. Maybe I was just wearing down. The game was getting the best of me. A month of bad beats and a 20K downswing could get you thinking like that.

Fuck it. I was only down a couple of hundred bucks for the night, which almost felt like a win. I got one of the clear plastic racks and began stacking my chips.

"You leaving?" Lawyer Dan asked. "Must suck to have a real life."

"That's what they tell me."

* * *

The F train went above ground after the Carroll Street stop. Around a curve, at the high point of the El tracks, you could look out the window and see the Manhattan skyline, the place you'd just left behind. For me, that was the best part of the trip.

Brooklyn was a place to heal the pain and losses of Manhattan. Inside this fluorescent-lit moving steel box, I thought about the advice I gave Max. Though I'd walked away almost even, I still felt the hammer coming down.

Off the train at 4th Avenue and 9th Street, north along the avenue, down a few blocks to 5th, past the bodega where Sam knew me as *Daily News*-coffee-one-sugar. We lived on a quiet tree-lined street, on the second floor of a brownstone fronted by a small iron-gated yard similar to every other house on the block. I let myself in the front door and made my way past a couple of strollers parked in the vestibule, then up the creaky dirty white uncarpeted linoleum steps. The aroma of an hours-ago dinner lingered in the hall; something heavy on the garlic. At least it wasn't fish. When the Kleinman's cooked fish, Laura looked at me like it was my fault and started talking about moving.

Inside our apartment, pitch dark. Stepping gingerly, I felt my way toward the back of the living room. My foot hit something soft and fleshy, and though I did a sort of hop-step, it was too late. With a bloodcurdling yowl, Milo the cat went skittering off across the floor.

"Fuck," I muttered, heart pounding stupidly.

A sleepy voice from the room beyond: "Nate?"

"Sorry," I hissed. "Fucking cat."

Now Hannah was up, crying softly. "Mommy?"

"Great," Laura said.

I walked back toward our bed, still in the dark, and opened the door to Hannah's room. "Don't worry, I'm dealing with it."

A football-size glowing purple gummy bear dimly lit her small room. When Hannah saw me, she threw back her covers. "Daddy? You are back from work?"

"Yeah, sweetie. But it's very late and you need to go back to sleep."

"I don't wanna go back to sleep."

I needed to nip that idea quickly. "Honey, it's the middle of the night. Mommy and I are sleeping. I want you to go to sleep, too."

I braced myself for the "*I don't want to.*" Mercifully she just said, "Will you sing me a song first?"

"Of course I'll sing you a song."

"The Monkees song?"

"Sure," I laughed, "if that's what you want." I cleared my throat and sang, off-key but heartfelt. *"Here we come, walking down the street..."* And right then, in the midst of singing, looking at my little girl's chubby barely illuminated face, I found myself choking up, overcome by a sense of love so powerful it actually hurt. How had I gotten here? How had this happened? How had I, Nathan Fischer, who had never wanted responsibility for anybody or anything, been given charge, by a perverse God, of this defenseless, sweet-smelling, 40-pound fucking miracle?

4

A Marriage is a Living Thing

I n my Williamsburg days, I liked to lie in bed in my underwear on mornings I wasn't at my studio or working construction, listening to Radiohead and reading up on poker strategy.

One of the first books I ever read was called *Play Poker, Quit Work and Sleep Till Noon!* As a primer, it was pretty much useless since among other failings it was devoted to the archaic game of five-card draw. But the title made me smile, and the fantasy it promised turned out to be real.

These days, though, the irony of the "Sleep Till Noon" part wasn't lost on me, because I couldn't remember a time since Hannah was born that I'd slept past seven in the morning. Nearly four now, she was still at an age where she woke up earlier than any human should. Laura had the brilliant idea of drawing a crayon clock for her, with the little hand on the seven and the big hand on the twelve, and it had proven useful in training Hannah not to bug us the minute she woke up. But 7 a.m. was still rough, especially on weekends. Especially since I might've just gotten home an hour before.

Every morning, Hannah sidled up to one side of the bed or the other and, with her little fingers, jabbed awake whichever one of us was nearest, her sweet innocent face unintentionally mocking our crabby morning frowns. Even though only one of us needed get up, once I was up, I was up. So even though it was Laura's turn to deal with Hannah on mornings like this one, all it really meant was that I got to drool on my pillow for a few extra minutes while Laura was changing and dressing her.

When I did finally groan and grunt my way out of bed and wander out to the bathroom, wearing my paint-stained DiFara's T-shirt, Hannah glanced up from Elmo on the TV long enough to say, "Daddy, where are your pants?"

Through the open bathroom doorway, I saw Laura leaning toward the mirror, inspecting her face.

"Can I get in here?" I asked.

She looked at me, annoyed.

"I gotta pee," I explained with a croak. "It's either here or the kitchen sink."

Wordlessly, she exited. I squeezed by her and closed the door behind.

"Hannah," I heard her say, "that's enough Elmo. Turn it off, please. Your oatmeal is almost ready, and then you and Daddy are going to Poppa Leo's. I want you to wear that blue dress your grandma sent."

"You sure you don't want to come with us?" I yelled through the closed door. She either didn't hear me or chose not to answer.

I kicked aside the little yellow plastic footstool in front of the toilet and took aim. The footstool along with Elmo's "Potty Time" video and a kid-sized "transition" toilet seat were part of our efforts to get Hannah off diapers. The journey was not going smoothly.

After flushing, I followed the sound of voices to Hannah's room, "the den" as it was called by creative Brooklyn realtors, a room big enough for a toddler bed, a bureau topped by a changing pad and not much else. Laura dangled an ironed blue dress over the open top drawer.

Hannah crossed her arms, her lips forming an expression to match.

"The pink one," she said.

"But this one looks so nice on you."

"No!"

"How about this one?" Laura plucked another dress, also not pink, from the drawer.

"Nooo!"

I watched this negotiation, glad I wasn't part of it. "Did you hear me?" I said to Laura.

"What?"

"I said why don't you come with us?"

"You know I have my class on Saturday mornings. Anyway, you'll have a better time if I'm not there."

"Says who?"

"You do realize that every time you and I go to your dad's, we get into a fight."

"We do?"

She lowered her head a couple of degrees keeping her eyes trained on me as if to say, How do you play poker if you can't even take note of something obvious like this?

After breakfast, I rinsed the dishes while Hannah sat by the window conversing with her dolls. Drying my hands on a red-and-white-checked dishtowel looped through the stove handle, I said, "Hannah, honey, where are your sneakers? Let's get you ready to go."

"I don't want to wear my sneakers," she said. "I want to wear my party shoes."

"Where are your party shoes?"

"I don't know."

I spent five minutes rummaging around her room for them. That was when Laura appeared in the doorway, yoga mat slung over a shoulder.

"I'm going."

"Do you happen to know where her party shoes are?"

"I gave them away. She needs new ones."

"Could you please explain that to her?"

"I'm gonna be late for class."

"Just do me this one favor before you go?"

Laura knew she owed me this much. I trailed after her to the living room, curious to see how she'd explain to Hannah the fact that the party shoes were gone forever. There was a moment where I thought it was going to be okay, that she'd pulled it off, but then full comprehension dawned and Hannah began to wail, exercising her lungs so loudly I was sure the Kleinman's could hear her from downstairs.

"Hey bunny," I said brightly, talking over her tears, "I know you're disappointed, but the good part is that if you put on your sneakers right now, Mommy can walk us to the subway. We can all leave together!"

This was like telling her that even though the cake was gone, the empty cake box might also taste good. She howled even louder.

By the time I tied on her matchbox-sized sneakers and we left the apartment, Laura and I were both fried. Hannah, on the other hand, was now as happy as a drunk in a brewery, her tantrum magically forgotten. She skipped along in her Keds, holding our hands, as we swung her over and around the smeared and crushed chicken-skin colored ginkgo berries that had turned the sidewalk along our block into a shit-smelling minefield.

"Just so you know," I said to Laura, tapping the shoulder bag. "There was only one diaper left."

"I'll pick up some more on my way home."

"On Amazon, they're like half the price."

"I forgot to order them, sorry. You could have done it too you know."

40

"But you always do it. I take out the garbage and the recycling, you order the diapers."

"Oh Jesus." Laura looked skyward. "Meanwhile, Nathan, she's almost four years old."

"Is it almost my birthday, Mommy and Daddy?"

"That's right, in a little over a month."

"Precocious in some ways..."

Laura and I exchanged a look and a smile, and for the first time all day, I felt as if we were actually on the same side, allies not antagonists.

Then we were at the subway entrance, and she was asking me if I could give her some cash to get her through the day.

"Um, sure," I said, "What do you need?"

"Forty?"

I extracted the roll from my pocket and peeled off not two but four twenties. This was almost like a standing joke between us, our version of Lorraine Bracco asking Ray Liotta for spending money in *Goodfellas* and holding her fingers an inch apart when he asked "How much?" The difference being that my entire roll was about the size of one day's shopping for Lorraine Bracco.

"What?" Laura said.

I shrugged. "Just us. These conversations."

"We were gonna be different."

"So we thought."

"It makes me a little sad."

"You are sad Mommy?"

"No, honey," Laura said. "Not sad, depressed. There's a difference."

"Hey," I said. "Why don't you come with us? Seriously. It won't be that terrible."

"This is my favorite class. And I'm already late." She kissed me quickly, brushing her lips against mine.

I took Hannah's hand and headed down the subway steps. Behind us, I heard a faintly apologetic "Bye" drifting down over the rumble of an arriving train.

* * *

"What's the matter, your wife doesn't like me anymore?"

My father leaned back and flipped up his palms, an old-mobster-on-a-milk-crate gesture, except with him it was closer to old-Jew-in-a-rest-home. We were sitting on a pair of rusted white-metal chairs in the small garden in the rear of his ground-floor one-stop-further-out Park Slope apartment. I could hear a radio from somewhere, that stupid Kars for Kids jingle.

"She just needs her alone time now and then. You know how it is."

"So you're saying it's you she doesn't like."

"Yeah, Dad, it's me she doesn't like."

"Go ahead, make jokes. Just don't take her for granted."

"I'm not."

"You got a good broad there, Nathan. Don't fuck it up."

"What's going on, Dad? You bored?"

"Forget it. You gotta be half an idiot to take marriage advice from me anyway."

"You're right about that."

"Still. I know a few things."

He was dressed in classic geezer-on-the-corner garb: white wife-beater T, Bermuda shorts and a scuffed pair of loafers on his sockless feet. His face was tanned, probably from sitting outside like this, and there were more lines than there used to be, less hair on top of his head (but annoyingly still more than mine). He was handsome in a weathered-character-actor way. His dark eyes had a warmth and kindness that had charmed numerous women and conned not a few men (including me) into believing that he had their best interests at heart. For a man in his mid-70s, he looked a good ten years younger.

"What I'm trying to say is that a marriage is a living thing," he said. "You gotta feed and water it just like a plant."

"You have to kill one off before you learn that?"

He let this slide, just said softly, "Maybe you do."

Hannah dug with a spade in one of the flowerless flowerbeds that ran along the edges of the yard—the irony of which I felt tempted to point out in light of my dad's marriage metaphor. Instead, I shaded my eyes and admonished my daughter to be careful. She kept digging.

"You ever think about making another one?" my father asked, nodding toward Hannah.

"Dad!"

"I'm just asking."

I looked at him, trying to figure his angle. "We might have talked about it," I said at last.

"It's okay to tell me stuff. I'm your father for fuck's sake."

"Look, the thing is, Laura thought she might like another. I was on the fence. But it's moot. According to the doctor, I don't have strong swimmers. Hannah was basically pure luck."

"The best luck," he said. "I'm just saying you should do something nice for your wife every now and then. Make her feel appreciated. Women need that."

"Sons too."

"Hey, I'm not trying to bust your balls. I learned the hard way. Little things can make a difference."

It killed me to admit that he had a point. But it had been weeks since Laura and I had done anything fun.

"What's the real problem anyway?" he asked. "You been losing at poker?"

"Poker's okay."

"Okay doesn't sound very good."

"It's okay. Could be better, could definitely be worse. Point is, it's not a problem."

"From your perspective anyway."

It had been less than fifteen minutes and I'd already had my fill of him. If not for Hannah, who hadn't spent any time with her grandpa in over a week, I would have bailed. On the other hand, he had given me my escape route.

"You know, Dad, I'm beginning to think you're right. Maybe I'll go surprise Laura, take her out for brunch. If I leave Hannah with you—"

"She and I will find plenty to do together. Right, sweetheart?"

Hannah looked up from her digging. The morning sun cast sharp angles of light and shadow across the concrete and the flaking green wooden fences. A few pairs of Dad's boxers hung from a clothesline strung between two scrawny trees.

"Hannah, honey," I said, "Will you be okay if I leave you alone with Poppa Leo for a little while?"

She nodded, only half-listening.

"Leave her," Dad said. "It's fine."

I couldn't stop myself from wondering what Laura would say. Would it be worth whatever brownie points I got for trying to be a good husband? Or would bad father trump all? I should have asked my dad the answer to that one, but instead, I said, "Hannah, if I leave you here, will you be a good girl and do what your grandpa says?"

"Okay," she said in her little chirp of a voice.

I locked eyes with him. "Dad, please don't make me sorry I'm doing this."

"Have I ever let you down?"

In spite of myself, I laughed.

* * *

I arrived at Laura's yoga studio about fifteen minutes before her class was scheduled to end, ducking into the Starbucks across the street to wait for her. As I sat by the window sipping a large latte, I thought about how stupid it was to leave Hannah with Dad. Trying to prove I was a better husband than he was, I had done the one thing Laura might literally kill me for. As if playing cards wasn't iffy enough—given the fact that I'd sworn that the last person on Earth I'd ever emulate was him.

Throughout my childhood, he had never held a steady job or gone to an office, operating instead in a world of get-rich-quick schemes and hustles. He'd promoted boxing matches and auto shows, scalped tickets, and done other even sketchier things that he never talked about. Children and bad habits to support eclipsed whatever qualms he might have had about getting involved in shady doings.

I was twelve when the feds busted him for tax evasion. Two guys in dark suits led him out of our Cobble Hill apartment in handcuffs at six in the morning while my mother and my sister wept and I just stared in disbelief.

During his trial, I became obsessed with comic books, reading them, collecting them, even trying to draw my own. It was the beginning of my life as an artist. I loved the Marvel characters, identified with their troubled personal lives, the idea that you could be a superhero and still be fucked up.

But I read all the others too, whatever I could get my hands on, even *Richie Rich, Little Lotta* and *Archie.* The characters in *Archie* all laughed with *yuks* and *hyuks.* For a while, after the trial was over and Dad went to prison, I developed a fake laugh based on *Archie.* When something struck me funny, instead of a genuine laugh, I verbalized the *Hyuk* I'd seen in dialogue bubbles, making it sound something like *hyoik* and uttering it twice. *Hyoik hyoik.* Walking around, a wounded idiot kid, I laughed my affected *hyoik hyoik* without ever understanding how weird it was or how sad.

In the three years that followed his arrest, I only saw Dad the one or two times a month when my mom borrowed a neighbor's car and drove me and Lana up to the prison in Otisville. What I most remember of those trips was the four of us in a large noisy space like a school cafeteria, sitting at a table, guards nearby, Dad in his orange jumpsuit, Lana and I dressed like we were going to temple. I was as happy to see him as Mom was miserable. Sometimes I looked around at the other families and exchanged a nod of solidarity with another kid, wishing he and I were on a basketball court somewhere or just hanging out on a stoop together. Once, when it was time to leave, I bit down on my lip so hard it started to bleed.

I didn't care what my father had done. I just wanted him back, wanted everything to be the way it had been. Instead, my mother, sister and I were forced to move, farther out into Brooklyn. In Park Slope, Lana and I were forced to share a bedroom that was smaller than the rooms we'd had to ourselves in the old setup. Mom had tolerated the drinking, the carousing, the horse playing. But prison was the deal-breaker. No one blamed her when she filed for divorce.

About a year and a half into my father's prison stretch, Mom met a guy named Jim who was divorced and had three kids of his own (though they didn't live with him). Next thing I knew, we were all moving in with Jim on the Upper Westside of Manhattan. Jim wasn't a bad guy. He told corny jokes but was handy around the house, good at fixing leaky faucets and drawers that got stuck and things like that, and he treated my mom well. Though not rich, he made a decent living selling ad space for the local NBC station, enough that we were able to go to Fire Island for a couple of weeks every summer, which was nice. Later, when I was off in college, Jim got a better job although it meant my mom and him moving to Los Angeles, where they still lived.

My father, meanwhile, had gotten paroled and found a job selling "pre-owned" cars. I had changed a lot in the three years he'd been gone, but Dad, as far as I could tell, and despite the job, had not. He still played the ponies and drank, told funny, bawdy stories about the old days, knew the batting averages of every Yankee, smoked Camel unfiltered, hung out with guys named Louie, Deke, and Tugboat. And had a knack for charming the ladies.

* * *

The door to Chakra Yoga opened and out came Laura, followed by a man and another woman. They were all wearing street clothes, yoga mats slung over their shoulders. Standing out front, they talked, faces animated, bright. The guy was tall and slender, annoyingly relaxed looking. He wore jeans and a dress shirt with the sleeves rolled up. His tousle of dark hair and prominent nose seemed at odds with his otherwise compact features. He said something and Laura and the other woman laughed, throwing their heads back.

I stopped at the Starbucks door, trying to figure out what I was seeing. I watched Laura and the guy say goodbye to the other woman and head off down the street together.

For a few moments, I remained frozen. Then I opened the door and started after them, staying a couple of hundred feet behind, on the opposite side of Smith Street. My head was spinning, heart beating so fast I could barely breathe.

If anyone was in the wrong here, it was not me, and yet I felt like a creep and an asshole for following them and not saying anything. I had trained myself not to let my emotions get the best of me, to step back and assess before acting. But that did little to mitigate the feeling that I should announce myself, not skulk after them. Plus, what were they doing exactly? They were just walking. I hadn't caught them kissing or holding hands. His arm wasn't around her. There was daylight between them. And yet I couldn't keep my thoughts from going to bad places.

This wouldn't have been the case if Laura and I were still having sex regularly. If I weren't out at poker four nights a week. If my painting career were thriving. If we weren't exhausted by our three-year-old. My dad was right. We were like that plant: not getting enough sunlight and slowly withering away.

As I watched my wife and the tall handsome yoga man stop outside Café LuLuc, considering, it seemed, whether or not to enter, I knew I needed to take action. If they went inside and I followed, it would be even weirder and stalkier. So I half-heartedly shouted Laura's name, feeling self-conscious and strange. A passing truck drowned out my voice. I tried again. "Laura!"

This time she turned, squinting at me as if I were someone she recognized from *America's Most Wanted*.

"What are you doing here?" she said when I was within earshot. "Where's Hannah?"

"I left her with Dad. She's fine."

"You left her?"

"She's fine," I repeated, then turned to acknowledge her companion. "Hi, I'm Nathan."

"Uh, this is David," Laura said, clearly flustered. "David, this is my husband." The word "husband" sounded strangely formal to me as if she were saying, "This is my cardiologist."

Up close, David's blue eyes immediately struck me with their intensity and intelligence. I extended my hand. He took it. His forearm was tan and sinewy. He didn't seem at all unnerved or uncomfortable, and I found myself irritated not to be able to get a quick read on him. I also wondered about the impression I was giving off. As jarring as *husband* sounded to me, *jealous husband* was worse.

"I don't understand," Laura said. "Why did you leave Hannah with your dad?"

"I wanted to surprise you after class. Maybe go out to brunch."

She looked genuinely puzzled unless it was all an act, which given the circumstances I didn't discount.

"I just thought it'd be nice for us to spend a little time alone," I went on. "And Dad offered to babysit."

"I think I'll be on my way," David said abruptly. He turned to Laura. "We can have our talk another time."

"Oh." Now she was actually flustered. "But—"

David turned to me. "Your wife let me read some of her novel. We were planning to talk about it."

I shot Laura a look. She let *this* guy read some of her manuscript?

"David's an editor," she said. And then as if further explanation was needed, "At Random House."

"You should consider yourself privileged," I told him, casting another angry glance at her. "Laura doesn't usually let people read her stuff."

"It took a bit of persuasion," he said. "Anyway, she and I can arrange another time."

"No, no. I don't want to get in the way here. You guys go have your talk." I nodded agreeably as if I'd hit upon the only sensible solution. "I'll see you later, sweetie."

"Nathan, wait—"

"Yes?" I said hopefully.

"Can you please call your dad first?"

"Hannah's fine," I said, ticked by her question and the implication that I had exercised poor judgment. But off her look, I decided I better make sure. I hit my dad's speed dial, then turned away, covering one ear with my hand. Ten rings in, I gave up, trying his cell number with the same result. He probably didn't even have the damn thing turned on.

"He's not answering?"

"I'm trying again."

Another eight rings. Still nothing. "They must be out back. The reception there is shitty."

"Nate."

"What?"

"I can't believe you left her with him."

"I'm heading back there. It's not like she's alone watching TV while he's at the corner bar."

"Don't even say that."

"She's *okay*. Stop worrying."

"Can you please go back there?"

"I am. I'm going." Despite my anger, I made a show of kissing her quickly on the lips.

"Nice to meet you," David said.

"Yeah." I gave him a curt nod. And that was that. I sulked off toward the subway, sneaking a surreptitious backward glance as I crossed the street. But by then they'd apparently gone into the café because the sidewalk was empty.

5

Televisions in the Ceiling Showing Horses

M aybe he couldn't hear me from back in the garden. I leaned on the buzzer again and glanced at my watch. Slightly over an hour had passed since I left them. I pictured him collapsed in a flowerbed like Don Corleone, Hannah prancing around happily near his body, surrounded by dangerous gardening implements. Maybe patience was not the best course of action.

I rang Ray the super's bell.

At almost the same moment, a vibration in my pocket. Assuming it was my dad, I swiped, too late seeing that it was Laura's name on the screen.

"Hi, how's it going there?"

Fuck.

"Hello? Nate?"

"Yeah."

"Everything okay?"

"Sure, fine." I peered through the glass panel of the door, cupping my free hand against the cool thick pane to block the reflection of the trees and sky and houses across the street.

"So your dad didn't go to a bar?"

"That was a joke."

"Can I say hello to Hannah?"

I was a shitty liar away from the poker table but the truth did not seem like a good option. "Hang on." I lowered the phone. "Um, Hannah, do you want to say hi to Mommy?" Momentary pause, then: "She's kind of involved in what she's doing."

"She won't say hello?"

Before I could respond, the vestibule door opened, and I found myself facing a slender Italian man with an elaborate high gray pompadour.

"Hey, Nathan! You here to see your old man?"

"No, I, uh—hold on a second. Listen, Laur, I'll call you back."

"Why? Who is that, Nathan? What's going on?"

"It's Ray the super. He's here to fix a…leak. I can't talk. I'll call you back." I flipped the phone shut.

"A leak?" Ray said.

I waved him off. "I'm trying to find my dad. Have you seen him?"

"I think I heard him and the little girl in the hallway a while ago. That one's gonna cause you trouble someday you're not careful."

"She already is."

Ray spit out a laugh, nodding knowingly.

"Did it seem like they were on their way out?"

"Could have been. Not for nothing, Nate, but it means a lot to him, you bringing her by. He gets all choked up."

"Is that right?" I had a hard time picturing this. Almost as hard a time as I was having *not* picturing what my wife was doing right now.

"Your dad, he keeps a lot to himself."

"Yeah?" I snapped back into the moment. Ray's tone was giving me a bad feeling. "He probably hasn't said anything to you, but I thought I should let you know he's a little behind on the rent."

I felt a surge of heat along my scalp.

"No big deal," Ray said. "The landlord's a good guy. I just don't want your dad should have problems."

"How far behind is he, Ray?"

"The landlord, he's forgiving. Up to a point."

"How far, Ray? How much?"

"Coming up on three months."

"Three months!"

"I'm upsetting you."

"No, I appreciate the heads-up."

"He don't need to come up with all of it at once."

I reached into my pocket for my roll, slipped off the rubber band and started counting off $100 bills, each one I peeled adding to my aggravation, putting me in mind of the cash I'd given Laura earlier.

"You have my number, right? In case you need to reach me?" I moved my head from side to side, trying to ease the tightness in my shoulders. The vertebrae in my neck crackled like Pop Rocks, the base of my skull liquid and slightly crunchy. I handed Ray a couple of thousand. "This'll square him for now, right?"

"A hundred percent."

"Please. Make sure he pays going forward."

"I'll do my best, Nate."

"I'm gonna go outside and wait for them."

"What about the leak?"

"Leak? No, that was—" I started to explain but ended up just saying, "Some leaks you can't fix, Ray."

Ray looked at me like he might even understand, then shrugged and

53

let himself back inside.

My phone was vibrating again. Laura. I let the call go to voicemail. I suppose it was a good sign that she was thinking about Hannah even if, as it seemed, her concern didn't extend to me.

I slumped down on a nearby stoop, hands deep in the pockets of my quilted blue cotton jacket. My head and whole body felt numb. I'd never wanted any of this, had known instinctively that I'd be bad at it, that marriage would be a test I'd fail and that parenthood would make me feel inadequate—not because I wouldn't care but because I'd care too much

Once, when Hannah was two, Laura and I rented a car and drove up to Vermont to visit a college friend of mine. During our stay, on a shopping expedition to a big supermarket outside Brattleboro, we lost track of her for a few moments while we were discussing whether to get steaks or pork chops for dinner. We turned around and she was gone, vanished into thin air. It couldn't have been more than fifteen seconds. How far could she have wandered?

Not finding her right away, panic set in. I raced up one aisle, down another. Terrible things happened in places like this, huge well-lit caverns of banality. My breath stuck in my throat. Down at the end of one aisle, I saw Laura, equally panicked, her expression making it clear that she was going through exactly what I was. I sprinted toward the automatic glass exit doors. Out into the hot barren parking lot. Someone was unloading groceries into the back of an SUV. A white-haired woman walked slowly toward the entrance. The sky was flawless blue, the over-heated air absolutely still. I ran up and down the rows of cars, looking for…what? A rust-eaten Chevy with a meth-crazed predator at the wheel? Maybe I was already too late, had wasted too much time inside. In one horrible flash, it struck me that I might never see my daughter again.

On the verge of tears, I made my way back into the chilled fluorescence. When Laura saw me, saw my expression, all hope drained from her eyes.

And then, in a kiddie shopping cart that had been made to look like a red racecar, came movement, a childish giggle. Hannah grinned up at us, unaware of the living hell we had just been through, oblivious to the hideousness of the preceding God knew how many minutes when we were certain she was gone forever.

I finally caught sight of my father and Hannah coming down the block, his big mitt wrapped around Hannah's little hand. She broke free and ran toward me.

"Daddy!"

I crouched down, bracing myself. "Hi, Sweetpea."

She sailed into my chest, practically knocking me over, smelling faintly of urine.

"You came back!"

"Of course I did, silly girl! What were you and Grandpa doing?"

"Well," she said very earnestly, "we went to this store where there were televisions in the ceiling showing horses."

"Horses?"

"And I picked the pink one. And it won!" She dug a bunch of crumpled dollar bills out of the pocket of her fleece and waved them at me. "See?"

"Huh, that's terrific." I looked up past her as my father drew near, his shoulders swinging as if to help him walk, his bowed 70-year-old legs giving him the rolling gait of an old seaman.

"Dad, you took her to OTB?"

"Yeah, kid picked a winner," he said. "Paid six-sixty for a two-dollar bet. She had a great time."

"Laura will be so thrilled."

"How'd it go with her anyway? You're back sooner than I thought."

"Yes, I am."

"So?"

"So nothing."

"Oh, and guess what else, Daddy?" Hannah said. She stuck out her tongue. It was purple. "Poppa Leo got me a ring pop."

I just glared at him.

"What?" he said in all innocence.

"Is there anything you did with her that won't have my wife pissed at me, Dad?"

"What's wrong with a little candy?"

"Just do yourself a favor. Keep your mouth shut and don't mention this when you see her."

"Is that what you do?"

I refused to take the bait. "Hey, Hannah, say goodbye to Grandpa. We need to get going."

"Aw, come on," my father said. "I'm gonna make a pot of coffee. I'll get some nice pastries from down the block."

"Tempting as that is, we really gotta go. C'mon, Sweetpea."

"Bye Grampa."

I took her hand. "And next time, Dad? Before you take one of your little field trips, ask, okay?"

Hannah and I started down the block.

"You always liked it when I took you!" he yelled.

* * *

Laura wasn't home when we got back, but the bathroom floor was puddled and a damp towel hung on the back of the door. I reflexively grabbed my phone to call her, but then remembered that I still didn't feel like talking to her.

Hannah and I drew with crayons for a while, then did a puzzle. Then we played a game of her invention called "family" in which, in a real stretch, I took on the role of Daddy and she played the part of my little girl. We were deeply involved in our pretend world, meaning Hannah was playing and I was sitting on the couch in a semi-stupor, when Laura came home a little past four, lugging a big nylon bag of laundry. Her hair was still damp, a darker shade of red than usual, almost brown.

"Hi, Mommy!"

Laura smiled, dropping the laundry.

"Daddy's pretending to be Daddy."

"Oh is that what he's doing?" Laura said. "I couldn't tell. How was your day with Grandpa?"

"Grampa and I saw horses on TV."

"Really?" Laura cut me a look, wiping a thin film of sweat from her forehead with the back of her hand.

"Poppa Leo took her to OTB," I said.

"Oh. Well that's lovely. I thought you said that he hadn't done anything like that."

"I said he didn't take her to a bar."

"So a strip club would have been okay too?" Laura sat on the chair opposite the couch.

"Hey, it's not like I knew he was gonna take her there." Strange that I felt like I had to defend him. I realized that the only reason I was unhappy he took Hannah was that I knew Laura would have a knee-jerk reaction. It wasn't as if the experience would damage the kid for life.

"I'm just curious. Were you planning on saying anything? Or were you just hoping I wouldn't find out?"

I cleared my throat. "Truthfully, Laur, I wasn't really thinking about it. And if not for you bringing it up, I still wouldn't be thinking about it."

"I mean, have you ever seen the kinds of creeps and losers that hang out in those places?"

"You mean guys like my Dad?"

"Who takes a three-year-old child somewhere like that?"

She didn't wait for an answer. Instead, she got up and lugged the laundry bag into our bedroom, dumping the contents onto the bed. I stayed on the couch, watching Hannah continue the family game solo. Eventually, I asked her if she wanted to watch, which of course she did, so I popped a DVD into the VCR, then made my way back to the bedroom, where Laura was folding laundry. I stood there, watching her.

"I can't believe *you're* pissed at *me*."

She shook out a pair of jeans, the sound like the rustle of a flag on a gusty day. Then she laid them on the bed, folding one leg onto the other and smoothing them with the flat of her hand.

"Is it really because I left her with Dad? Or is this just your way of keeping the focus on something other than your little meeting?"

"What are you talking about?"

"You know exactly what I'm talking about."

"You're jealous, aren't you?"

"I mean, you've never even mentioned this guy to me, and now I find out that you're showing him your book?"

"He's an editor."

"I know. At a major publishing house." I picked up a blue cotton T-shirt.

"You *are* jealous."

"What if I am?" The T-shirt was wrinkled and still warm.

She laughed. "Well, whaddaya know."

"I'm glad you find this so amusing."

She started shaking out another pair of jeans.

"Look, if you don't want to talk about it, just say so."

"There's nothing to talk about, Nate."

I balled up the T-shirt and threw it at her. She was startled momentarily, then retaliated, picking up a sock and throwing it at me. I ducked out of the way, then grabbed her around the waist, wrestling her to the bed while she squealed and laughed, saying, "Nate, cut it out." Her laughter continued as I tried to kiss her. But gradually she stopped and started kissing me back. "Quietly," she whispered, breathing rapidly. "Hannah's out there."

* * *

In the beginning, we used to do it everywhere. In coatrooms. Bathrooms. On couches. Chairs. On top of tables. In the shower. Bent over the kitchen counter. We did it once on a sand dune at the National Seashore on the Cape in the middle of a blazing hot day at the height of the summer tourist season.

Lately, when it happened, if it happened, it was way less adventurous, almost always confined to our bed, but somehow, surprisingly, still good. And when I wondered aloud why it didn't happen more often, Laura agreed, saying she wondered the same thing. Then days passed and turned into weeks without us figuring out the answer.

* * *

In the morning we took the subway into the city. It was the middle of November but the air felt like spring, the sky a deep rich blue. We walked around Washington Square Park, toting Hannah's diaper bag and her stroller, which she refused to ride in.

The sound of a trumpet from one end of the park mixed with the snare beat of a plastic bucket drum from the other. We walked past a tattooed man with a pigeon on his head, a guy with a rainbow Mohawk, a singer who sounded like Screamin' Jay Hawkins. The fountain was turned off, but a three-deep crowd there had formed a circle around some act I couldn't see.

In the playground area on the north side of the park, Laura settled onto one of the benches while I retrieved Hannah's shoes from the sandbox. Except for the memory, the sex of the previous afternoon might never have happened. I hadn't brought up the editor again and neither had she.

I took a seat on the bench next to her, still holding Hannah's shoes. Laura looked straight ahead, keeping a watchful eye on our child. In profile, the classical lines of her face, her graceful jaw, her elegant nose, the perfect dark crescent of a nostril, made her seem as beautiful and removed from me as a painting protected by glass.

I thought about the first time I'd ever seen her, in the now-defunct Barnes and Noble bookstore on Astor Place. I was talking to this guy I knew from the clubs, Howie, who I'd randomly bumped into while looking for a reissue of John Fante's *Ask the Dust*. Howie was fifty with a thick New England accent. He was decent company if a bit of a bore, able to recite bad beat stories for hours without taking a breath. This day he was actually ranting about politics not poker—specifically, Republican plans to "repeal and replace" Obama's recently passed healthcare. Laura glanced at us as she passed and seemed somehow to sense my predicament—or at least the simpatico smile she flashed allowed me to think so. That and her red hair were the things that immediately attracted me. I had a weakness for redheads.

"Buncha fuckin' grandstanders," Howie was saying. "They know they're never gonna do anything yet they persist in pawsturing—you listening to me?"

"Sorry," I said, nodding in Laura's direction.

"Ah, you fuckin' horny bastard," he said, suspending his rant momentarily to look at Laura's retreating backside as she disappeared around a corner. "Don't you know what I'm saying is more important than some wet dream of a broad you're never gonna see again."

A few minutes later, contrary to Howie's prediction, Laura reappeared, this time on her way out of the store.

"Personally," Howie was saying, "I think Obama undervalued his hand. I knew he was never gonna have the balls to push through the public awption. But he folded without anyone even raising him. A real fish move if I've evah seen one. Not to speak of the fact—"

"I'm going after her, Howie."

"What?"

"I'm going after her," I said, motioning in the direction she'd gone. Part of my motivation was to get away from him. I pursued her toward the exit, admiring the way her khakis hugged her nicely rounded ass. Outside, she turned east in the direction of Lafayette Street. Was I really going through with this?

I closed the distance, catching up at the corner before the light changed. No need to be nervous. She'd smiled at me, hadn't she?

"Hi," I said, for some reason holding up a finger.

"Yes?" She looked slightly perplexed and alarmed.

Fuck. Maybe I'd gotten it all wrong. I'd imagined the smile, the look of understanding.

Close up, I saw she was even prettier than I'd realized. A heart-shaped face and enormous eyes, bright, clear blue and unwavering. Christina Ricci as a redhead.

"I just wanted to tell you," I said, "that you have the nicest smile..."

And there it was. The smile. Again.

"And, um," I stammered. "I don't know what you're doing right now, but I was hoping that maybe you'd let me buy you a cup of coffee."

To my surprise, and without hesitation, she said, "Sure."

"Really?"

And so, with me talking nervously the whole way, we walked along St. Mark's to Café Orlin.

"Do you do this all the time?" she said when we were sitting at a table by the window. "Pick up girls in bookstores?"

"Is that what just happened?"

"Kind of."

"Actually, I never do this."

It wasn't a lie. I had never picked up anyone in a bookstore before. But I had picked up Jocelyn Nesbitt in a laundromat and Carrie Sager while standing on line to buy tickets for a U2 concert and Beckie Kristeller on the Staten Island ferry. I wasn't hopeless when it came to meeting women. The relationship part was another story. It didn't help that through most of my 20s, I went for the difficult, skittish types who promised maximum pain. By the time I hit thirty, warier and wiser, I tried to steer clear of the obvious train wrecks, but in the process became skittish myself, hard to pin down, a bit of a cad.

When I'd met Laura I was trying to evolve past such behavior but not doing such a great job of it. She had her own issues. Her father seemed to be the main source, at least as she interpreted it. He was a behavioral psychologist who treated her and her sister less like his children than like lab rats. They had discovered ways to hide from his cold assessments, her sister becoming obsessed with chess, Laura taking refuge in books. She read during meals, walking down the street, in the playground, under her desk in school. Wherever she went, she always brought a book. It carried over into adulthood. I still found books in the bathroom with their pages so curled and rippled it seemed probable she had taken them with her into the shower.

Her love of reading led to writing. There was a university award at Colgate, then later, residencies at Ragdale and the Virginia Center, stories published in online journals. The week we met, she had just sold a story to a little magazine called *Nuked*, and on our third date, I stayed over at her place and she read it to me aloud in a voice that quavered slightly, like the air over a highway on a hot summer's day.

Disturbing and beautiful, the story centered around an eighteen-year-old girl working as a cashier at a porn shop, who gets revenge on her sadistic employer by locking him in a storeroom overnight, only to find out the next day that he's died without his nitroglycerin pills.

I could only imagine then the dark corners of the psyche that had produced it. Even so, I was beguiled, the more so because she read it to me as we faced each other on the cozy Indian print-covered couch in her tiny Rivington Street apartment, our legs interlaced like fingers.

Off the page, Laura was less revealing, the facts not always adding up to a picture I fully understood. She was coming out of a two-year thing with a hotshot novelist who lied and cheated and was full of himself but also charming and seductive with a great apartment in Chelsea. And though she swore it was over and the only reason he remained interested involved his wounded ego, I had my doubts.

Especially when, a month into things, he persuaded her to have dinner so that they could "resolve some nagging questions." By then I had totally fallen for her and thought she had for me, and couldn't understand why she'd agreed to see him. She assured me it wasn't a big deal. To show her I was cool and mature, I pretended to believe this. It was tricky; as I mentioned, I was a lousy liar away from the poker table. But apparently I succeeded because she had no idea how much I didn't want her to go.

The night of their dinner, Charlie Bascombe and I went to see *The Bourne Supremacy*. It helped a little, but even as Jason Bourne snapped bad guys' necks and dove headfirst through flaming windows, I couldn't seem to stop thinking about her or stop that other movie playing in my head. After *Bourne*, Charlie got me shitfaced on Old Grand-Dad at Montero's. But when I got home and she still hadn't called and Charlie was gone, I began to unravel. What had made me think she'd want me, not him? How could I have been so stupid?

Masochistically, wanting to get a better idea of what I was up against,

63

I watched a YouTube video interview clip of my rival, his smug self-confidence well-concealed by an annoyingly self-effacing modesty. The fucker! He had a full head of hair. Family money. A father who had never gone to prison. He even had a cool name: Damian Troy Reilly.

I began pacing my tiny apartment in a rage of jealousy, waiting for the call that never came. There was no hope of my going to sleep. No hope of anything really. I was pathetic. I got into bed and lay there with my brain on fire. I tried reading. I tried TV. At five in the morning, I fried a couple of eggs that I couldn't eat, and turned on the television again, and turned off the television, and looked out the window at the dark empty street, and knew that if I called her right then I would never see her again.

At 9:30 in the morning, unable to stand it any longer, I swallowed my pride and picked up the phone. It was a new day after all. There were people in the street. People who had slept, who had no idea that there were people like me who hadn't.

To my astonishment, she answered, annoyingly cheerful and oblivious. "I'm sorry I didn't call last night," she said. "It was late. I was afraid I'd wake you."

This confused me. Was she really being considerate? Had I really spent a sleepless night of agony and torture because she hadn't wanted to disturb me? Had I lain there, watching a pornographic tape loop of her and fuckhead rolling around naked and sweaty because she was worried about interrupting my R.E.M cycle?

I tried to keep my anger and craziness bottled up until I could make sense of things, but when she asked me how my night had gone, my grunted "all right" was so strangled with resentment that it came out like the last-gasp death rattle of a dying man.

"Are you okay, Nate?" she said. "You sound strange."

I tried, but my anger was too close to the surface, too unruly to

64

contain.

"I just...I don't understand, Laura. Did you not have any idea of what I might have been going through? Did it not fucking occur to you that I might have been going nuts here?"

A long pause, and then: "Oh my God." Genuine surprise. "No," she said. "No, I had no idea."

"Well, I was."

"Oh, Nate."

Well played, man, was all I could think. *Letting her see your hand this way. What a fish move. Parading your insecurity like a float in the Macy's Day Parade.* And the worst part was, I still wasn't sure where I stood with her. I had let my imagination run wild and I still didn't know what she was thinking or what had happened. I mean, maybe she *had* slept with him. Maybe she'd been about to tell me she was still in love with him. Or maybe the sex had sucked and she'd remembered why she'd gotten out. Or she hadn't slept with him but had considered it. Or...what difference did it make? The real point was that whatever else had happened, she hadn't been thinking about me, and no matter how much she reassured me, in my unconscious, that sleepless night left a scar.

We fell into a steady two-nights-a-week routine after that. It was fine but oddly inert. I was vaguely aware that things were different, though I'm not sure I could have articulated how.

"You're bored with me, aren't you?" she said one night, sitting on my green couch watching a video of *Ferris Bueller's Day Off.*

I hit the pause button and looked at her. "Why would you say that?"

"You told me this is what happens to you, what you always do."

"What am I doing?"

"I don't know. You're just. Here."

I frowned.

"Just keep watching the movie, right?"

I turned off the TV. "Laur, seriously, what's the matter?"

"No, it's okay. I get it. The thrill wears off. You warned me."

She was right. I knew and yet hadn't been able, couldn't seem to stop what was happening from happening. This sideways momentum.

I looked at her: sad-eyed but with a laugh that could light up her face in an instant. I thought about her gorgeous, haunting stories, and that she liked me and found me sexy. She hadn't been scared off by the poker or the instability. She actually seemed to want this. Want me instead of the hotshot novelist.

Why was that? Because of the time I held on to her all night long while she hung over the toilet rim puking her guts out from stomach flu? Or the time I insisted she take my umbrella in a rainstorm at the end of an evening when we were peeling off in opposite directions? Maybe it wasn't anything I did, just a smell I had or the way our bodies fit together, or the way we looked at each other when we were talking, as if we had never truly seen another person before. No, it didn't add up. Love never did. Unless you threw out logic. Which was hard for me as a poker player.

And so I wavered and went back and forth and did my best not to blow it even while looking for reasons to break up. Our needs weren't so terribly different. We both wanted patrons, helpmates, not fellow wretches, not people like us. What if she couldn't make it as a writer? If I couldn't make it as a painter? What then? There was that ever-present sadness in her eyes, clear and cool and inviting as they were. Was I supposed to fix that? What would happen if her dreams went unrealized? If mine did?

On the heels of breaking up with the novelist, she'd found a new therapist who had already advised her, given the general outline of the story, to ditch me. I knew if our trajectory didn't change, she would follow the therapist's advice. But I couldn't seem to give her the certainty she wanted and expected from a boyfriend. I couldn't shed the ambivalence once it set in. For a while, she put up with me going through the motions and didn't bail. But then when she did, I wasn't surprised. It felt like confirmation of what I'd always known was inevitable. I didn't even try to stop her.

Until the morning I took that taxi to her door.

* * *

"Hey," I said, and Laura turned, eyes blacked out by dark Wayfarers, hair up in a messy bun that gave her a movie-star-without-makeup look.

"Hey yourself," she said.

"So when *are* you gonna let me read your book?"

"At some point."

"I don't understand. What are you afraid of?"

"I said I'll show it to you. Just not yet."

"Is there something in there that'll upset me?"

"Dude, back off."

"I don't get why you feel okay showing it to someone else but not me."

"He's an editor."

"You don't think I'm capable of reading it critically?"

"You're not objective."

"I can be objective."

"I don't think you're objective enough to say that."

"Haha."

"I'm not trying to change the subject," she said, looking over my shoulder, "but maybe you can tell me why those people on the other side of the fence are pointing at us."

"What?"

"Those people. Do you know them?"

I turned, irritated. On the outside of the fence, D.J. waved at me. He had his arm around a girl.

"Do you know them?"

"It's D.J." I got up and walked toward the fence, realizing as I drew closer that the girl was Caitlin, the cashier from the Fish Tank. There was also another guy, an Internet wizard everyone knew as Florida James. He was with a girl too. It took me by surprise—D.J. and Caitlin. The four of them looked like they were part of a fashion shoot, wool-knit hats, shades, colorful slouchy sweaters.

"Didn't I tell you the little girl in the sandbox looked like Nate's kid?" I heard D.J. say.

"What are you degenerates doing out in broad daylight?" I said, coming up to the fence bars.

"On our way to see a movie. Wanna come?"

"Which one?"

"*Get Him to the Greek.*"

"I'm pretty sure that's not family approved."

"My folks took me to see *Heathers* when I was her age."

"Yeah and look how you turned out."

"She's adorable," cooed Florida James' girl, a pretty twenty-something in an off-white shirt jac, black jeans, and plain black baseball cap, nodding in Hannah's direction.

"Is that your wife over there?" Caitlin asked.

"You should've dropped by last night," D.J. said before I could answer. Two days of beard shadowed his squarish jaw. His thick dirty blond hair was combed back in a casual sweep.

"What'd I miss this time?"

"Only one of the greatest games in history. Danny the Jeweler was there. Doc Larry. It was nuts. But this guy—"

Florida James shrugged modestly.

"—was not only killing it in real life, he had a laptop going at the same time and finished second in a PokerStars tournament for eighteen K. He's a monster."

"So James," I said, "maybe you can tell me. Why can't I seem to win online?"

"Maybe because you suck at poker," D.J. said.

"If you're serious," James said, "why don't you come over sometime? We'll play together. I'll see what you're doing. We can talk through stuff."

"I might take you up on that."

Laura finally got to her feet and wandered over.

"Hey Laura," D.J. said.

"Hey D.J.," Laura said coolly.

"Honey, this is Caitlin. James. And…"

"Sarah," the other girl said.

We stood there talking for a while through the bars of the fence. Then Hannah called for Laura, and D.J. said they'd better get going if they wanted to make the movie. I watched them wander off, half-wishing I was going with them.

Back on the bench, Laura said, "So that's D.J.'s girlfriend?"

"I guess."

"She's cute."

"I suppose."

"Make you pine for the good old days?"

"Terribly."

"Come on, it's fun having crushes on pretty girls."

"Laura, I don't have a crush on her."

"It's okay if you do. I'd understand."

"Well, I don't."

"Okay."

"I feel like you're the one who's trying to tell *me* something."

"I'm not."

I looked at her appraisingly. She lifted her sunglasses and returned the look. There was a warmth there, a directness in her gaze. Enough to persuade me to let it go.

6

The Outward Signs of My Foolishness

E leven thirty at night, half an hour from my usual curfew. A couple of mopes had just made a clean getaway, booking good-sized wins. A couple of other monkeys were on the brink. You could tell they wanted to leave but didn't want to do it right after raking big pots, so they were sitting there pretending to play even though they were in full lockdown mode. I wanted to say, Cut the shit. Get up and go. Just don't yank my chain like your money's actually still in play.

I was in a cranky mood, another crummy night taking its toll, making the hole I was in seem even larger than the money, and leading me to think, in profound ways, about time and existence and what the hell I was doing with my life. I knew one thing: I would never be able to reclaim the hours I'd lost here, hours that could have been spent with my daughter, my wife, my friends, and my work, my real work.

I rarely had these thoughts when I was winning. But during a prolonged downswing like the one I'd been going through, it was all too possible to believe that my assumptions were wrong, that I had merely developed elaborate rationales and constructs surrounding my skill and mastery and level of control over my destiny. Maybe poker was my drug, my way to avoid confronting my inability to truly connect or commit, to live passionately or feel deeply, to be open to hurt and pain.

It was so easy to kid yourself, to not really take a clear-eyed look at who you were, and not just as a poker player. So I had to ask myself…was I living a lie? The Fish Tank had palm prints and dents on its metal door from where guys had whacked or kicked it in anger as they stormed out. Maybe I was more like them than I cared to admit, another guy blaming luck and refusing to look at the harder, bigger truths, the roadblocks I'd put in my own way.

Even when I was winning, my monthly nut kept eating away at the bankroll, putting me always on the brink. Twenty-five hundred on rent. Eight hundred for my studio. Two hundred on various phones. Ninety to Con Ed. Four-eighty to Visa. Six-fifty on health insurance. Quarterly bills from Hannah's preschool. Unexpected expenses like my dad's back rent. I was one epic bad run away from ruin. Was I in the midst of that run now? It wasn't as if I didn't know what one looked like. I'd seen plenty of guys go broke. Typically, the ones who went bust were the ones you'd expect. Guys like Boston Bill or Spaghetti Tony or Spanish Pedro who almost never won. Guys whom every time you saw them they were losing. One K, 2K, 5K, whatever.

Most worked or hustled real jobs to support their habit. Boston Bill sold sports memorabilia; Spaghetti Tony owned a restaurant in Little Italy; Spanish Pedro ran a numbers racket uptown. Still, no matter how much they pulled down on the outside, they could only lose so much before they had to check into the poker hospital. Sometimes they'd be out of action for a few weeks or months until they could recoup.

Sometimes they never made it back. Either they really went belly up or they joined GA or got married or found religion or died. Eventually, you'd hear something about them, but until that happened it might be months before you even noticed they were gone. Somebody said, "I saw Spanish Pedro the other day," and suddenly it was, Oh, yeah, that guy, I'd forgotten all about him, where's he been?

Then there was someone like Joe the Cleaner, who had to sell his two dry-cleaning stores after the other pros and I had—for want of a better phrase—taken him to the cleaners. Dead broke now, Joe still came around just to hang on the rail, hoping that someone would take pity on him, throw him a bone, get tired of looking at his hangdog sorry-assed face. It was money down the drain, but that didn't stop guys from staking him to a couple-three hundred dollars. It was like a tithing. Maybe someday somebody would do the same for them when they were down and out.

Before Joe lost his dry-cleaning stores, I actually tried to set him straight. I took him aside one night and said, "Joe, I'm only telling you this because I like you and it's hurting me to watch. You keep playing with us, you're gonna throw away everything you ever worked for, everything you ever dreamed about. I'm not supposed to say this to you. It's money out of my own pocket. But you need to stop playing with us. You need to find a home game somewhere and gamble for nickels and dimes." It hadn't done him any good or made me feel any better. I wondered now if someone were to take me aside and say the same thing, would I listen?

I knew that playing at these stakes, I'd never build up my bankroll high enough to eliminate broke from the equation. I'd only be able to do that by playing bigger. But I couldn't play bigger unless I built a bigger bankroll and I couldn't build a bigger bankroll unless I played bigger. It was a classic Catch-22. What if my best move, as D.J. said, was to strap it on and take a shot at Eddie's game?

Not that D.J. was necessarily the guy I wanted to go to for advice. I mean, what did he know from kids and wives and being a responsible adult? He went bust it was a minor hassle, not a major crisis.

I tried to picture myself explaining to Laura how I'd lost everything, the thought instantly conjuring an image of my father, alone in his crummy little apartment, everyone who once cared about him gone, except for me.

No. I wasn't going to make the same mistakes he made. That wasn't going to happen. Whatever else he'd done, he'd marked out the roads not to take.

* * *

Thanksgiving came and went and the weather turned cold. The days leading up to Christmas dropped away like the leaves from the trees. In our neighborhood, they strung the brownstones with colorful lights, pasted paper snowflakes to the windows, turned front yards into playpens for plastic Santas and elves.

Real snow fell at the beginning of December, a full-out storm that lasted into the night, speckling the air, dotting the bright halos around the street lamps and turning the sky a ghostly purple. A blanket of white entombed cars and piled up on the sidewalks and stoops. But when the temperature suddenly started rising during the early morning hours, the snow melted away like a dream. By afternoon it was mostly gone save a few small pockmarked little mounds. Hannah wept.

I tried to explain things to her. The laws of physics and all. But I could hear my words. How meaningless they seemed. Laura told me to let her be sad. It wasn't the worst thing. It was how she felt.

* * *

On nights I didn't play, I usually made dinner while Laura got Hannah ready for bed. Particularly now, when I still couldn't face going to my studio, I found myself taking extra pleasure in cooking. It gave me an outlet, a way to use my hands and work with different textures and colors. Not that I was doing anything fancy. On occasion, I got ambitious and made something difficult like paella or coq au vin, but mostly I just cooked good simple food: a roast chicken, pasta marinara, vegetable stir-fry.

Tonight was one of those. I opened the door of the toaster oven. The fragrant sweet potatoes oozed dark bubbly syrup from holes I'd poked with a fork. I flipped the sizzling pork chops and gave the zucchini a stir. On the radio, a writer I'd never heard of reminisced about her days in a Vermont commune smoking pot, taking acid trips and Sufi dancing.

"Do you want to say goodnight to Hannah?" Laura called from the other end of the apartment.

"Be right there." I wiped my hands on a dishtowel and creaked my way over on the old plank floorboards. She was sitting on the edge of Hannah's bed. "Can you keep an eye on things for me in the kitchen?" I asked.

"Sure." She got up.

I knelt down by the side of the bed. "The chops'll be ready in five minutes," I said as she left.

Alone with Hannah, I sang to her and said my goodnight. But when I tried to get up off my knees, she grabbed my sleeve and said, "Just a little bit longer, Mommy—I mean Daddy."

"Sweetie, I can't. Dinner's cooking and I need to deal with it. I'll see you in the morning."

"Please, Daddy, just one more minute?"

"Okay, one minute."

I stayed on my knees by her bed. She rolled onto one shoulder and cheek, touching the tip of her thumb to her lower lip. When sleep came, her breathing slowed to almost nothing. I just stayed there, staring at her, wondering if anyone could look at her and not see the beauty I saw. At last, I got to my feet, my knees aching from the hard floor. "Goodnight, sweetie," I whispered. "I'll see you in the morning." I leaned over and kissed the top of her head.

Back in the kitchen, I hoisted the cast-iron pan and slid the chops onto plates while Laura set out the napkins and silverware. I dished the zucchini and the potatoes. Laura lit a candle. I opened a bottle of white wine. She turned down the lights.

"Are you listening to this?" she asked.

"I was but you can change it if you want. Or turn it off."

"Can you believe this woman smoked pot at the age of ten?"

"Well," I said with a shrug, "she did grow up on a commune."

"Why? How old were you when you first smoked pot?"

"I don't know, eleven or twelve?"

"Really?" Laura looked at me, slightly aghast.

"I ran with a fast crowd."

"You ran with crowds at the age of eleven?"

There was an edge to Laura's voice that made me uneasy.

"Can we turn that thing off and sit down to dinner?"

She changed the channel to music. An old Jackson Browne tune, "Somebody's Baby."

Neither of us spoke as we sat there salting and peppering, pouring wine, buttering our sweet potatoes, cutting into our chops.

"So what are you gonna do when Hannah's eleven or twelve?" Laura asked at last, breaking the silence.

I took a bite of pork and chewed on it for a while, trying to delay my answer, sensing trouble. "What am I going to do?" I looked up and met her eyes.

"I'm afraid that you're going to be overly permissive because of the way you grew up."

I saw where this was going and I didn't like it. "Hannah's not even four, honey. Do we really have to have this conversation now?"

"What's wrong with now?" she said. "Why can't you just say what you're going to do?"

"Because it won't be an issue for seven years?"

She took a sip of wine, dabbing at her mouth with a napkin. "I'd just like to know how you think about it."

"I don't think about it."

"I'm asking you to try."

I stabbed at a zucchini medallion with my fork. "I don't want to argue about things that are years away."

"Why does it have to be an argument?"

"I just feel like we're coming from different places on this."

"You make it sound like it's the distant future," she said, "but it isn't as far off as you think."

"Fine," I said, balling up my napkin. "You want to know my feelings? How I'm gonna be? I'm not going to be a fucking hypocrite. I'm not going to be one of those parents who says one thing but in his own life did another."

"You're going to tell her that it's okay if she takes drugs?"

"We're talking pot here, right?"

"Pot is a drug. And by the way, it's not the same pot you smoked when you were a kid."

"You're right," I said. "It's not. But that's not even the point. Our job is to educate her so that she makes intelligent choices and—"

"You're not answering my question."

"I'm trying. Maybe if you'd listen—"

"I am listening—"

"Fuck, Laura!"

She glared at me as if I'd just slapped her.

"What? I wasn't saying 'fuck you,' I was just saying 'fuck.'"

But it was too late.

She pushed away from the table, leaving her pork chop half-finished.

"Laura, come on. I'm sorry."

Instead of getting up and going after her, I finished eating. I could be stubborn too. And she'd been the one to start the goddamn conversation in the first place.

By the time I cleared the table and did the dishes, she'd turned out the light in the bedroom. I approached her side of the bed and whispered her name, but either she was asleep or more likely pretending to be. I certainly wasn't ready to climb into bed, not with her lying there like a loaded bear trap, so I stayed up for a while, in the middle room, checking my email and surfing the Net. When I started to get sleepy, I stripped down to my underwear, laid my clothes on the windowsill, and got into bed. I reached over and put my hand on her hip, but she rolled away so that her back was to me and we were no longer touching.

The inside of my chest felt tight and airless, a small clenched ball of rage. How could she understand me so little? How?

It didn't matter that I knew she was probably awake and thinking the same thing. She could be just as pigheaded as me. I thought of what other couples said about never going to bed mad. Christ, we went to bed mad all the time. All the fucking time.

* * *

Doyle Brunson wrote in Super/System that if you had a fight at home or were experiencing any other kind of emotional disturbance you should stay away from the poker tables. His blunt advice: "Never play when you're upset."

I prided myself on my ability to control my emotions and compartmentalize my feelings. So trouble at home didn't stop me from going to the club the next night, as usual, the first of what proved to be several questionable moves. In fact, my only good decision was to quit after losing most of my original buy-in of twenty-five hundred.

From behind the desk, Caitlin took one look at me and knew. I handed her three hundred dollars worth of red chips, along with four one-dollar white chips, which I told her to keep.

She counted off three bills and handed them to me.

"Well, that was a supposedly fun thing I'll undoubtedly do again."

"Sorry," Caitlin said. "Tough lineup tonight?"

"It wasn't them, it was me."

"Weren't feeling it?"

"Laura and I had a fight."

"Oh." She squinched up her face. "That sucks. Sorry."

"Yeah." Suddenly I felt like talking. "You know how sometimes afterward, you can't figure out whose fault it was and that makes you feel even worse?" Clearly, she did know. She said, "My shift's over in fifteen minutes. If you want a shoulder to cry on."

I looked at the clock behind her. Eleven forty-five.

Fuck it.

Twenty minutes later, we were sitting in a window booth at the 24-hour diner down the block. There weren't a lot of people near us, which was good, because right after we ordered, I noticed she was crying.

Not sure what to do, I sat there and watched.

"Jesus," she sniffled. "Look at me. This is pathetic." She dabbed at her tears using the neck of her faded green long-sleeved T-shirt, which was at least a size small and showed off the contours of her breasts. "This is so embarrassing."

"Don't worry about it."

"I mean, I'm the one who offered you a shoulder to cry on."

"That's all right. I actually don't need to cry."

She almost smiled. "You'd think I'd know better," she said. "It's not like he gave me any reason to expect things from him."

"D.J."

"You must think I'm an idiot."

"Why would I think that?"

"Crying over someone like him."

She stared down at the tabletop, embarrassed, and her blond hair fell across her sad pretty face. After a moment, she looked up, brushing hair away, moving a saltshaker around the Formica in small circles with one hand. I thought about what Laura said, about me having a little crush on her. Maybe it was true.

"So what'd that asshole do anyway?"

"Do you really think he's an asshole?"

"Let's just say, I wouldn't want to depend on him."

"Isn't he your friend?"

"Not the question."

"We were having such a good time. I don't get it…"

"He's just one of those people. Doesn't mean he's a bad guy."

"What does it mean?"

"I don't know. I wish I could tell you something more useful."

"Like what I should do?"

"Yeah like that."

"What *should* I do?"

I found myself looking at her, this extremely attractive young woman with her wounded eyes. What I wanted to say and what I actually thought I should say were at such opposite ends of the dial that it occurred to me that I probably ought to disqualify myself from saying anything at all. Which is what I did, by shrugging and looking stumped.

Later, after we paid the check, I walked with her to the corner of Sixth Avenue and 28th. It was noisy. Traffic sounds and rushing tires, car headlights everywhere.

"Which way are you?" I asked.

"Uptown. Hell's Kitchen."

"Brooklyn for me."

"Oh. Well."

"I'm taking the subway, though, so it really doesn't matter where I get on. I'll walk you."

"You don't have to do that."

"I know."

We started walking up Sixth and already I was aware that this was no longer what it started out to be. Or maybe it was.

"How long have you lived up here?" I asked.

"A couple of years."

We kept walking. The sidewalks were still populated but not thronged the way they were during the day. Macy's loomed up ahead, its windows still ablaze though the store was closed.

I found myself oddly aware of my body, the awkwardness of talking while walking, as if I'd never walked and talked with anyone else before and had to figure out how you did it, how you looked over at that person and kept your stride without bumping into things.

I asked questions, casually, like I did this all the time, like I wasn't married and out of practice and it wasn't different than when we had a desk between us and a reason for my being near to her.

She had grown up in Buffalo. Gone to SUNY Purchase. Gotten a degree in English and moved to the city to get an advanced degree in lit from NYU, maybe eventually teach.

"What about you?" she asked.

"Where did I grow up?" I didn't know what we were talking about. What I did know was that beneath all this banality lurked desire, a longing for connection. And weirdly, as I thought this, I actually did bump into something, a newspaper box, with the point of my hip. I kept walking, pretending I was okay even though it hurt like hell.

When we reached her apartment building, a desolate glass-door tenement on West 49th Street next to a barbershop, Caitlin turned to me and said, "Well, this is me."

We lingered there in the glow from the light over the doorway. Did I see in her eyes an invitation—or was it just my own desire reflected? I leaned in and she didn't flinch. There was no tell, no signal from her that this was unwanted. No reason to stop. My mouth found hers. Right away it was different from kissing Laura. Caitlin tasted different. Her mouth was wetter. Her tongue was more forceful. With my hand in the small of her back, I pulled her close, gripping her ass with my other hand, pressing her against me, our hips grinding together until it got too heated and she turned away.

"What's wrong?"

She looked at me, blurry and bruised. "I better go."

I kept my hold on her, our eyes locked, unwavering. "I like kissing you." My voice was thick, stupid.

"Yeah, me too."

We started again. Hotter. Heavier.

"Nathan," she said, once more pulling back. "You should leave. Really."

"You're not going to invite me up?"

"I want to, but no."

"Not that I'm saying I'd go."

This drew a laugh. "I've always really liked you."

"I guess it's funny the way things happen, isn't it?"

Another, more wistful laugh. "You should go home, be with your family, get some sleep. That's what you guys always tell me is the move when you're on tilt."

She extracted herself from my arms, opened the glass front door, shot me a parting smile halfway between regret and desire.

82

"Doesn't mean you have to listen," I said as the door swung shut behind her.

I watched her walk down the fluorescent-lit hallway in her long flouncy skirt and ankle boots. She turned a corner toward the stairs and disappeared from view. I stood there a moment, drunk on her kisses, before turning and heading back toward the subway. I was glad no one was around to notice the outward signs of my foolishness: my tented pants, the goofy guilty smile, and the funny way I was walking because of the pain in my hip.

7

The Objective Distance Necessary for Optimal Play

Our apartment was dark and smelled of sleep. I made a beeline for the bathroom, closed the door, turned on the light, and only then took off my jeans so my belt buckle wouldn't rattle and wake anyone.

Reaching into my boxers, I looked at myself in the mirror, then turned away, thinking dirty things about Caitlin. Quietly, I squeezed and rubbed myself until I came, letting out a soft groan, grabbing for some toilet paper.

Slipping into bed, I kissed Laura's shoulder through her silken nightgown. Maybe I'd have felt guiltier if Caitlin had invited me up. If I hadn't had to imagine her naked body. I put my hand on Laura's hip, which was warm and round, pleasingly supple. Sometimes when I was in bed with her, I had to move away because so much heat came off her body.

Tonight, the warmth was tolerable, and I kept my face near the nape of her sweet-smelling neck, with my hand still on her hip. She twitched and quivered slightly as she reentered deep sleep, like a house settling and ticking at night after a day of baking in the sun.

Lying there, I thought again about my strange evening, the stupid fight that had started it, my continuing poker downswing, how it felt to kiss Caitlin. It was possible I had more of my father in me than I wanted to admit.

Maybe I'd always known that and that's why I'd resisted taking the plunge for so long. In poker, getting married to a hand meant that you'd lost the objective distance necessary for optimal play. As I tried to get comfortable next to my sleeping wife, I kept thinking about my father. Had getting married caused him to lose the objective distance necessary for optimal play? Is that why he had fucked up his life so royally? Was I going down the same road? And what about Laura? The idea that she might be in love with someone else was exquisitely painful whatever my own ambivalence. It made me feel vulnerable and pathetic. When I looked coldly and objectively at how I must appear to her, to the world, it was not as a man of strength but as a man of defects, staking my future, our futures on something as uncertain and sketchy as a gambling game. I was not dynamic or interesting as I wished to believe, but a failure and weak. Why would she want someone like me?

And then it was morning, the sky overcast through the large windows that bracketed the bed. Laura seemed not to have changed positions at all throughout the night. She lay in the exact same pose, with her back to me.

I slid out from under the covers and walked stiff-legged to the bathroom. My erection made peeing difficult. The angle was tricky and the stream thin and uneven. After flushing, I confronted my puffy face in the mirror. I looked tired and old, a red crease marking my forehead, my lips noticeably thinner than they used to be. I thought again of Caitlin and remembered a passage out of Celine about how, as you got older, you became uglier and more repulsive, unable to hide your unhappiness. I splashed some warm water on my eyes and cheeks to wash away the crust and the feeling that I'd just walked face-first through a spider web.

The bathroom door swung open while I was still looking at myself. Hannah marched past me, lowered the kiddie toilet seat and plopped herself down. Potty training had finally kicked in now that she was four. It was a brave new world. She was growing up and I was growing older. As if to underline this, she let loose a veritable hissing gusher of pee in contrast to my earlier tortured trickle. Regarding me sleepily, she said, "Excuse me, Daddy, I need my privacy."

I laughed at her sense of privilege. I had been there first, after all.

"It's not funny," she said with a pout.

"I'm leaving, sweetie." I smiled and gave her the privacy she wanted, closing the door behind me.

Laura was wide awake, staring up at the ceiling.

"Good morning."

"I didn't hear you come in last night."

"It was late."

"Does that mean things went badly?"

"Ehh."

Her face clouded, and I instantly regretted my lapse, attempting to undo the damage. "Just a little frustrated," I said. "Treading water again. You know."

"Mmm," she grunted skeptically. "Is treading water just a euphemism for losing?"

"It means I broke even."

She brushed a strand of hair away from her eyes. "Are you taking Hannah to school?"

"I was planning to."

"Because we owe them money."

"Jesus, already? I thought we were paid up."

"The bill's in the living room."

"Ugh."

Tuition for Montessori preschool now stood at over 20K a year. Alternatives were limited. The local public school—which by all reports wasn't the greatest—didn't have pre-K. We'd discussed putting Hannah in daycare, which would have been cheaper, but the advantage of Montessori was that it secured her a spot in kindergarten for the following year if we could figure out a way to keep paying—or get financial assistance.

The problem was, even adding Laura's Groupon earnings to my poker money, the math remained impractical. It didn't help that neither of us wanted to acknowledge how impractical. What I knew was that if we *did* wind up having to pull Hannah out of Montesorri, somehow it would be my fault. I'd be the guy who hadn't figured out a way to take care of his kid. Maybe that's why, after throwing on a T-shirt and a pair of pants, I began disassembling Hannah's toddler bed at seven-thirty in the morning on a school day.

"You're doing that now?" Laura said, standing in the doorway of Hannah's room while combing her hair.

"I got a text from UPS. They're delivering her new bed this afternoon. So it needs to be done."

"My big girl bed?" Hannah said with excitement, coming up behind her mother, traces of toothpaste at the corners of her mouth. She saw her old crib mattress leaning against the wall and went over to it, knelt down, hugged it and began weeping. I looked at her and then at Laura, wanting to cry, myself. I was thinking not only about how quickly Hannah was growing up but also how quickly things could change.

Through her tears, Hannah said, "Do we have to give it away, Daddy?"

I still had the screwdriver in my hand. "We don't have room to keep it, sweetie."

"It isn't fair."

"I understand. It's hard making changes."

At school, we forded the usual noisy crush of kids and their grownups. I nodded at familiar faces, trying and mostly failing to remember names, ashamed that, aside from footing the bills, I wasn't more involved in this world that was at the center of my daughter's life. It was easy to recognize the Wall Street dads. They were the ones in pinstripe suits and power ties who looked like they'd been awake for hours. Me being a painter didn't impress them much, but playing poker for a living? That was sexy. I wondered if they'd still think I was cool if they knew how close to the edge I was. Hell, maybe they'd think that was even cooler.

On the way to the bursar's office, I bumped into the mother of one of Hannah's classmates, who asked me if Laura had mentioned anything about my donating a painting to the annual art auction.

"Not a word."

"Do you think you could? It's for a good cause."

"Yeah, okay, sure."

"Thank you!"

Cathy in the business office, who took my check, proffered no such gratitude, oblivious to the physical pain it caused me to hand it over.

* * *

When I got back home, I found Laura in the kitchen slicing an avocado to go along with two poached eggs.

"That was quick," she said. "I'm sorry. I would have made some for you."

"That's okay." I opened the refrigerator and poked around.

"Do you want half of mine?"

"Nah, but thanks for offering." I decided to have the same thing I gave Hannah, almond milk and granola. "You told one of the parents that I'd donate a painting to the auction?"

"Oh, yeah, Nina. Did you see her? I hope you're okay with that."

"Just took me a little by surprise."

"I'm sorry. I should have mentioned it."

I poured the almond milk on the cereal and put the box back in the fridge.

"So what's your plan?" she asked.

"My plan?" The way she said it felt like a test.

"For the day."

"I was thinking I'd head over to my studio. How about you?"

"Find someplace to set up my laptop."

"Why not stay here?"

"I feel like getting out."

I spooned some granola into my mouth, wondering if she was telling me the truth. Not that I occupied the high ground in that department, especially after last night. There was so much we weren't telling each other. As if we didn't know how. Or where to begin. The thing about us was that we'd always talked easily. Maybe we didn't open up veins or bleed on a regular basis, but we actually liked *conversing*. Sure, she tired of my sometimes-extended political rants, my obsession with poker. Just like her literary-world gossip bored me. We weren't always in sync, but who was? The point is we were compatible. We got along. We generally agreed on what was important, what was beautiful, what was funny, what was sad. Yet I had my doubts, especially lately, that these things were enough. Sometimes I felt as if we were just skating across the surface, everything important and meaningful trapped below the ice. And the longer things went on this way, the more impenetrable and thicker the ice became.

It was easy to point to my doomed show as the place where the chill began, even if deep down I knew the conditions were there from the start. I'd hoped that having a child would give us courage, help push us into the uncomfortable spaces we instinctively avoided. But that hadn't really happened. If anything, Hannah served as a buffer, something to focus on that wasn't us.

Meanwhile I was turning into one of those guys you sometimes hear about, who loses his job but continues to don a suit and head off to work each morning as if nothing were wrong. Except instead of a suit, I wore a T-shirt and jeans, and instead of losing my job, I'd simply lost my way.

Judging by the number of similarly attired slackers hiding behind computer screens and lattes in cafes around Brooklyn, I wasn't alone. Which is not to say that all my time in the wilderness had been misspent or wasted. I'd read ten books in two months, mostly novels. I'd gone to Gagosian, Matthew Marks, the Met, the Whitney, Asian and noir film festivals at BAM and Landmark Sunshine. But on the flip side, I'd also become embroiled in pointless comment wars on *The Huffington Post* and a blog devoted to pro football, getting as worked up over the Jets' chances in the upcoming season as about income inequality and climate change. In a weird dislocating way, everything seemed to carry the same weight—Facebook feeds that juxtaposed someone's vacation in Boca with an earthquake in Haiti, or a celebrity's plastic surgery with mass rape in Congo.

I worried constantly about how to make this crazy world a better place for Hannah, but I couldn't even seem to get a handle on my own small problems. Years from now when my daughter asked me why I stopped painting, why her mother and I couldn't make a go of it, what would I tell her? Would I be like the deluded Willy Loman—"I am not a dime a dozen!" Or Brando—"I coulda been somebody..."—blaming bad luck and timing for how things went, the standard fallback for a gambler? Or would I just blame the world's insanity and my failure to adapt?

The truth is it *had* snowed on the night of my opening; the economy *had* sucked; a couple of collectors who had bought pieces of mine in the past *had* lost most of their money to Bernie Madoff; Richard's assistant *had* checked into a psychiatric ward the day he was supposed to take care of the mailings and publicity.

But was that really why nothing sold? Or was it just that the paintings sucked? That I had failed to make sense of what I was seeing or, as Pollock put it, "paint the truth of my life." Was that going to be the history? The one I told my daughter? And when the time did come for telling her, would I mention the part where I got drunk at the sparsely attended post-opening dinner and told Richard that next time, instead of jetting off to St. Lucia with some bimbo while his assistant went mental, maybe he should actually do something to help promote me? Would I admit that my public tirade might have been a factor in why Richard hadn't given me another show or even talked to me since?

Laura turned on the water in the kitchen sink and rinsed off her plate. "Are you going to be home tonight or are you playing?"

"Working."

"Working," she said. "Right."

She wiped her hands on a dishtowel then made her way toward the bedroom. I followed, watching as she picked up her tan knapsack, slung it over one shoulder and did a quick appraisal of herself in the mirror above the dresser, turning to assess herself in profile.

"Hey," I said, going over to her, pulling her towards me and laying a kiss on her like I meant it.

But she just waited for it to end, and said, "No offense, sweetie, but I'm, uh, already kind of in my work head. Also, you should brush your teeth."

I pretended to be unfazed by the rebuff, but after she left, I actually did brush my teeth and swish around some mouthwash for good measure. I gathered up my stuff: my old Dell laptop, a sketchbook, a pair of Ray-Bans, my pencils, and headed off to my usual barista encampment. But halfway there, I changed my mind. It wasn't just Laura. I was disgusted with myself. I couldn't bear the thought of another day in my self-imposed limbo. If I didn't use my hands or make something soon, I was pretty certain I'd lose my mind.

My studio was on the third floor of a warehouse down by the Gowanus Canal. I creaked my way up the steep wooden stairs, inhaling the familiar smell of oil paint and roach poison, trying to ignore the knot in my stomach. Opening the door, I was greeted by a flood of sunlight across a gray concrete floor that was dotted and encrusted with paint. The pieces from my ill-fated show lined one wall. A couple of unfinished canvases leaned against another. I took it as a positive sign that upon seeing the new work I didn't instantly want to throw up.

One, in particular, held my attention. It was large, five by six feet, dominated by a bald guy in a T-shirt and khakis, who could easily have been me, holding a cell phone, standing in the middle of a jungle. The light of the phone illuminated his face. He looked at the electronic device the way you might look at an apple you were thinking of eating. The paint was thick and textured and the palette was almost the opposite of the muted colors of the older work.

I went about setting up my paints and brushes. I hooked up my computer to the boom box. For a long time, I just stood there, trying to find my place, looking for a way back in. Gradually, I began to see a point of re-entry. I picked up a brush and as soon as I did, blood started to pump through my body. I found myself thinking about Fast Eddie Felson at the end of *Color of Money* when he's just about to crack open a new rack and young Vincent challenges him, saying, "Yeah? What makes you so sure?"

Unlike Fast Eddie, I didn't say it aloud, but I felt it. *Hey, I'm back.*

* * *

The elevator doors opened on the sixth floor. Before I could brace myself, three Airedales the size of goats tore out of an open door, coming right at me. One slithered through my legs, but the other two jumped up, yapping, drooling and raking my chest with their sharp-quilled paws while I tried to fend them off.

Richard watched from the mouth of the doorway down the hall.

"Jesus, man, call 'em off," I said, laughing.

He affected a stern I-am-master-of-the-dogs look, then whistled through his teeth, loud and shrill, but without apparent effect.

"What the fuck," I said as I paddled my way past them.

"Come on, Nate," Richard said, ushering me into his apartment. "Don't be such a pussy. They're just being friendly."

He was wearing a straw weave hat that looked like something Huck Finn would have worn rafting down the Mississippi. I noticed now that I was closer that he was sporting a black eye and an ugly gash on his cheekbone. "What the hell happened to you?"

He loosed a throaty sound of disgust. "Fuckin' Kimora."

"She did that?"

"With the stiletto heel of her fuckin' shoe."

I tried not to laugh.

"Psycho bitch," Richard said with a dismissive wave. "I'm done with her."

"I've heard that before."

"Hey, you and Laura broke up plenty of times."

This was true. But Laura had never fucked a bellhop under my nose or assaulted me with a Jimmy Choo.

Richard caught my look. "She pulled some shit on you. Don't pretend she didn't." He led me into the open kitchen area of the apartment. There was a Viking, a Sub-Zero and a wooden island with expensive-looking stools surrounding it. I took a seat at one of them, while Richard opened the refrigerator door.

If it weren't for the dog-hair-covered cushions strewn around the floor, the half-empty cans of dog food on the counter, the dirty dishes in the sink and the gamy overripe pet-shop smell, Richard's apartment would have been the model of a successful guy's bachelor pad.

Unfortunately, the apartment was a pretty fair representation of Richard himself. On the surface, he had it going on: He was handsome, ran a successful gallery, had a house in the country and liked dogs. Look a little closer and the cracks were visible: scraggly Van Gogh beard, wild bushy eyebrows, crooked teeth, odd twitches of the mouth and left eye, and a tendency to drink and eat to excess.

We'd met ten summers before during a residency at Yaddo. He'd primarily been a painter then and a pretty good one. The two of us had chased after the same woman during our month there, a beautiful young poet named Celine Hardaway, who was amused by our pursuit but kept us at arm's length. By the time she ultimately hooked up with a woman sculptor, Richard and I had bonded over our laughable and futile rivalry.

We had a number of other things in common, including our badly-behaved fathers and our ambitions. Ten years later, Richard still liked to think of himself as an artist, but he had channeled most of his creative energy into starting an art-moving business and a gallery. Though the art-star dreams still nagged, the gallery, in particular, seemed to suit him, making use of his painterly eye and his need to curate and collect. The only thing really stopping him from becoming the next Gagosian or Castelli was impetuosity and excess. Whether it was food or drink or drugs or women—even art, for that matter—Richard never knew when to stop, when enough was enough.

And though he was not totally blind to that part of himself, he was still somehow puzzled when it led him toward fatness, drunkenness, pissed off girlfriends and overdrawn bank accounts. In many ways, he was no different than the dogs he loved so much. He had virtually no sense of time or responsibility, no sense of proportion or any real ability to empathize with others' needs. Though he was sloppy in his show of affection for his artists, throwing them big expensive parties and sticking with them through lean times, he was careless about their basic requirements, such as getting paid on time so they could keep up with necessities like rent and food.

"I think a celebration is in order," he said, reaching into the refrigerator for a bottle of Cristal.

I laughed and shook my head. "I haven't eaten today."

"Come on. To mark your reemergence amongst the living."

"And all this time I thought you were the one who'd died."

He untwisted the wire hood from the bottle. "I would have gotten in touch, Nate. I figured you needed your space after what happened."

"Yeah. Whatever."

Ignoring my demur, he grabbed a couple of flutes from a cabinet, then popped the Cristal cork, which thwacked off the ceiling and bounced along the kitchen floor. He tilted a flute and filled it.

"None for me," I said. "Seriously."

"Come on, man. We're making up here."

I moved my head side to side, feeling the by-now-familiar little crackling pops along my neck. "Fine. Fuck it."

He poured the second flute and handed it to me. "We've known each other too long to hold grudges." He clinked my glass and we drank. "But just for the record? You really did act like a prima donna."

I almost spit my mouthful of champagne. "Are you fucking kidding me? You want to get into this? Because we can."

"Easy, easy." Richard held up his hand. "Jeez, you're so touchy."

I took a breath, reminding myself why I was there.

Lifting my glass again, and with as much affection as I could muster, I said, "Okay, how's this? Go fuck yourself."

Richard laughed loudly, for which I was grateful. Even at his worst, he was usually able to laugh at himself.

"So that email I got saying you weren't going to be able to store my work much longer?"

"I shouldn't have sent that," he said. He poured himself more champagne and topped off my glass. "Look, we're here now, that's the important thing."

"We're here now," I agreed, not wanting to appear too eager to discuss business. "And I'm sorry to hear about you and Kimora."

"Who knows? Maybe it's for the best. Sometimes I think she's not a very nice person. She certainly doesn't have any maternal instincts."

"I didn't know that was a priority for you."

The corner of Richard's mouth twitched. "And she's fucking selfish. I was in bed with a fever last week and I asked her to walk my dogs. You know what she said?"

I shook my head, waiting for the punchline.

"She told me to hire a dog walker." He barked out a quick laugh. "Can you believe that? A dog walker! Man, I really know how to pick 'em."

"Maybe you ought to find someone who'll take care of you instead of one of these chicks who needs a daddy."

"Is that how girls see me?"

"You didn't know that?"

He pulled out his phone. "Shit, I've gotta go take care of something at the gallery," he said. "You mind walking me over? We can talk on the way."

Back when I first agreed to let Richard handle my work, the mingling of business and friendship wasn't a major issue. But he had a knack for blurring the lines. If I were more successful, I definitely wouldn't have put up with it. But I needed him more than he needed me, so the balance was out of whack. The truth was he liked holding power over me. Maybe it lessened the sting of watching me continue to make art while he turned his focus to business.

"What about you and Laura?" he asked as we rode the elevator down to the lobby. "You guys doing okay?"

I nodded, not wanting to get into it.

Outside, we walked up Tenth Avenue, past a storefront gallery, a parking garage, a cuchifrito joint, and an auto stereo store. It was a neighborhood in that awkward stage of transition where the contrast between the old and the new lent it the Frankenstein look of random body parts sewn together. We turned the corner onto 25th and the long row of galleries there.

"So what about it, Richard?"

"What about what?"

I waggled my hand between us. "Me. You. The gallery."

He laughed awkwardly. "Things are tricky right now. Finn and I aren't seeing eye to eye." Finn was Finn Begstein, Richard's gallery director, who had discovered Polly Lymarin, among others, and was now, according to Richard, swinging his dick around. "He's threatening to leave and take all my artists with him if I don't make him an equal partner."

"Not all. I'll stay with you."

Richard smiled weakly. "I'm kind of over a barrel."

"It's your gallery, for Chrissakes."

"Tell that to him."

"So where does that leave me?" I stepped around an unscooped pile of dog shit, half wondering if Richard was the scofflaw.

"The best I can do right now is bring a piece or two of yours to one of the art fairs. Here or in Miami. If we can sell something, that'll give me some leverage."

"You can't give me a show? It doesn't have to be a solo."

"I definitely want to see what you're working on, but I can't promise anything at this point."

"Because of Finn."

"He's taking a bottom-line approach to things."

"So I'm fucked."

"I'm just saying it's just tricky right now."

"Meaning I should start looking for a new gallery?"

"No one's saying that."

We arrived at the glass door to the Genome. Inside, lining the walls, were large canvasses of ordinary pastoral landscapes invaded by flying saucers.

"Come on in, hang out a while."

"I can't," I muttered. "But thanks. You know, for the champagne and everything."

"Hey," Richard said, cuffing my shoulder. "We'll figure this out. It just might take a bit of time. I'm glad we were able to clear the air a bit."

"Yeah," I whispered.

* * *

I wandered downtown along 10th Avenue. At 20th Street, I climbed the stairs up to the High Line. I'd only been on it once before, with Laura and Hannah on a beautiful spring afternoon when the air was warmer and lighter. I remembered carrying Hannah on my shoulders, solid planks underfoot, feeling the heat of the sun on my face, appreciating the beauty of the city from that vantage point—Jersey across the river, high blue sky, shadowy clouds, leafy trees and buildings near and far, some windows so close you could look in, and the Hudson right there, nearly close enough to touch. The parade of people, foreigners, locals, children, adults, everybody seemingly in a good mood...

I stopped and sat on a bench, looking out across the river between buildings. Maybe I needed to rethink everything. Marriage, art, poker. My whole damned life.

I could start from scratch. Just blow the whole thing up like my dad did. But with more intentionality. Like, on purpose.

How would that be? To scorch the earth. Leave nothing standing. Deal a new hand. More than a new hand. Totally new game. What would that be like? Could I even imagine? Did I have that big an imagination?

I watched a beautiful red tug push a barge south toward Brooklyn. I could be a tugboat captain. Spend all my time on the water, be my own boss just like now except with a salary, nobody running me or telling me what to do. Who was going to fuck with a tugboat captain? *I'm the goddamn captain*, I said, maybe aloud, the boat going blurry as my fantasy carried me along...then coming back into focus, vibrantly red against the leaden blue of the river.

Did I have the balls to rethink myself, recast my idea of who that self was? For a moment, I felt the possibility, and the weight eased up.

* * *

I found Laura lying crossways on our bed, staring at the ceiling. She didn't look at me or move.

"You okay?"

"I was spinning my wheels staring at the computer screen, so I came home. I didn't sleep very well last night."

"Me either."

She took a deep breath, turning to her side, facing me now.

"Is it just that you didn't sleep?" I asked.

She shrugged, picking up the clock from the end table to get a closer look. "How about you? Why are you home?"

"I went to see Richard."

"After all this time."

"Yep, after all this time."

"And?"

"And nothing. He…" I spit out a laugh. "Maybe he'll be able to squeeze me in a couple of years from now if things break right."

"Is that what he said?"

"It's what it felt like."

I noticed that Laura's eyes were red around the rims.

"What's going on? Seriously. Are you okay?"

She looked at me without saying anything.

"Have you been crying?"

She shook her head, then buried her face in the comforter.

I sat down on the edge of the bed, put my hand on her back. "Laura?"

"I'm pregnant," she whispered without looking at me.

8

A Bunch of Sleep-Deprived Degenerates

The fact that we'd had sex just twice in the last two months made Laura's disclosure feel like one of those good-news bad-news jokes. Except I'm not sure what aspect of it actually qualified as good news. She must have sensed me doing the calculations, factoring in my procreative shortcomings. "I think it was that night we stayed home and you made those fish tacos from that *Times* recipe."

I nodded. At least she remembered, too.

I leaned closer, pressing my unshaven cheek against her neck, holding her awkwardly. Her hair had a sharp animal smell.

"Do you have anything to say about this?" she asked. "Any reaction at all?"

"Give me a chance. God. I mean don't you think it's incredible that the one night we had sex—"

"You're saying this qualifies as a bad beat?"

"That's not what I'm saying."

She looked at me in anger, but then her lips and chin began to tremble and I realized she was near tears. "What are we going to do, Nate?"

I took a moment, fighting back the impulse to laugh. "I guess we're going to have another baby."

* * *

In the last few days leading up to Christmas, I spent money recklessly, wantonly, buying Laura a necklace for $600, a silk top for $200, a cashmere throw for $350, four new hardcover novels, a digital camera. I spent $200 on stocking stuffers. An American Girl doll for Hannah cost another $100, the outfits and accessories another two bills on top of that. I dropped another couple of hundred sending gifts to my mother and my sister. I got Dad an expensive bottle of single malt.

Sitting on a crowded subway with shopping bags full of expensive crap, I remembered my mother trying to soften the blow of Dad's arrest by buying me and my sister a Christmas tree, something that Dad, who was in no way religious, had always refused us on religious grounds. But with him in jail and unable to object, Mom paid a guy from a stand down the block forty bucks to haul a five-foot dried-out Norwegian spruce up our four flights of stairs. For weeks, I breathed in the piney aroma of that tree and looked at its fat triangle of lights in our darkened living room, getting a small thrill of guilty pleasure from knowing that it was my father's absence that made the tree possible.

* * *

The day after Christmas, I was awakened by what sounded like the buzzing of a bee or someone playing the comb in a jug band. I squinted at my wristwatch through sleep-swollen eyes, feeling a throbbing in my sinuses. Seven-thirty. Laura was still asleep next to me, her body wrapped in the comforter, which she had wrestled away from me sometime during the night. In sleep, she was like a lustrous apparition, an otherworldly goddess. I remembered how in our first days I looked at her in the morning and felt as dumbfounded as if I'd woken up next to Angelina Jolie or a young Audrey Hepburn. That was how beautiful she was and how unlikely it seemed that she would let me have sex with her.

In life, some people are dealt better starting hands than others. Laura was dealt two aces: smart, beautiful and talented—oh, wait, that's three aces. But ask her and she'd tell you that her aces felt like deuces. It didn't matter how the world perceived her. Deuces was how she saw herself. More than once it occurred to me that I'd been the beneficiary of her warped perception, that if she'd really known the value of her hand, she'd have aimed higher. But maybe that was me, selling my own hand short.

The vibrating buzz again. I got out of bed and staggered to the window, where my pants were draped on top of the wooden radiator cover. Out the window, the morning already had the cold gray-white gloom of a coming storm. I dug my phone out of the pants pocket. The face of it was lit, a line of text:

"You need to get over here."

It was D.J.

"Where?" I typed back. "Why?"

I opened Hannah's door a crack and peered in. To my surprise, she was still sound asleep, her hands stretched straight up over her head in a pose of utter surrender. I wondered if I'd ever slept that way, that free and unburdened and open to the world. She was still so near to being a baby. I feared losing that. Yet now here we were about to go through it all over again with a different child. What if my relationship with Hannah changed?

The phone began vibrating again. A call this time.

I made my way quickly to the other end of the apartment and into the kitchen before answering.

"Yo."

"Dude, you've gotta get your ass over here." In the background, I could hear poker chips and voices.

"Do you have any idea what time it is?"

"This might be the greatest game in New York poker history. It's been going since yesterday."

Despite the early hour and the intrusion, I felt my pulse pick up.

"That's what you say about every game I'm not at."

"This is different," D.J. said, "You need to get over here."

"You sick fucks actually started playing on Christmas?"

"It's all Jews and atheists. Russian Eddie is throwing a party. He's stuck sixty. Lenny Garfinkle is in for thirty. Fonzie and Little Moishe are here. There must be a hundred and fifty on the table."

"In a five-ten?"

"Started out five-ten, then went to ten and a quarter. Now it's quarter-fifty."

"Fuck. And you're playing too?"

"Of course I'm playing."

"That's fucking huge."

"I'm in for twenty. I got twenty-five in front of me."

I let out a whistle. "Holy shit."

"I'm telling you. I wouldn't be a friend if I let you miss out on this."

"D.J., it's not that I don't appreciate you thinking of me, but I can't."

"Why the fuck not?"

"For starters, it's seven-thirty in the morning, I'm with my family and it's Saturday morning, the day after Christmas."

"What do you care? You're a Jew."

"Who married a shiksa."

"Tell her you've got a business opportunity. This is your business, dude."

"Do you have any idea what a disaster it would be if my bankroll took a major hit?"

"I'm trying to do you a solid here. I'm not going to twist your arm."

"I appreciate the thought," I said, pressing the red end-call button.

After breakfast, Laura and I did a bit of housekeeping, bagging up the ripped and torn wrapping paper and breaking down gift boxes while Hannah played with her new American Girl doll.

"Do we have a plan for the rest of the day?"

"I dunno. What do you want to do?" I asked disingenuously. Fucking D.J. and his game. It was like a mosquito buzzing in my ear.

I'd need fifteen thousand at a minimum—especially if guys were already sitting behind twenty and thirty. Even with that, which would be most of what I had, I'd be undercapitalized. I knew what you called it when you went into a game that way—you called it taking a shot.

Or stupidity.

It was what my father had done countless times. It was what gamblers did.

"Nate!"

"What?"

"I just asked you a question. Did you not hear me?"

"Yeah. No. I'm sorry. What?"

"I said, do you want to take Hannah to a movie?"

"Oh. Yeah. Sure."

There was a 12:30 showing of *Rango* at the Cobble Hill Cinema. We loaded up on water and snacks from the deli across the street, using Laura's canvas tote to smuggle them in. At the ticket window, I turned to her, putting on an expression of queasy uncertainty. "What if...I didn't go with you guys?"

"What?"

"I just got a text from D.J. There's an incredibly juicy game going on."

"Right now?"

"Since last night." I studied her reaction to see if she understood the significance. It was clear she didn't. "The point is," I went on, "I'll be coming in fresh against a bunch of sleep-deprived degenerates."

Laura returned a watered-down facsimile of my hopeful smile. "Sounds delightful."

"It's…" I thought of D.J.'s expression, "a business opportunity."

"Right," she said in a flat, unimpressed tone. She put out a hand. It was clear I was to deposit money in it for their tickets.

I peeled off a couple of twenties from my roll and handed them to her.

"Thanks for understanding," I said.

"Yeah," she said. "Sure."

I kissed her, then bent to kiss Hannah. "Bye bunny rabbit. You can tell me all about the movie later."

* * *

Back at the apartment, I counted my reserve bankroll. It was made up almost entirely of $100 bills. There were two hundred and eighteen of them, along with forty-eight $20s, for a total of $22,780. I counted off a hundred and fifty of the $100 bills, secured them with a rubber band, and put the rest back in a hollowed-out hardcover copy of *The Carpetbaggers*. My heart pounded. This was nuts. It was irresponsible.

Fuck it. I opened the book back up and grabbed the remainder of the hundreds, adding them to my roll. There was no point in playing scared. You either went for it or you didn't. As I stuffed the huge roll in my pocket, I was seized by an over-the-cliff sense of exhilaration.

And in that moment, I almost felt as if I'd already won.

9

The World I'm Waking Up To

A single crowded table lit up like a stage at the back of the club. I made my way past the darkened rows of empty tables, all jittery and buzzed. D.J. nodded and a couple of others acknowledged me, though no one said anything. A hand was underway, a mess of green and black chips scattered in the center of the felt. Little Moishe, a harried-looking Orthodox Jew, had a stack of twenty-five black hundred-dollar chips pushed out in front of his cards. His opponent, a sweet-faced nebbish known as Jersey Joe, shifted his gaze between Moishe and the board, an unrevealing assortment of five random cards. I quickly calculated about thirty-five hundred in the pot, not counting Little Moishe's unanswered bet.

"You want a call?" Joe asked.

"Depends on vot you have," Little Moishe said.

"I got shit, as usual. I'm just thinking it might be better than your shit."

"In dot case, if I vere in your shoes, I'd probably raise."

"Maybe I should," Joe said.

It was impressive, given the amounts of money involved and the fact that they'd been up all night, that Moishe and Joe were still able to banter.

Another minute passed. "What the fuck," Joe said finally, counting out twenty-five hundred. "It's only money." He pushed out the call.

Little Moishe sighed. "You're good. I've got only an ace." There was no ace on board, so he meant he only had ace-high.

"Ace what?" Joe asked.

Suddenly hopeful, Little Moishe said, "Ace-ten."

Joe took another look at his hand. After a moment that perhaps stretched out too long, he flipped over ace-queen.

Little Moishe was incensed. "Vot da fuck vas dat? You tryna to slow roll me?"

"I had to look."

"Unbelievable. You sonovabitch. How da fock you make dot call?"

Jersey Joe shrugged, trying not to smile as he raked in and stacked the massive pile of chips. D.J. caught my eye, as if to say, *You see what's going on here? Why I called you?*

The dealer scrambled the cards, then scraped them together for another shuffle.

Mike K., an ex-boxer and one of the owners of the Lucky Seven, nodded in my direction. "You come to kibitz or play?"

"Can't I do both?"

"This is a little out of your league, Nathan, isn't it?" Lenny Garfinkle said.

"Why do you say that?"

Lenny was in his fifties and retired. He'd made a fortune in the medical-supply business and played poker strictly for entertainment. When he lost, which was most of the time, he still managed to project an attitude that in the game of life he was so far ahead of you that your little victory against him at cards barely counted.

"It just seems to me like you could get hurt," Lenny said.

"I'm touched that you care, Lenny."

"Who says I care?" Lenny laughed. He looked like a suburban country-club swell with his full head of white hair and bright red V-neck sweater over a starched white shirt and khakis.

I took the empty seat at the table between Mike K. and Fonzie.

The dealer, a long-haired kid called Stevie Drummer, said, "How much you behind?"

I looked at the stacks. D.J. hadn't been lying. There was easily a hundred and fifty thousand on the table. "Ten thousand," I said.

"Chips!" Stevie yelled across the floor to the guy behind the desk.

"Gimme your money, I'll take it up," Mike K. said, rising from his seat.

I counted out the ten grand from my roll and handed it to him. It was a slightly sick feeling, seeing my roll nearly halved like that. Mike K. headed off toward the desk.

Stevie dealt to all the stacks including my nonexistent one. The action folded around to me on the cutoff. I picked up my cards by one corner, lifting them only high enough to get a peek, cupping them with both hands. King-queen suited. My heart pumped. I hadn't really wanted to get a playable hand so quickly, but what the fuck could you do?

"Raise," I said. "One and a quarter."

"Comes right out firing," Russian Eddie said.

It folded around to Lenny Garfinkle on the big blind.

He looked at his cards and tossed out three black and two green chips, a reraise to $350.

I felt as if Lenny was trying to test me right off the bat. Obviously, I couldn't fold. I had a decently strong hand, plus position. But already

I was being made to grapple with the size of the stakes. Could I play my regular game or would I be too intimidated? Should I make a statement out of the gate, raise back, make it clear I wasn't going to be bullied.

Lenny was a pure psycho, though. If I sent in a four-bet, Lenny was capable of firing right back at me with nothing just because it would give him a thrill—and then I'd have to fold because I wasn't going to Defcon Four with just king high. Calling was the prudent play.

"Here, this'll make it easier," Fonzie said. "Until your chips come." He slid me nine pink $1,000 chips and ten black $100s.

"Thanks, Fonz." I threw four of my newly acquired black chips in the pot and received $50 in change.

Stevie pulled in the chips, extracting a couple for the house cut, then burned a card and spread the flop. King, queen, deuce, with two hearts.

I tried not to betray anything, but I could feel my heart banging away under my flimsy blue T-shirt. I'd flopped a monster. Adding to my excitement, Lenny led out right away for $500.

I took a moment to consider. It was perfectly reasonable to assume that Lenny was just making a standard continuation bet, trying to take down the pot with nothing. If that was the case and I raised, Lenny would undoubtedly fold. The other possibility was that he had a real hand like ace-king, even aces. Either that or he had a straight draw or flush draw or some combination of the two. There was one other possibility: he'd flopped a set of deuces or (less likely given my hand) a set of queens or kings.

All these thoughts ran through my mind in speeded-up time as I tried to decide on the correct play. Calling made the most sense, because apart from the flush and straight draws, the only turn cards I was really afraid of were an ace or a deuce. I was almost certainly ahead at this point and if I raised and Lenny folded, I was losing value by denying Lenny the chance to fire another bullet on the turn. On the other hand, if I raised, it would allow Lenny to make a mistake with a worse hand. In the end, that was what swung the balance: Lenny's propensity for overplaying hands and making ill-advised bluffs.

"Raise," I said as if slightly annoyed. "Eighteen hundred."

Before I could even put my chips out, Lenny said, "All in."

The speed and decisiveness of his declaration, in combination with his smug little smile, threw me. This was exactly what I had hoped would happen, but now that it had, a speck of doubt entered my mind. I glanced down at my chips. I was almost certainly going to call the bet, but I wanted to slow down and think things through. I had eight thousand left, after all. Eight thousand real dollars that could purchase food and pay rent and tuition. Lenny couldn't possibly have a set, could he?

No, as far as I was concerned, he either had aces, ace-king or a flush and/or straight draw. That or he was just pushing an out-and-out kamikaze bluff. But even Lenny wasn't that sick, was he? Either way...

"I call," I said. But before the dealer could deal the final two cards, I stopped him. "Are we doing anything?"

It was common in big hands like this to do business after all the money went in, to spread out the risk a bit by dealing the final cards more than once, each outcome settling a third or a half of the pot, depending on what the players agreed to. I was always amenable to business as a way to spread out the risk.

Unfortunately, Lenny wasn't. The more pain he could inflict on you the better. "Deal it once," he said.

"You sure you don't want to run it a couple of times?" I said, perhaps a bit more plaintively than intended. I had a sudden and overwhelming sense of dread.

"Once," Lenny instructed the dealer.

Stevie Drummer burned and turned a four and I felt the beginnings of relief. I watched as Stevie paused dramatically before he burned and turned the river. And boom there it was, the one card I didn't want to see—a miserable rat-fucking ace. Lenny immediately turned over his hand, an ace and a king, just as I'd thought.

It was like a freak accident, a finger lost in a paper shredder, a knife dropped on a barefoot. I stared at that ace, trying to take it in and absorb it. Then searing pain and I wanted to scream.

Mike K. arrived back at the table while Lenny was still stacking. "Ten thousand," he said, handing me a rack with ten pink chips in it.

"Actually, you can give them to me," Fonzie said.

"You're kidding," Mike K. said.

"Unfortunately, he isn't," I said.

"First hand?"

I nodded with a feeble laugh.

"Should I go back to the desk?"

Good question. Losing ten gees the first hand was about as clear a sign to quit and go home as you could get. I still had $12K left in my roll. If I took off a couple of days to lick my wounds and get over my momentary lapse of sanity, that would be sufficient capital to go back to grinding the $5-$10 game. The only requirement was for me to swallow my pride right now in front of these assholes.

"Give me ten more," I heard myself saying.

"Ten more it is," Mike K. said, heading back to the front desk.

And that was how it happened. That was how you went over the cliff.

* * *

The funny thing was, down to my case money, my luck started to turn. It didn't happen right away. At first, it was just a few small pots. Then in a hand against D.J. of all people, I hit a five-outer, catching two pair on the river to beat D.J.'s overpair. When I counted my stack afterward,

I was up to fifteen thousand eight hundred fifty, and the knot in my stomach began to loosen a bit. It was amazing how a little love from the poker gods could change your outlook.

Russian Eddie, as advertised, was in some kind of desperate death spiral, raising and reraising indiscriminately. I watched him put several horrific beats on people, the kind that filled those of us not involved with a kind of sick glee because we knew it could just as easily have been at our expense.

Eddie was a curiosity. Mid-thirties, handsome but not chiseled, more the slightly doughy best friend of the leading man, with soft blue eyes, full lips and a smile that had been lasered white, he was a bit of a playboy, yet also oddly self-deprecating and insecure. At poker, he seemed resigned to losing and at the same time faintly resentful of it, as if a bargain had been struck between him and Lady Luck, then canceled without his consent. No one knew what he did for work, yet his funds appeared inexhaustible. He frequently disappeared for stretches of time, during which photos of him ziplining, scuba diving and hiking in exotic locations appeared on his Facebook timeline. Even if on a particular night he went broke, which happened with regularity, the next night or the night after he was back in action, his roll mysteriously replenished. Even on those rare occasions when Eddie grew morose losing, I never felt the weight of having caused him true pain the way I did with some of the other fish.

As the hours passed, the club began filling up. By five in the afternoon, there was action at almost every table, chips clicking and the feverish buzz of eighty voices in an enclosed space. By seven, I'd actually managed to climb out of my hole, all the way up to $25K, putting me in the black.

Sometimes the best move after a long fight back to even or slightly above was to call it a day. I'd noticed that when I continued playing after digging out, I had a tendency to drop down again. Maybe it was a coincidence, maybe it was a letdown; whatever it was, I'd seen it happen often enough that I'd begun forcing myself to go home when it happened. In this case, I wouldn't have been leaving even, I'd have been leaving up five grand, which was nothing to sneeze at. But I kept looking at Russian Eddie and his monster stack and thinking, *Isn't this why I took a shot in the first place? Not just to book a win, but to try and change my circumstances?*

So I stayed, biding my time, waiting for the moment. My stack went up a little, then down, then up again. Some of the players from the smaller games drifted over to watch, including the kid Max, who hovered over my shoulder kibitzing until Little Moishe complained and Mike K. said, "All right, clear the rail."

Max objected. "Hey, I'm on the list for this game. I can't stand here and watch?"

"Ven you get a seat, you can votch all you vont," Moishe said.

Still, Max lingered, asking in a loud voice if anyone was planning on getting up soon. I was thinking of asking him how much he'd pay for my seat when Moishe said, "Please, Mike, can you make this patzer go avay?"

"Jesus Christ, Max, will you get the fuck out of here already?" Mike said.

In the midst of this little drama, I got involved in a hand with Russian Eddie, who tossed in a preflop raise of $150 from middle position. Holding tens on the button, I reraised to $400. When Eddie made it $900, I flat-called rather than get into a raising war. Like Lenny, Eddie was perfectly capable of four-, five-, and six-betting with any two cards. It was better for me to see a flop with a hand like pocket tens.

"Why do you want to mess around with me?" Eddie said. "You've seen what's been happening to other people."

"Oh, you know me, Eddie. I like to live dangerously."

"I just don't want to see you get hurt, Nate."

The table laughed while the dealer spread the flop.

Suddenly, I was looking at three cards that made me want to get up on the tabletop and dance. There was a beautiful, hard-to-believe ten, giving me top set, along with a harmless five and deuce. Even better, Russian Eddie tapped the felt. I'd played with him often enough to know that a check could only mean one thing. If he'd missed or had a pair under the ten, he'd have come out firing. The check screamed big hand. Definitely an overpair. Probably aces or kings.

Confident that a check-raise was coming, I bet $1,400 into the $2,000 pot. Sure enough, Eddie took a moment to consider, before announcing, "Raise." He pushed out $1,400 to match my bet, then assembled an additional $4,000 and moved it gently past his cards.

The chips stayed out there in front of me as I pretended to think about what to do. In fact, I *was* thinking, but not in the way Eddie might have imagined. I was thinking about the best way to get him to put in the rest of his money. I was thinking about what a $30K win was going to feel like. And I was thinking about what I'd be able to do with it.

I was convinced by the size of Eddie's raise and his body language that he had aces. Which meant that it almost didn't matter what I did, because he was never folding. In the end, I decided to reraise but not go all in. I made it another $5K on top.

"Really?" Eddie said. "I've got a very big hand, Nate. Did you really flop a set?"

I shrugged.

"I don't think you'd bet a set on that flop. I think you've got jacks or queens. You have jacks, Nathan?"

I smiled.

"Fuck it," Eddie said. "I'm all in."

"I call," I said instantly.

It was at that moment, as Eddie's face fell, as he realized how fucked he was, that a commotion began up toward the front of the club—loud voices and sudden movements, followed by an odd hush that rolled back toward us like a wave.

Turning, I saw people diving for the floor, and in the same instant, I saw why: four figures in black ski masks, brandishing handguns and sawed-off shotguns.

One of them hurled a chair against a wall and yelled in a booming angry voice, "THAT'S RIGHT, MOTHERFUCKERS! THIS IS A ROBBERY! Everyone the fuck on the floor right now!"

I hit the carpeted floor as if pulled by gravity, blood pounding in my ears and chest. A ratcheting metallic burp, the sound of a shotgun being pumped, *Chiilllliiiip-Liiiiipppp*—something I'd only ever heard in the movies.

"FIRST MUTHAFUCKA WHO DOESN'T DO WHAT I SAY IS DEAD!"

The moisture in my mouth evaporated. I was afraid to breathe. Maybe if I closed my eyes then opened them, all this would go away, would turn out to be a bad dream. I tried, but couldn't seem to blink away the scene before me, change it back to what it had been. Time moved in slow motion. I found myself wondering, Why? Why had I put myself in this situation? For what? The money? What would happen to Hannah if I didn't come home?

D.J. glanced at me over the bodies between us and hissed, "How's this for a bad beat?"

I stared at him, livid. Did he think this was a fucking joke?

From the other end of the room the voice boomed:

"OPEN THE DRAWER, BITCH!"

"Okay, okay, just don't—"

Crack!

"DID I ASK YOU A FUCKING QUESTION?"

No response.

"I DON'T WANT TO HEAR NONE OF YOU MUTHAFUCKAS SAY SHIT, UNDERSTAND? I WANT YOU TO EMPTY YA MUTHA-FUCKIN' POCKETS AND START PUTTING WALLETS, JEWELRY, WATCHES, EVERYTHING ON THE FLOOR. AND NO FUNNY BUSINESS OR I WILL CAP YOUR STUPID ASSES!"

I unstrapped my watch and placed it along with my wallet and my roll, the two thousand I had left, on the carpeted floor near me.

Feet approached. A pair of red-and-white Nike high-tops. I pressed my face against the floor, which smelled sour, like dirty sweat socks. The Nikes were so close to me I could see the scuffs in the leather. Dizzy, I tried not to look up. Across the floor through a tangle of limbs, I caught D.J. trying to stick his roll down the front of his jeans. What the fuck was he doing?

Suddenly a deafening boom. The noise echoed and reverberated, sucking up every other sound, obliterating every thought that came before it.

"What the fuck, man!"

"It was a accident. He was reachin'! the muthafucka was reachin'!"

"What did we talk about, man? Damn!"

"I tol' you. He was reachin'."

"Fuck it, fuck it! It's time! Let's move the fuck out!"

Hands continued to shovel money and valuables into garbage bags.

"LET'S MOVE IT MUTHAFUCKAS!"

I pleaded silently for them to go, for it to be over. Finally, the feet started toward the door at the back. I heard them pounding down the stairs, the sound growing fainter.

"Are they gone?"

People started to get up around me. Except for D.J.

I caught my breath, got to my feet, went over to him.

"D.J.!"

He didn't move. I was stabbed by a cold shot of dread.

And then he rolled over, grinning, waving his roll.

"Fuckin' asshole." I was shaking now, trembling, as what happened—what could have happened—hit me full force.

That was when I heard a groan from nearby. A guy still down.

Max.

Vinnie the dealer knelt by him, looked up. "Somebody call an ambulance!"

Max's eyes were open but with a faraway look. His hand pressed against his belly and blood oozed through his fingers, staining his blue dress shirt.

I felt like I was going to throw up, bile rising in my throat. There was blood all over Max's shirt, pulsing out between his fingers. Looking at his face, it was as if I were seeing him for the first time. Seeing his sweetness, his vulnerability. Guilt washed over me for any unkind thoughts I'd ever had about him.

An involuntary sob shook my body and came out of my mouth in a jagged whimper.

In the distance, a siren. It could have been the cops or an ambulance or just a random unconnected sound of the city.

One of the bouncers moved through the room, yelling, "Everybody clear out! Go home!"

Vinnie the dealer ignored them. He took off his T-shirt and pressed it to Max's belly, trying to stanch the bleeding, taking charge while a small group of us stood there gaping. "Somebody call nine-one-one!" he commanded. The T-shirt was already soaked through with Max's blood.

Vinnie had run with street gangs, stolen cars, done a stretch in prison. There were tears in his eyes. "It's okay, Max," he soothed, voice breaking, cradling Max's head in his arms. "Just hang in there, buddy. You're gonna be all right."

"They don't know," Max mumbled.

"What?"

"They don't know," he said again.

"What's he saying?" someone asked.

Vinnie shook his head.

Mike K. approached, flanked by one of the bouncers. "Help me get him downstairs." He grabbed at Max's wrists.

Vinnie knocked his hands away with a swipe. "What the fuck you doing?"

"What's it look like I'm doing? Trying to get this motherfucker out of here."

"The fuck you are."

"In case you forgot," Mike K. said, leaning toward Vinnie menacingly. "You work for me. You don't wanna help, get the fuck out of my way."

"Maybe you didn't hear me, Mike. You're not taking him anywhere."

The boxy-headed muscle-bound bouncer made a move toward Vinnie, but Mike called him off. "Fuck these guys, Santiago. They want to be heroes, let 'em." He started toward the back stairs. "Come on." The bouncer, after a hard stare, turned and followed.

The place had cleared out. It was just me, D.J., Vinnie and poor Max.

"You guys should go," Vinnie said. "The cops'll be here any minute."

"We're not leaving you here by yourself."

"Go," Vinnie said. "You don't need this."

"What about you?"

"Don't worry about me."

"He's right," D.J. said. "We'll be here all night. And you got a family to get home to." He grabbed my elbow and moved me toward the rear exit.

"It's not right to leave Vinnie this way."

"Nothing we can do, brother," D.J. said, pulling me along. Over his shoulder, he said, "You're a fuckin' mensch, Vinnie. For real."

Vinnie nodded, but you could tell he wasn't listening. All his attention was focused on Max.

Out on the dimly lit street, players milled around in small groups, smoking and talking, as if waiting for something, seemingly unaware that someone had been shot. I felt even worse about leaving Vinnie.

Two cop cars screamed up the block, light bars flashing. They slammed to a stop, and the cops rushed inside the building.

Somebody said, "Do you think they'll ever reopen? Or is that it? I pocketed some chips. I want to redeem them."

"I think the whole thing was a scam. They robbed their own club."

"A guy was shot!" I said. "It wasn't a fucking scam."

"Is that true? A guy was shot?"

"Yeah, I saw it," another one said. "One of them in the masks got spooked. He was stepping over a guy and the gun went off."

"So it was an accident?"

"Does that sound like a fucking accident?"

One of the waitresses heaved and sobbed uncontrollably. A uniformed detective approached our little cluster and asked if we'd been in the building. We all shook our heads, no, lowering our gazes.

"Why you crying?" the cop asked the waitress.

She couldn't answer.

The cop turned to one of the other players and asked them why she was crying. His back was to us, and as D.J. and I looked at each other, we both realized the time had come to get out of there. We headed down the block together toward Seventh Avenue. All I wanted was to get home to Hannah. But then I thought of Laura. What the hell was I going to tell her?

As we passed by Paddy's Irish Rose, D.J. said, "I need a drink," and when he said it, I realized I needed one, too. So we ducked in and took a seat at the bar. The place was almost empty. Just us and a couple of stare-ahead drunks on the other side of the horseshoe. I ordered a whiskey, which I supposed was what you did after getting robbed and seeing a guy shot. I was still shaking.

"We should have stayed."

"Nothing we could do."

"I keep thinking about his face, about the blood…"

"Dude."

"I mean—" I held up my hand. I didn't want to say it. I couldn't say it.

"I know," D.J. said. "I saw."

The bartender set our glasses down then poured from a bottle of Jim Beam. We downed them like water.

"Again?" the bartender asked.

We nodded and he refilled them.

"On top of everything, after something like this they're going to shut it all down," D.J. said.

"Are you serious, D.J.?"

"That's what's gonna happen."

"What the fuck's the matter with you?"

"I'm just saying—"

"Max is lying up there with Vinnie and that's your concern?"

"It's not the first thing…but it's one of them."

"You're a sad sick motherfucker."

"We still gotta eat. You gotta eat."

I took a sip of whiskey. "Is that what you were thinking about when you pulled that dumb move for a few lousy bucks while a guy was pointing a shotgun at us?"

"It was ten thousand. And it was a calculated risk. Like I make all the time. Like you make all the time."

"Not that kind of risk."

"It was an accident. Max was an accident. You heard them. It wasn't because of anything I did."

"You know that for a fact?" I gave him a hard look.

"What do you want from me? I understand you're upset. I realize you were about to take down a fifty K pot off the Russian. It's shitty luck."

"You're such a prick."

"You want half my roll? Will that make you feel better?" D.J. took his fat roll out of his pocket.

"Stop it."

"I'm serious."

"Fuck you."

"Come on, Nathan. This has got us both messed up."

"Yeah, whatever." I pushed away from the bar. "I'm going home. I'll catch you later."

"Really?" D.J. said. "You're just taking off?"

I kept going.

* * *

Halfway across the Brooklyn Bridge, I realized I had a problem. I waited until the cab made it to the Brooklyn side and was coming down off the ramp before I said anything.

"Uh, driver, um, I don't know how to put this in a good way, but I, uh, I don't have any money on me."

"You what?" the driver asked in thickly accented English.

"I said I don't have any money."

He hit the brakes, pulling off to the side. Turned and glared.

"I'm sorry," I said. "I was robbed."

"Why did you not say anything sooner?" His dark brown eyes appeared hot and magnified behind a pair of steel-framed glasses.

"I guess I'm not thinking very clearly."

"You are telling the truth? About this robbery?" Surprisingly, there was a tone of compassion in his voice.

"Yeah," I said, and my voice cracked and I struggled to fight back tears.

"I will take you home then."

I was embarrassed by his sudden generosity. "I can send you the money. If you give me your address."

"That will not be necessary."

His name card identified him as Ramesh Pandit. He drove me to my door, once again refusing my offer to send money. "I believe in karma," Ramesh Pandit said. "It will come out all right."

Letting myself into the apartment, I made straight for the bathroom, flicked on the overhead light, emptied my bladder, studied my face in the mirror, looking for answers. Pouchy bags under my eyes, a twitch like a tiny heartbeat playing beneath the left one. Leaning in closer, I began to sob out loud, my eyes going all squishy, my mouth twisting, the sound like a car engine weakly trying to turn over on a cold morning. As my crying jag continued, my vision darkened and blurred and my sobs morphed theatrically into a kind of crazy laughter. "It'll all come out right," Ramesh Pandit said. But would it? Should I track him down and get him to say that to Max's family and friends at the funeral? Or Laura when I told her I'd lost all my money? Excuse me. All *our* money?

On my way out of the bathroom, I caught a whiff of my own stink and stopped short. I lifted an arm and sniffed, shocked by the smell. I'd come back from poker with sweat funk before, but never anything like this. I undressed and showered, soaping my pits thoroughly, digging my fingernails in, clawing at my skin as if to scrape away the last 24 hours.

Still slightly damp, I slipped under the covers, my foot brushing Laura's leg. She stirred and rolled away. Could she sense, even in sleep, the buzzing crazy energy right next to her?

Closing my eyes, I was confronted again by a slideshow of horrors. I tried to force myself to think about something else, but couldn't. The night's shocks were too vivid, my worries too real. They revolved around money and what I was going to do now, and about the world I'd wake up to if I could ever fall asleep.

III

2011

10

Tell Me What I Have to Do

Hannah sat on the floor playing with an array of garishly colored plastic pony figurines. She trotted one of them across the woven red rug toward the yellow pony I held in my hand.

"Pinkie Pie," she said with great seriousness, "come see what Fluttershy is doing."

"What *am* I doing?" I asked in a squeaky voice, brandishing the yellow pony.

"You're wanting to tell me a secret really, really badly," Hannah explained patiently. "And if you don't, you might explode."

"Oh, right," I said. "Of course."

Laura emerged from the bathroom in a cloud of steam, her head and body wrapped in towels. "I'll take over as soon as I'm dressed," she said. "But you can leave now if you need to."

"I'm not going."

"Again?"

I didn't want to have this conversation in front of Hannah. I nodded toward the bedroom and Laura took my cue. As D.J. had predicted, all the New York poker clubs had shut down in the wake of what was now being classified as a robbery and murder. Max died in the hospital less than 24 hours after being admitted. I'd been on my way to visit him when I heard the news from Vinnie. In the several days since, some of the clubs had been raided, others simply closed preemptively to avoid the heat. At first, I told Laura that I was taking a little break from poker. But I'd known that wouldn't fly for long.

Telling Hannah I'd be right back, I followed Laura's wet footprints to the other end of the apartment and watched as she plucked a white T-shirt out of a dresser drawer and lifted her arms to put it on, letting her towel fall to the floor. She was all curves suddenly, ripened by pregnancy to a bursting fullness.

"So?"

There was no way not to tell her, so I just spilled it. "The clubs got shut down."

She stood there in her T-shirt, hair wet and stringy, staring at me. "All of them?"

"Every single one."

I could see her trying to make sense of this as she opened another drawer and took out a pair of jeans. "What the hell happened?"

"There was a robbery."

She waited for the rest.

"And, um..." I rubbed my jaw with an open palm. "They shot someone."

"They shot someone," she repeated dully.

I nodded.

"Jesus Christ, Nate."

A sudden wail from the other room. Laura and I exchanged a look, then rushed back to find Hannah with her head stuck in the space between the chair seat and one of the horizontal slats underneath.

"Daddy," she moaned.

Partially from the release of tension, I laughed. I couldn't help myself. Laura did too. "How did you manage that, bunny?"

"It's not funny," she said angrily through her tears.

By gently twisting her head sideways, I extracted her fairly quickly and easily. She continued to sob, throwing her arms around me and burying her face against my chest.

Later, after we gave Hannah her dinner and sang her to sleep, Laura wanted to talk about the shooting again.

"I can't," I said. "Not right now. I'm sorry. I'm just really, really tired."

To my relief, she let it drop.

* * *

The next morning, a Saturday, I took Hannah to the Rumpus, a café in the neighborhood that had a play area with brightly painted miniature tables and chairs, a wooden kitchen range, an assortment of pull toys and a battered selection of books. I was sitting in a comfortable easy chair sipping coffee when Laura marched in and stuck *The Times'* Metro section in my face. It was a story about the murder.

"Why didn't you tell me there had been other robberies before this?"

"I didn't want to worry you."

"Is there anything else you're not telling me?"

"No."

"You weren't at this club when this happened were you?"

I didn't say anything.

"Oh my God, Nate!"

If I'd been as easy to read at the poker table as I was with Laura, I'd have gone bust long ago. "This is exactly why I didn't tell you."

"You could have been killed! This could have been you!" She stood there, waving the newspaper at me, actually hitting me with it. People nearby stared at us.

"How could you put yourself in a situation like that?"

"Do you honestly think if I thought it was dangerous I would have been there?"

"There were three previous robberies!"

I looked away, trying to avoid her gaze. Three little Park Slope moppets were cooking up a feast on the wooden stove—and I realized that none of them was Hannah. Springing up from my chair, I scanned the room.

"What is it?"

I didn't answer, just quickly made for the front room. Rounding the corner by the bar, I spied her wandering down the hall near the bathrooms.

"There you are!" I could feel my heart pounding. "What are you doing? Do you need to go potty?"

She shook her head. I took her hand and led her back to the play area. The other little ones were plating plastic slices of pizza and wooden cupcakes. "Just let me know next time you go somewhere, okay?"

"Okay, Daddy."

Laura seemed a bit calmer when I sat down again. "How can you not have known it was dangerous?" she said in a more modulated voice.

"I didn't think about it in those terms. I certainly didn't think anyone would get *killed*. Anyway, you don't have to worry. I'm not going back."

"Damn right you're not."

"Did I not just say that?"

"You're a father. You're not just some dude who can do whatever he wants."

"I know I'm a father. Jesus."

She took a deep breath and her expression softened. "I'm sorry if I sound harsh. It scares me. What if something had happened to you?"

"I'm okay," I said, taking her hand. "Nothing happened. And nothing's gonna happen."

* * *

But I wasn't okay. I was having trouble sleeping, waking up several times each night from nightmares about the robbery. Laura said she could hear me grinding my teeth, and I must have been; in the mornings, my jaw ached and my bad mood felt permanent.

I wish I could have talked to her about what was really going on with me. My fear was that if I did it would only push us farther apart. If I'd had the money, I would have gone back into therapy. The cheap alternative was Charlie Bascombe, who I could still always count on when I needed a good listener. Back in our Williamsburg days, when he and I shared a studio space, our friendship had grown naturally out of our similar journeys, both of us young, single, poor and ambitious. Like me, Charlie was still struggling to break through as a painter. It hadn't helped that he suffered a series of serious physical problems—caused either by the materials he worked with or Lyme disease—and that there was a two-year period where he'd been so sick he was almost unable to work at all. And though he hadn't given up or had his spirit crushed, it had definitely taken a toll. Charlie and I didn't see each other as much as we used to, but he still had a knack for helping me stay sane in darker moments.

When I confided my troubles, he said, "It always cheers me up hearing about somebody whose life is even more fucked up than mine."

Right away, I felt a little lighter.

"What are you doing to take care of yourself?" he asked. "Is Laura helping?"

"She's trying. In her way."

"You gotta talk to her, man."

"I wish it were easier."

"Newsflash, buddy. You're no fucking picnic yourself."

"Hey, I'm not that bad."

"No, apart from the fact that you're an ambivalent neurotic mother-fucker who plays poker for a living, you're quite the catch."

"Sometimes I think I should have just stayed single in Williamsburg."

"Then you'd be like me. The picture of health and happiness."

"At least you're not letting anyone down."

"True. But like I keep telling you, one of the main things keeping me sane is our Mondays at Zabloski's. You really need to start coming again, see the old gang. Even Polly showed up last time. It'll do you some good, I promise."

"Polly came?"

"All the way from her loft in Tribeca."

"Fucking Polly."

"Hard to hold success against her. It's just tough waiting for our turn to come."

"You still waiting?"

"Aren't you?"

"I'd even settle for winning the World Series of Poker."

Charlie laughed. "Anyway, I'm sure she and a lot of other people would be happy to see you. You need to be around folks who understand. You're dealing with some heavy shit, Nate."

"I wish I were. Dealing."

"I'm just saying you're not alone, pal."

* * *

Laura tried to be patient with me while I figured out the next move. She didn't know I was paying bills with my credit cards and taking out cash advances for daily expenses. Or that I'd lost my entire bankroll. She just knew vaguely that things weren't good. I tried to stay upbeat. I'd think of something. Hadn't I always?

D.J. had been to one of the new places that sprang up in the wake of the shutdown, a one-table joint in a doorman building. The game sucked balls, he said, but at least it was safe. I decided I'd be better off giving online another try. So many idiots were making a living online. This one guy I knew, a total fish in live ring games, had made over a $100K the past year multi-tabling $1-$2 on Stars. My lack of success had to be due to bad luck and variance, didn't it?

Yet, I kept losing online, the same way as before, the bad beats continuing all through the first month of 2011. It was crazy. If there was one card I didn't want to see, or two running cards, those were the cards that appeared. I hated being one of those guys crying, "It's rigged," but I was stumped. Beyond the pain and aggravation, the monotony of playing on a computer was deadening. I might as well have been doing data entry.

Between living expenses and online poker losses, I'd gotten myself twenty grand deep into credit cards, the weight of which became tough to manage, particularly since I felt compelled to keep it to myself.

Further eroding my spirits, Laura had enlisted David, the annoyingly handsome book editor, as a kind of literary 12-step sponsor, talking with him on the phone and having coffee with him whenever she needed encouragement, which seemed to be frequently. On the other hand, if I tried asking her about the book, she snapped at me, as if I were prying or getting up in her business.

* * *

In February, I heard from Richard, who after five minutes of small talk got around to the real reason for the call.

"I'm working on getting you a show, but I thought you might like to earn a little dinero for yourself in the meantime and do me a solid in the process."

I was instantly wary, especially since the "working on getting you a show" sounded like prime Richard bullshit. "Is this like the time I lent you ten grand for what was supposed to be one day and didn't get paid back for two months?"

"You made money on that loan."

"Not the point."

"Relax, pal, this doesn't involve any outlay of cash. I just need you to bid on something for me. Chrome's having a fundraising auction. It'll be easy money."

"This might seem like an obvious question, but why don't you bid on whatever it is yourself?"

He laughed abruptly and mumbled something about owing money from the previous year's auction.

"Another obvious question. If you still owe from last year, how are you gonna make good on this?"

"You remember the flood in the warehouse where I was keeping my old work? I just got half a million in a settlement."

"They settled? Maybe I should set fire to my studio."

"It was a flood. And for your information, I'm still messed up over it."

"You sound pretty distraught."

"The point is, fuckhead, I'll give you ten percent of the winning bid."

"Why not just pay off what you owe in full so you can bid yourself?"

"It works out better for me to keep things on the installment plan with them. Plus, I don't really want anyone to know I'm buying this piece."

"And why's that?"

"It's a Polly Lymarin."

"What the hell, Richard?"

"The thing is, not even Polly can know it's me."

At this point, I'd heard enough. "Look, I appreciate the thought, but I'm gonna pass. Find someone else." I knew the game Richard was playing, trying to buy a piece for under-market value from an artist that might be leaving him for a higher-profile gallery. But it wasn't just that. The bullshit about owing money from the year before and paying in installments? That set off alarms. He needed me to beard because he *couldn't* bid on Polly's piece. They wouldn't let him while he still owed money. Typical Richard—overextended but still wanting more. No, it was a clear and hard pass for me.

"Come on, Nathan. You're one of the only people I trust enough to do something like this."

"That in itself is an argument against doing it."

"It'll be worth your while."

"In my next life or this one?"

* * *

After you've played poker for a living, it's hard to think about going back to a straight job. Assuming I could even get a job on a construction crew, was I really going to be happy pounding nails for a thousand bucks a week when I'd been making three times that in a few hours at the poker table? It wasn't just the hours-to-pay ratio, either. I needed to make way more than a grand a week if I had any hope of digging out of my hole. So despite my promises to Laura and myself, I asked D.J. for the address of the one-table club in the doorman building on 24th Street.

I went on a Tuesday night, telling Laura that I was meeting D.J. for a drink. It was a nice new building over a Whole Foods, with a majestic canopied entrance and revolving brass-framed doors.

I gave my name to the uniformed concierge who, after calling upstairs, directed me to the second elevator bank. Riding up to the 16th floor, I checked myself out in the mirror, nodded a practice hello, tried on a smile. It was weird getting back on the horse again. I felt self-conscious and slightly ashamed.

A short blond guy with a gym-pumped physique let me in.

"I'm Doug. You're D.J.'s friend."

"Yeah."

Doug led me past a small kitchen area into a narrow living room the major portion of which was occupied by a red-felt-covered table. Seven faces turned to look at me, all a bit wary. To my surprise, I knew only a couple of them but not well enough to remember their names. I thought I knew everyone in New York poker.

"How much you want?" Doug asked.

I looked at stacks as I took a seat. No one had more than $800.

"I'll take eight hundred," I said. I'd withdrawn two thousand on overdraft from my bank earlier in the day.

Whatever my misgivings, it felt good to be back in a real game. The familiar shuffling sounds of the cards and chips. The dealer's simple directives. *Thirty dollars. Raise seventy-five. Forty-five more. Next hand. Blinds up everyone. Action's on the three-seat.*

Most of the players were business types. Real estate. Financial services. Insurance. They'd played regularly at a now-defunct club on Wall Street. Before long, they started talking about the murder, transfixed when I said I was there and that I knew the guy who was killed.

Every time the doorbell rang, we all looked anxiously toward the door, peering at the black-and-white closed-circuit monitor to see who it was. I found myself thinking about the mood of the city in the months following 9/11, how riding the subways I'd look at my fellow passengers with suspicion and fear, wondering if they had a bomb strapped to their body.

I got stuck five hundred early, my aces cracked by a small set, and despair set in. Just getting even in this shitty little $5-$5 game of nits would be an accomplishment; I'd probably need a cooler going the other way. Instead, I was dribbed and drabbed out of another few hundred, and by the time I left, I was in a sour mood with no intention of ever going back.

* * *

"All right, Richard. You win. Tell me what I have to do."

I listened to him explain the dynamics of the auction, asked him some questions, got some answers, felt sick inside.

"Aren't they going to wonder how someone like me is bidding on an expensive painting?"

"If anyone wants to know, tell them you came into an inheritance."

"What's the estimate?"

"Forty to sixty."

Fucking Polly. A few years ago we'd been on equal footing. Now I was running weird angles to try and pay the bills and she was getting profiled in *ArtNews*. On the plus side, if the painting went for sixty, my ten percent would net me living expenses for a couple of months.

"I just want to make sure you're not going to leave me high and dry here, Richard. You definitely have the money?"

"You'll get paid. Don't worry."

There was a moment in which sanity almost prevailed. A long moment of hesitation. Then I heard myself say, "Okay, I'll do it."

* * *

The following Friday, wearing a slightly frayed topcoat over my one suit, a baggy black-linen thrift-shop special, I showed up at the Chrome Gallery just after the doors opened at 6:30.

Three well-dressed people sat at a table inside the door checking a list. I gave my name and received a numbered paddle along with a pamphlet of the auction items. In the main space of the gallery, a large well-lit concrete-floor open area, collectors and patrons in suits and cocktail dresses milled about looking at the art on the walls. Waiters in white shirts and black slacks circulated with trays of goat cheese and basil crostini, confit duck spring rolls and smoked-salmon seaweed cones. I made my way to the white-linen-covered bar table and ordered a scotch and soda, scanning the room for Richard.

"Nathan, what are you doing here?"

It was Polly Lymarin. She'd cut her hair short and bleached it blond. She wore a black leather jacket with a white silk scarf tied around her neck. She looked every inch the rising art star.

I was unnerved to see her but tried not to show it. "Hey, Pol."

"Look at you in the suit."

"Yeah." I could feel my face getting hot.

"You have a piece in the auction?"

"What? Oh, no. No."

"I'm here as a favor to Gary. But I'm feeling kinda weird about it."

"Why?"

"I don't know." She did a creepy-crawly shiver. "I'm thinking of ducking out during the actual auction part. What about you? What's your excuse?"

"Well," I said, trying to figure out what to tell her, "I'm, uh, I'm actually here to bid on one of the pieces. In fact—"

"What? Oh shit," Polly said, looking past me. "There's Gary. I gotta go. Sorry." She made her way toward the back of the gallery where Gary Schell, the director of the Chrome, stood watching.

I breathed a sigh of relief, then saw Richard frantically waving me over from behind a pillar, making a zip-the-lip motion with pinched fingers.

When I got close, he yanked me by the arm, spy-movie style, into the shadows. "What the fuck?" I said, swatting his hand away.

"What did you say to Polly?"

"Nothing. Jesus, Richard. Why didn't you tell me she was going to be here?"

"I didn't know. Anyway, no need to panic, it's fine."

"I'm not the one panicking."

"The main thing is not to let on that we're here together."

"You don't think Polly's going to figure it out? What the hell is she going to think when I start bidding on her painting?"

"You gotta make something up. We discussed this. This is what I'm paying you for."

"And what about Gary? You think we're fooling him?"

"As long as they don't know for certain, that's all that matters. Just be sure to keep your distance from me."

"It might help if you weren't manhandling me. Fuck. I can't believe I'm involved in this shit with you. Every time we do something together, I wind up regretting it."

"You're not backing out, are you?"

This got the wheels spinning. "I'm thinking about it."

"We had a deal, Nate."

"I decided I don't like the terms. I want fifteen percent."

Richard laughed. "You bastard."

"I'm happy to walk."

"I'll give you twelve."

"Fifteen or I'm out of here."

"Fine. You win. Fifteen."

"Just so we're clear, how high are you authorizing me to go?"

"Up to a hundred."

"A hundred!"

"You think it might go for more?"

"More?"

"Let's make it one-twenty. Polly's about to blow up big."

"Bigger than now?"

"I've heard some things."

"What things?"

"You've gotta keep this under wraps," he whispered so low I could barely hear him. "I think Sikkema Jenkins is gonna sign her. Let's make it, one-thirty..."

"You're insane, Richard."

"Just make sure you get it."

"Whatever the price?"

"Just get it."

I tried to lie low after this encounter, looking at various pieces hanging on the walls, most of them by artists I knew. Lexi Stoyanoff. Dan Goldbaum. Charlie was right, it was a lot like when one of my poker buddies broke through, won a big tournament. I'd think about the difference between them and me. Was it attitude? Mindset? Luck?

I did my best to avoid Polly, but she caught up with me while I was getting a refill at the bar.

"Did you say you were bidding on a piece, Nate?"

I decided my best response was to come clean.

"Yeah, and just so you're not surprised, Pol, it's your piece I'm bidding on." I lifted my paddle to demonstrate.

"Jeez, Nathan, really? What'd you do, win the lottery?"

"Kind of. I won a few hundred thousand in a poker tournament."

"A few hundred thousand? Bullshit!" Polly let loose her seal bark of a laugh. "You and your poker games. Holy shit! Is that for real? That's crazy!"

"Pretty crazy."

We grinned at each other and I remembered why I liked her. It was impossible to hold it against her that she'd been anointed and I hadn't.

"Wow, a windfall like that, I hope that's giving you some time to paint," Polly said.

"Definitely."

"That's good. I'm glad to hear that, Nathan."

Before the auction started, I positioned myself down near the front. It wasn't a formal sit-down auction. Everyone just stood near one end of the gallery while a couple of the assistants carried out the piece that was up for bid and Gary Schell did his impression of an auctioneer, holding a wireless mike as he prowled the small makeshift stage. He was actually good at it, persuasive and charming as he talked up the gallery and made humorous appeals for people to empty their pockets.

My heart rate accelerated when Polly's piece, the last of the evening, was paraded around while Schell extolled its virtues. Once the bidding began, I didn't raise my paddle until the price had reached thirty thousand. By then there were two interested buyers, a mop-topped guy wearing a bowtie and a redhead in a black dress. I laid back, waiting to see how far they'd go.

"Thirty thousand, can I get thirty-five?" Schell asked.

When I was sure the second bidder had dropped out, I raised my paddle.

"I've got thirty-five now. Do I hear forty?"

I looked at the guy in the bowtie. He pursed his lips slightly. Schell repeated his plea. No response. This was going to be easy.

Just as I was getting ready to do a mental victory dance, a bald guy in a herringbone tweed suit jumped in.

Fuck. I raised my paddle again.

"I've got forty-five," Schell said, his eyes darting from me back to the bald guy.

It was on.

The bald guy wasted no time going up to fifty.

I raised my paddle again. And just like that we were at war, the bid ratcheting up rapid-fire to a hundred thousand in a matter of moments. The room was electric.

Glancing back, I caught Richard's eye. He didn't look happy but neither did he give a signal of surrender.

"I'm at a hundred and ten thousand. One hundred and ten. What about one-twenty? Can I get one-twenty? One-twenty here. Do I have one-thirty? One-thirty. One-thirty. Can I get one-forty? Yes, I have one-forty. One forty. Do I hear one-fifty. Am I all done at one-forty?"

I looked back for Richard again, but this time couldn't find him. Someone had moved in front of him.

"Okay. We're done at—"

I lifted my paddle.

"Check that," Gary said. "I've got one-fifty! Can I get one-sixty? One-sixty, yes? I'm at-one fifty. One-fifty. One-fifty? Am I all done? All done?" He looked at the bald guy, who shook his head. "Yes! I'm all done at one-fifty. Sold at one-fifty. Number One-forty-two!"

Thunderous applause. I felt a rush of adrenaline, aware of everyone's eyes on me. I glanced back again. This time I spotted Richard. He looked ill.

Total strangers came up and congratulated me, patting me on the back. Polly found me. She whispered that she was flattered and a little freaked out. Had I lost my fucking mind?

I saw Richard heading toward the exit and followed as soon as I could get away, meeting up with him in the darkness under the unfinished part of the High Line along 24th Street. A raw wind carried plastic bags and other trash in eddying swirls along the curb. I was still buzzed.

"Let's walk," Richard said. "I don't want anyone to see us together."

At the corner of Tenth Avenue, we turned downtown.

"What the fuck happened in there?" He looked around nervously under the arcing glow of the street lamps to see if anyone was nearby or listening in.

"What do you mean what happened?"

"Who was that fucking bald guy?"

"I have no idea. Why? Do we have a problem?"

"He must have been a shill. I saw Gary chatting him up earlier. I'll bet he's a friend Gary brought in to bid things up."

"Richard, I'm going to ask you again: Do we have a problem?"

"Didn't you see me? I drew my finger across my neck when it hit one-forty."

"Look, shithead. You told me to get the painting whatever the price. I got the painting."

"But a hundred and fifty thousand!"

"I don't care if it was two million. You said, 'Get it.' I got it."

"What did Polly say to you? I saw her talking to you after."

"She told me I should get my head examined. Which I should. And by the way? You owe me twenty-two five."

"As soon as I get the settlement, you'll get your end."

"As soon as you *what*? You told me you already had the fucking settlement."

"No, I said I won the judgment. I didn't say I collected."

"Bullshit."

"Hey, you just made over twenty-two thousand dollars."

"The fuck I did! Where is it? Do I have it?"

"You will."

"And it's not just my money I'm talking about. You end up stiffing the gallery, I'm the one on the hook for it! I'm the one screwed! This is my name and reputation in the art world."

"I get it. Calm down."

"Calm down? Fuck you! You don't come up with this money, I swear I'm taking you down with me!"

"That's not going to happen, Nate. Relax. They'll get their money, and so will you. Let me buy you a drink."

I snorted, wondering how it was that I didn't just haul off and clock the guy. For some reason, I didn't.

11

The Man You Spent Your Energy Trying Not to Become

Since my credit hadn't yet been compromised, I was able to take cash advances on the card offers that arrived in the mail almost every day, using some of that money to make payments on the outstanding balances. At some point, I knew, it would catch up to me. But for the time being, I could maintain a semblance of normality, life proceeding as always. Except for the little matter of Laura's pregnancy. Four months in, she was Superwoman, going a hundred miles an hour, trying to finish her book, getting Hannah's room ready to accommodate a baby brother (when she wasn't saying that we needed to move), writing copy and still doing yoga.

I hadn't told her about my credit-card kiting, though I'm certain she must have suspected. I rationalized this by telling myself that I was protecting her. But it wasn't her, it was me. I was petrified of what she would do if she found out. Even more so in regard to my little escapade with Richard, about which I'd also managed to keep her in the dark. And thank God, because Richard hadn't paid one cent of the over twenty grand he owed me. Worse, Chrome was dunning me for the hundred and fifty he owed them.

When I lost my shit with him again, over the phone, Richard acted like it was no big deal, like shirking bills was standard operating procedure, which for him it was. Of course, I had no one to blame but myself. I knew what I was getting into. And yelling accomplished nothing. He simply and calmly explained that his damage settlement was taking longer than expected. "Chrome will just have to wait."

"Why don't *you* fucking tell them then?"

"Unfortunately, that's your job, Nate."

I wanted to hurt him so bad. And I might have if we were in the same room and I didn't need him to make good on what he owed. It was my ass on the line after all, not his. "You're such a fucking liar, dude. I asked you straight up and you didn't blink when you told me you had the money."

"I thought I'd have it by now."

I looked out the kitchen window at the bare trees in the neighboring backyards, the dishwater-gray sky. "You make it sound like you represented things truthfully," I said, biting off every word. "You told me you *had* the money. I never would have done this if you'd told me you didn't."

"You must have misunderstood. Anyway, it doesn't matter. You're gonna get paid."

"You're not the one they're dunning."

I felt Laura's presence behind me. When I turned, I saw she was holding up the bill from Chrome that Richard and I were arguing over. Fuck. I'd left it lying on the dining table.

"I can explain that," I said, hanging up on him.

"I'm listening."

For one second I considered running a bluff, but folded instantly under her withering gaze. Big mistake.

"Have you totally lost your mind, Nate? What the actual fuck were you thinking?"

Yeah, definitely should have lied. "It was stupid," I said. "I'm not defending it."

"Are things really that desperate? How fucked are we?"

Before I could think how to answer, my phone buzzed again. A temporary reprieve. I reached into my pocket. It was Ray the super. Why was Ray calling me?

"You really have to look at your phone right now?"

"No. I just—"

"Go ahead." She stalked out of the room.

I went after her. "Laura, I'm sorry."

"And what the fuck is up with Richard? Why would he ask you to do that in the first place? What else is going on that I don't know about, that you don't trust me enough to share with me?"

"Nothing," I said, trying my best to sound convincing while resisting the urge to fight back by asking her the same question.

* * *

The next day, Hannah's little friend Malia had a party at Chelsea Piers. Laura offered to take her, but only on the condition that I relieve her halfway through. No point in us both suffering through the whole thing. Or bringing more toxic energy to this poor kid's birthday than absolutely necessary.

I arrived to find ten little girls sitting at a long narrow table eating pizza off of paper Elmo plates on top of a plastic Elmo tablecloth. Behind them, taped to the wall, was a vinyl Elmo cutout. Parents milled about, taking pictures with cellphones. In a corner of the room,

147

Laura sat with Kim, Tasha's mom, deep in conversation.

Kim worked as a certified life coach and was very good at asking probing questions. When she came over with Tasha for dinner one weekend, the evening turned into an impromptu marriage-counseling session after Kim asked Laura if she had ever been bothered by the volatile and dicey nature of what I did.

At first, Laura was philosophical. She'd known what she was getting into. It's not like I'd sprung anything on her. But gradually, Kim coaxed out the fact that my seat-of-the-pants approach to life had begun to wear thin now that we were parents. The romance of me being a gambler had faded; in fact, she'd begun to see it as a character flaw. Having identified the problem, Kim suggested no solution. She just set off her bomb and made her getaway with me and Laura feeling shitty about each other.

Ever since that night, I'd tried to steer clear of Kim. Now, however, after waving hello to Hannah, I had no recourse. As I approached them I thought I heard Laura say, "I hope I have the nerve," at which point Kim turned to me with a wide smile and a cheery, "Hello Nathan!"

"Hi, Kim."

"How ya doing, Mr. Poker Player?"

"Very excited to be at this party, I can tell you that."

"Oh come on, it's cute, don't you think? We've gotta appreciate these things while we can. We won't be doing this much longer."

"Well, actually..."

"Oh. Right." Kim looked meaningfully at Laura. "I almost forgot."

Laura wound up staying a while longer, even though she'd told me she'd leave when I got there. She and Kim kept talking, while I got collared by one of the dads who knew what I did for a living.

"You really make enough at poker to support a family?"

I knew he did something in private equity. "Why? How much do you make?" I asked. He looked at me slightly confused, uncertain whether or not the question was intended in earnest.

* * *

That night at home, with Hannah safely tucked away in bed, Laura changed into her nightgown and spent what seemed to me to be an inordinate amount of time in the bathroom. Then she slipped into our bed without a whisper, while I was in the middle room, surfing the Web.

Eventually, I got up and made my way from the darkness toward the small circle of light emanating from the little twisty-neck lamp on her night table. She was propped up on pillows, reading. I squeezed one of her feet through the covers. "What's up with you?"

She returned my gaze with a quick blank shrug, a dismissive jut of her lips.

"You okay?"

Another shrug.

"Are you *angry* with me?"

"I don't think we should have this conversation right now."

"So it's a *conversation*?"

The look in her eyes scared me. I knew Kim had gotten her all wound up, but there was more to it than that.

"I saw one of your credit card statements. In your files."

I took my hand off her foot.

"Is that something you were going to tell me about? The cash advance for ten thousand you just took out? The twenty-five thousand that you already owe?"

I brushed a piece of black lint off the comforter. "I can't believe you went through my stuff."

"Why didn't you just tell me, Nate?"

"I didn't want you to worry."

"Oh, bullshit!"

"I know you don't believe me, but I was trying to take care of us."

She bit her lip, seemingly fighting back tears.

"What?"

"I just don't understand how you think that's taking care of us."

I threw up my hands. "I'm doing what I've always done, Laur. Whatever I need to do, so we can pay the bills."

"It scares me."

"Which is why I don't tell you about it."

"This isn't working, Nathan. Don't you see that? It's not working."

I felt anger rising in my voice. "Fine. Tell me what you think we should do."

"You're not going to like it."

Suddenly, my head got heavy and I didn't want her to tell me.

"I'm taking Hannah."

"What? No!"

"We're going to go stay with my sister for a while."

I shook my head, shuddering, trying to breathe, only able to get air into my lungs in small jagged inhalations. "No," I said again.

"I'm sorry."

"Kim put you up to this, didn't she?"

"What?"

"You were saying something to her when I first arrived today. You were talking to her about this."

"I don't know how you got that. But this doesn't have anything to do with her."

"Laura, come on," I pleaded. "How's this going to help anything?"

She looked away, dabbing at her eyes with the back of her wrist. "I know you're going through stuff," she said, softer now. "I know that."

"Are you really leaving because I took out cash on my fucking credit card?"

"Don't make this bigger than it is, Nathan. I'm not *leaving* leaving…"

"*I'm* making it bigger?"

"Nothing is settled."

"Look, you want some distance, some space. Whatever. I get it. But there's no point in *your* leaving. I can go stay in my studio for a few days."

"I appreciate your saying that. I just—I don't know how long it's going to be…"

"We're talking about a few days or a week or two, we're not talking about forever. Right?"

"I just. I don't want to feel any pressure from you."

"Who's pressuring you? Just tell me this isn't permanent. I mean, Jesus, Laura, we're going to be parents again."

She started to cry.

"And what about Hannah? Have you thought about how you're going to explain this to her?"

Later, when I got in bed with her and my anger wasn't so close to the surface, I said, "Whatever's going on, Laur, we'll work it out."

She looked like she was about to cry again and I drew close to her and hugged her, feeling the roundness of her belly. She turned and hugged me back.

"Maybe you're not cut out for this," she said. "You know? I mean, not everyone is. And that's okay. I know you love us…"

"You're wrong. I do want this."

"I just need some time," she whispered.

I was still holding her a few minutes later when I felt her hand start to twitch and her breathing slow down. I whispered her name, but there was no response.

In the morning, she made breakfast as if it were a normal day. Watching her scramble eggs for the three of us, I thought for a moment that maybe she'd changed her mind, that it had just been a crazy pregnancy moment and she wouldn't follow through or that the whole thing had been a bad dream fueled by kids' birthday cake. But then, at the breakfast table, she told Hannah that Daddy was going to be sleeping somewhere else for a while.

Hannah closed the toy catalog she was flipping through. She said, "Daddy, where are you going?"

"I'm not going anywhere, sweetie. I'm just not going to be sleeping here." I reached over and brushed her hair out of her eyes. "I'm working on a big project so I'm going to be at my studio a lot until I finish."

Hannah curled her lower lip into an exaggerated pout.

"I know, bunny. I feel the same way. It doesn't mean I won't see you. I will. All the time. Just not at night for a while."

After breakfast, I washed the dishes. Swooshing a soapy sponge around a plate, I closed my eyes, wallowing for a moment in self-pity and shame. To my surprise, there was also something weirdly intoxicating about fucking up like this, about life gone wrong.

Nothing ever turned out the way you thought it would. Or maybe it turned out exactly the way you thought it would. There came a moment when you realized that the man you spent all your energy trying not to become was the man you had in fact actually turned out to be.

Before taking Hannah to school, Laura whispered in my ear that instead of going with them, I should stay behind and get whatever things I needed immediately, so Hannah wouldn't have to see me doing that.

I waited five minutes after they'd gone, then took down my rolling suitcase from the top shelf of the closet bedroom. I opened a dresser drawer and looked at a jumble of T-shirts and underwear, trying to figure out what to take. I knew it didn't matter. It wasn't as if I wouldn't be able to get anything I'd forgotten later on. But I still felt like I was doing it badly, failing somehow, and that I'd be reminded of that, along with all my other failures when I got to where I was going.

In the bathroom, I packed my toothbrush, razor, and mouthwash in a Ziploc bag and was about to add the tube of Crest then thought better of it. No point in being petty. I set the tube back down on the edge of the sink. Looking up at myself in the streaked toothpaste-flecked mirror, I saw more of my dad in my face than ever. The beginnings of pouches under my eyes and creases in my forehead.

After zipping my suitcase closed, I carried it to the door, hoping that Laura would come back before I left. Would she change her mind if she saw me here on the precipice? I waited for a while, then figured that she'd probably stopped someplace for coffee on the way home, just in case I was taking longer than expected. Maybe it was just as well.

12

One for the Couch

I trudged up the creaky stairs to the second floor of the old machine factory on 7ᵗʰ Street. Down at the end of a long hallway, with its worn and battered narrow hardwood floors, I put down my suitcase and dug for my keys.

All the months I'd dreaded coming here, now I could find a whole new kind of pain to associate with it. I opened the door and stood there for a minute, breathing in the smell of old paint and turpentine.

I'd occasionally slept here uncomfortably on the flat foam-cushioned couch. But never for more than a night and not in a while. There was no shower, so I'd have to bathe myself in the slop sink. The shared toilet was down the hall. The kitchen consisted of a coffee maker and a hot plate.

I took a seat on the couch and tried to breathe. It was okay. I was going to be okay. I just needed to talk to somebody. Hear a calming voice.

I started scrolling through my phone. Some of the names I didn't even recognize, random mopes I'd met on the bus to Atlantic City, names I couldn't attach to faces. I tried calling a couple of my real friends, like Charlie Bascombe. But when their voicemails answered, I didn't even bother to leave a message. How had this happened? How was it that I barely saw my close friends anymore? Was it just that we were all too involved with our careers and families? Or was it something bigger and more profound?

After college, we all swore that the inevitable slow erosion of intimacy with friends brought about by career and family wouldn't happen to us. We'd be different. Now we found out we weren't. Time *was* limited, and even the ones who had it, the single ones like Charlie, had other priorities that didn't allow much space for married people. Aside from the parents of Hannah's classmates, the company I kept consisted mostly of poker players. Was that really what I wanted?

Sitting on this sad foam couch, arms crossed, head falling back, neck cords tight as piano wire, I stared at the greenish paint on the ceiling. It was peeling, curling back like old skin, the diseased dull primer visible underneath. Goddammit, Laura, didn't you know that once things went this way, they usually didn't get better? I couldn't stop thinking about her and the editor. Bad enough that he was handsome, charming and employed. He was also in a position to be able to help her publish her book. All I seemed capable of doing was pissing her off and making her cry.

To stop myself from sinking further, I focused on her short-comings—her lack of generosity, her guardedness, her blue-eyed unknowability. Maybe not everything was my fault. Maybe if she could have given me a little more...

It was no use. I slumped forward until my chin touched my chest. I remained that way for several minutes, startled out of it only when my phone, still in hand, began to vibrate.

It was Ray the Super. Fuck. I'd totally forgotten about him.

"Nathan, Jeez. Didn't you get my message?"

"I'm sorry, Ray. I'm going through something here."

"I wish you would have called me back."

I didn't like the sound of that. "What's he done now?"

"The rent."

"Fuck, Ray, we discussed this. You were supposed to let me know."

"I'm sorry, Nathan. I would've. Nobody said nothin' to me."

"Forget it. It doesn't matter."

"He was able to get some stuff out of the apartment before the door was padlocked. He slept at my place last night."

"Christ. They padlocked his door?"

"Maybe if you could talk to Mancuso, get him some money…"

"The fucker locked him out?"

"He's normally a reasonable guy."

"Where's Dad now?"

"Out. He didn't say where he was going."

"Listen to me. When he gets back, have him call me. I don't care what he says, make him do it."

"I'll do my best."

* * *

Dad's troubles got me thinking about Mom and how I'd been neglecting her too. She and I usually talked at least a couple of times a month, but since the robbery, I'd twice failed to return her calls, afraid that she'd hear something in my voice and start in with questions. Now my guilt mixed with a little-boy need for reassurance prompted me to pick up the phone.

"I was starting to worry," she said.

"Sorry."

"Everything okay?"

I hadn't gone into this call thinking about exactly how much I wanted to tell her, but once I started in, the floodgates opened and I pretty much spilled everything. It wasn't as if I was unaware of the fact that I hadn't been able to do this with Laura lately, but the stakes didn't feel as high.

"Oh honey," she said, after I'd finished. "Do you want me to get on a plane? Should I send you a ticket to come out here?"

She lived for moments like this, for the opportunity to focus all her anxiety outside herself and reclaim the one role that had never failed to give her a sense of balance and purpose.

"I'm fine, Ma. I realize it might not sound that way, but I am."

"That's just like something your father would say."

After a long, loaded silence, she said, "Have you talked to him lately?"

"I might have."

"How is he?"

"The same."

I was actually thrown by her asking after him when I'd just been describing the disaster of my life.

"Well, tell him hello when you talk to him."

"I'll do that."

I was remembering now why I'd been leery of talking to her.

"I think the best thing you can do is give Laura some time," she said. "And maybe you ought to start thinking about getting a real job."

I sighed audibly.

"It's just a suggestion, darling."

Underneath everything, it seemed, she didn't understand me any better than any other woman I'd ever known. Or maybe I had the equation reversed: All the women I was attracted to understood me in the same way she did.

Figure that one out on the couch.

* * *

I spent the rest of the day making the studio livable. I swept the floors. Scrubbed out the slop sink. Bought an air mattress at Target. All the busy work actually helped take my mind off things. My father, despite my numerous attempts to reach him, and whatever telepathic energy Mom's inquiries about him might have sparked, never called back.

* * *

Just after seven-thirty, I was waiting outside Lupa on Thompson Street. Here came D.J. up the block, cigarette dangling from his mouth, grinning. "Just like the old days, huh?"

We were part of a crowd of about fifteen people waiting outside. Back when the Siena had been going strong, this was part of our routine: leave our chips on the table and cut out for an hour or so to have a plate of bucatini and a glass of wine. Returning to the club, we'd find our chips stacked high, just like we'd left them.

Only now, it would just be D.J.'s chips waiting.

"I gave the maitre'd our names," I said, as we bumped fists.

"I gotta be back in an hour or they'll give away my seat."

"Game juicy?"

"Like always. You should come play after."

"What about security?"

"Dude, nothing's safe, but they put in a second door at least."

I didn't bring up Laura until we were inside sitting down.

"Why did *you* leave? It's your crib too."

"Because, if I hadn't left, she would have."

"So?"

I debated whether or not to try and explain. D.J.'s grasp of human relationships was not, shall we say, very evolved.

"It's just better this way," I told him. "I didn't want to be a dick about it."

"You ran up a little credit card debt. Big deal."

"Have you even been listening? It's because I didn't tell her."

"No shit. She'd have gone ballistic."

"The point is, leaving was the move to make if I want to work things out with her."

"I'm just surprised that's what you want."

"Look," I said, surprised by my anger and my need to defend her. "I'm doing what I'm doing and I'm done talking about it."

"At least admit what she did is kind of fucked up. It's not like she doesn't know what's involved in what we do."

"The longest relationship you've ever had was, what, six months?"

"That means I'm not allowed to have an opinion?"

My phone, which I'd laid on top of the tabletop, lit up. Thank God. A reason to stop talking to this idiot. Better yet: It was Dad.

"Finally," I said, getting up and weaving between tables toward the door. "Where the hell are you?"

"I'm with Ray. He said you wanted to talk to me."

It was freezing out and I was in shirtsleeves. My breath came out in in wispy puffs. "Yeah, I want to talk to you. You were supposed to tell me if you were having a problem."

"I didn't want to worry you."

"Are you okay? Where are you staying? Can you stay at Ray's again?"

"I'll figure something out."

"What does that mean?"

"It means I gotta make a few calls. I'll be fine. Don't worry about it."

"You need a place to stay tonight, you can stay at my studio."

"There's a bed there?"

"An air mattress." I couldn't believe I was saying this.

"How will I get in?"

"I'll let you in. I can meet you there in a couple of hours."

"You don't need to put yourself out like that."

"Unfortunately, it doesn't involve putting myself out."

13

We'll Try to Do Better Tomorrow

"I'm actually surprised she didn't give you the boot sooner," Dad said, leaning back into the couch and kicking off his shoes. He poured himself a Dewar's. The bottle was the first thing he unpacked. "It's a wakeup call. It's not the worst thing."

"What would that be? The worst thing?"

"When it's too late to fix it."

I got up from the paint-spattered folding chair I'd been sitting on and found another glass by the sink. Dad reached out and handed me the bottle.

"I'm not in jail yet," I said pointedly. "So I guess there's some hope left for me." I sloshed some scotch into the water glass.

"Your mother put up with a lot," he admitted. "I'm not going to tell you otherwise."

"I think you're actually happy about this." I threw back a slug.

"You got me wrong. I want you to be better than I was."

"And yet here we are, two peas in a fucking pod."

"I'm not here to add to your problems."

"Oh for Christ's sake, Dad."

"Maybe this is an opportunity for us. I can help you."

Now there was a scary thought. I took another sip of scotch. "How about we talk about your situation instead of mine?"

It required some prodding, but I finally got him to answer a few questions. I discovered that Mancuso had ordered Ray to padlock his door without a court order or any paperwork. Not that it mattered. Dad wasn't interested in exploring his legal options or consulting a tenants' rights advocate.

"I've known Mancuso for fifteen years," he said. "He and I'll work things out. He's just being a sonofabitch to teach me a lesson."

"It doesn't mean he can lock you out."

"It's the way he does things."

"So you just kiss and make up and then move back in?"

"Assuming I can get him some money. You don't deal with that aspect of things, you sure as shit won't solve the rest of your problems."

I felt a scream building up inside because what he was saying was true.

"How'd you get in this spot anyway?" he asked. "You suddenly turn from a shark into a fish?"

It was crazy. I looked at him and was filled with contempt, yet I still wanted his approval. Before I knew it, I was describing the bad run I'd been on, capped off by the $50,000 hand I'd been on the brink of winning, the subsequent theft of my remaining bankroll, and of course the murder.

"Holy shit. You're lucky to still be breathing. That could have been you."

"That's exactly what Laura said."

"This happened when?"

"December."

"You never said a word."

"I learned from the best."

He ignored the little swipe. "You been playing since?"

"I've been trying to figure things out. The games dried up."

"That's where the credit card debt comes in?"

"It seemed like a good idea at the time."

"Let me ask you something," he said. "Do you really have an edge in poker or is that some bullshit you tell people?"

"You looking for proof?"

"Come on, I been around gamblers my whole life. They're all liars—"

"*They?*"

"All right, *we*. It's what we do."

"As a matter of fact, I keep records. Detailed records."

"Yeah? How much did you make last year?"

I wanted to say, "None of your business," but I also wanted to see his reaction when I told him the number.

"Ninety-five thousand. Cash."

He gave me a quick glance over the top of his scotch glass. Enough for me to see he was impressed.

"I guess Laura didn't have any complaints about that."

"It doesn't really matter now, does it?"

"Not when you're broke and out on your ass."

"I just didn't think I'd be in this spot."

"Nobody ever does."

"Any other words of wisdom for me?"

"I just want to help you," he said.

"Unless that little suitcase you showed up with is filled with cash in addition to scotch, I'm not sure how you can."

"Is that what you need? A bag of cash?"

There was so much I could have said about what I really needed. "A bag of cash wouldn't hurt."

He fell silent. I could almost hear the gears turning. I didn't want to give him any encouragement. At the same time, I was curious to know what he was thinking.

* * *

It's bizarre the way this had all gone down. The timing of it. My first night in the studio would otherwise have been spent in a purgatory of isolation, obsessing about the circumstances that had led me here. Instead, I had been spared that fate in the strangest of ways and by the one person in the whole world, other than myself, I could reasonably pin the blame on. Maybe the real surprise was that I found myself enjoying his company.

After turning out the lights, my father on the air mattress, me on the couch, I found my thoughts drifting to places I didn't want them to go. My father breached the silent darkness, pulling me out of my spiral.

"Did I ever tell you about my first night in prison?"

He'd never told me about that night or any other, the way some guys never talked about the war.

"You may not remember this, but after the arrest, I was considered a flight risk. I couldn't make bail, that's how high they set it. It took a while, but on appeal, the judge lowered it, and I came home for a bit before I went away."

"I remember you coming home. It didn't seem like it was for very long."

"It wasn't. And the idea that I was probably going away after... I mean, you know it's coming but you can't really face it or wrap your mind around it. The funny thing is, when it did happen, when I got off the prison bus at Otisville, I still felt that way. There I was in the freaking joint—bleak as shit—and I was convinced the entire time that a guard was going to come into my cell and tell me that it'd all been a big mistake, that the judge had had a change of heart. 'We know you're not a bad guy. You've got this family that loves you and needs you, and we'll let you out if you promise not to do it again.'"

I raised my head on an elbow and peered at his prone silhouette. The air mattress was positioned under the windows and I could make him out vaguely in the dim light coming off the street. "You really thought that?"

"Not only did I think it, I was convinced of it. And when it didn't happen, I developed a rationale for why. As the days went by, I became certain that they were going to tell me that the delay was intentional, a way of making their point, and now that the point had been made, they'd let me go home."

I heard a garbage truck outside, the clatter of cans.

"The hardest part of being there for me was when you and your mother and sister would visit. I dreaded those visits."

"You did?" Even as I asked this, I remembered how I had dreaded them, too.

"Made things worse. Made me more aware of the life I was missing. Just like I thought the guards were going to come tell me it was all a big mistake, I thought that after that happened and I got to go home, things would go back to being the way they were."

"That was all I wanted too. I was so mad at Mom that she didn't want that anymore. Almost as mad as I was at you."

"Yeah, well, your mother can't really be blamed."

"No." I thought about telling him I'd talked to her, that she'd said hello. Better to let sleeping dogs lie.

"You know the strangest thing about getting out of prison?" he continued. "The day before they cut me loose, all that time—and time in prison, I mean an hour inside feels like a whole day on the outside—but all that time just collapsed. I felt like I'd just gotten there

165

a few days before. Almost like I had dreamt the whole thing."

Neither of us spoke for a while. I'd never really tried to think about things from my father's perspective. I'd always been too angry. Like, fuck him, who cares what he's thinking?

A memory bubbled up of him taking me to the Golden Gloves at Madison Square Garden when I was seven. We sat so close to the ring that when one of the boxers took a punch, the sweat flew from his face and landed on me. The sound of the punches, kind of a dull thud, wasn't at all what I thought it would sound like, and the roar of the crowd, rising and falling, a cacophony of shouted encouragement—"Put dat jab out dere! Put dat jab out dere!"—held a barely contained hysteria that filled me with excitement and fear. Dad chain-smoked Parliaments and made bets with fans in neighboring seats ("Twenty bucks says the kid in blue beats the crap out of the other kid"). Sometimes he leaned over and whispered in my ear, explaining something that had just happened or was about to happen.

"Hey Dad, you remember taking me to the Golden Gloves when I was seven?"

"The Golden Gloves? Yeah, I think I remember that."

I could tell that he didn't.

"You know what I do remember?" he said.

"What?"

"The time you dropped the car keys down the VW's air vent when we had box seats to the Mets and Giants. I practically clocked you."

"Yeah, I definitely remember that."

"You were seven or eight."

"I started crying and that just got you madder."

"Christ, I'm sorry, kid."

"It's okay. I would have been mad in your place too."

"No excuse for it."

We didn't say anything for a while. Just lay there thinking our

166

thoughts.

"Well, good night, Dad," I said at last.

"Goodnight, kiddo," he said. "We'll try to do better tomorrow."

14

A Little Insane

T he smell of coffee. Light streaming in through the windows. My father walking around in red-striped boxer shorts and nothing else, his hairy paunchy belly hanging over the elastic band. I groaned my way into consciousness, leaning my head back on the hard square arm of the sofa.

Dad stopped his pacing to stare at a canvas leaning against the wall at the rear of the studio. It was one of a series I'd started of fingers in the pages of a book, parting the gilded top end. Holding a mug, he appeared to give the painting his full attention.

"What am I supposed to get out of this?" he asked without turning away from it. "Am I supposed to get something?"

"How does it make you feel?"

"It makes me feel uneasy."

"Yeah?"

"Because I'm not sure I'm getting out of it whatever I'm supposed to be getting."

I sighed, then, despite myself, laughed.

My father turned away from the painting. "Anyway, what's the difference between you and the schmucks who sell their shit for millions?"

"The millions, for one thing."

"So what is it? Is it talent? Is it marketing?"

"Dad, can we please talk about something else? I know you don't mean it, but this isn't helpful."

"Why don't you try listening to me sometime?"

I could only shake my head, incredulous.

"Because I been thinking about your situation," he continued, undeterred. "I got a guy you should meet. A businessman."

"Who buys art?"

"Not for art."

He proceeded to tell me about Kirill, a Russian mobster he knew from the joint, who happened to be in the money-lending business.

"Are you seriously suggesting I take out a loan from a Russian mobster?"

"It'll be more like an investment for him. He's always looking for opportunities. You need to start thinking outside the box. You've got a skill in an area he understands. If poker is pitched the right way, he might be interested."

I said I'd think about it.

But my father telling me to stretch my boundaries actually did get me thinking about how I needed to get back in action and fix my problems. It was just a question of where and by what means. Guys were making millions playing poker on the internet. I *personally* knew players who were killing it. So why in hell couldn't I?

* * *

"No good reason I can think of," said Florida James as we carried paper cups of coffee to the back of the Tea Lounge and sat down at a battered old wooden table. "Could be variance."

"Really?"

"It's possible."

Florida James flipped open his MacAir. Looking around the low-lit space, full of comfy couches and mismatched tables, I saw glowing white Apples everywhere.

"I'd put this whole place on tilt if I came in here with my Dell," I said.

Florida James forced a smile. He had a crazy bouncy Jewfro, a scraggly beard and big puffy pouches under rheumy pale-lager eyes. He stripped off his coat and hoodie to reveal a ratty T-shirt underneath with the word DEGEN on it.

"From what I've seen of you in cash games," James said, "your real strength is live reads. It hides some of your deficiencies—"

"Really? My deficiencies?"

"I've seen you raise in spots where a call was the stronger play. I've also seen you lose value by betting too much or not enough. Things like that."

"Remind me not to play with you anymore."

"Like I said," Florida James laughed, "I think you make up for it with your live reads. I mean you've made some calls and laydowns against me that are just sick."

"I remember one."

"The set of fours? I still don't understand how you got away from that."

I laughed. "Yeah, I can't really tell you about that one."

"Maybe that'll be your payment for this," James said.

He clicked away on his keyboard, registering for a sit-n-go. A moment later, sitting shoulder to shoulder, we watched as the digital cards fanned out like starbursts against the green oval of the virtual table.

"Online, you need to play more aggressively post-flop and try to really define hands since you don't get physical reads. Also, I'd play fewer hands, and definitely not from out of position."

Staring at the screen, James kept narrating his thought processes, making observations about his opponents' betting patterns and bet-sizing, assessing ranges and predicting responses. By the time we busted out in third place on a tough beat, I felt as if I'd actually learned a few things.

"Why don't you try playing one?" James said, turning the screen toward me.

There was an awkward moment where I thought about how to explain to him that I didn't have any money left in either of my online accounts. But then he said, "If you win anything we'll split it."

An hour and fifteen minutes later, after knocking out Crackpot, whose icon was a small picture of a cracked flowerpot, I turned to James and said, "That was almost too easy."

"Don't let it go to your head," James shrugged. "What's your screen name?"

"Artvark."

James tapped at the keyboard, transferring half the $1000 winnings to my FullTilt account.

That night, back at the studio, I ran the $500 up to $1000, playing a few $55 nine-player sit-n-go's while Dad watched television. A few times I yelled out loud when I hit a card or when one of my opponents did something stupid, and when this happened, Dad glanced over at me, frowning, perplexed.

I didn't believe that one session with Florida James had changed everything. It might have been as simple as variance finally having tilted back in my favor. Whatever the reason, though, winning made me feel as if order had been restored, that my entire world wasn't upside down, that maybe there was a way forward and some hope.

Over the next few days, I continued to grind up. When my online roll topped $4,000, I withdrew half of it so I could pay some bills. I worried that this might trigger the dreaded cash-out curse. In fact, not a day later, as I stretched out on the couch in my studio with my Dell balanced on my thighs and a carton of fried rice on the floor next to me, that worry became manifest.

I was playing three games simultaneously, two $109 sit-n-go's and the nightly $33 rebuy tournament. Not a heavy slate by online standards—Florida James routinely played eight screens at once—but about as much as I could handle without getting too jittery. The sit-n-go's proved frustrating. In one, I made it to four-handed (with the top three spots paid), then lost my stack when I moved in with KK and got called by A-3. In the other, I lost in even more annoying fashion, getting my money in with a set and losing to a runner-runner straight on the river.

Irritated, I quickly lost my stack in the nightly $33 and had to rebuy. You get a certain feeling you're at the beginning of a bad run, and I was starting to get that feeling.

The very next hand, I four-bet shoved with AK, got three callers and found myself up against AA, KK and QQ.

"What the fuck?" I was so enraged by the absurdity of yet another cold deck, and so fully expecting to lose, that I couldn't quite believe it when I hit a miraculous 10,J, Q, for a straight, quadrupling me up.

By the time Dad stumbled through the door of the studio sometime after eleven, I was among the big stacks and the field had been whittled down to a couple of hundred.

Dad weaved across the room and sat down behind me, on the arm of the couch, peering over my shoulder at the screen. I could smell the cigarettes and whiskey on his breath.

"You winning?"

"I'm doing okay."

"Ya must get sick of looking at that screen."

I didn't answer.

"Tough way to make money, laying on the couch..."

I continued to ignore him.

"You giving lessons?"

As much as I didn't want to think about turning into him, I really didn't want to think about him turning into me.

"Why'd you call that bet, for instance?" he asked, leaning closer. "When you don't have shit."

"It's called a float," I said, his persistence wearing me down. "I'm guessing he hasn't got much of a hand either. And I've got position."

The turn card came. The guy bet again. Again, I called.

"I don't understand," Dad said.

"Just watch. Watch what happens when he checks on the river." But when the river card was dealt, the guy jammed.

"Fuck!" I yelled, folding immediately. "Dad, will you please—I need to concentrate here."

"All right, all right. Chrissakes." He got up and stumbled around the paint-streaked floor, trying, it seemed, to figure out what he should do with himself. At last, he plopped down and stretched out on the blanket-covered mattress parked by the window.

I felt bad about losing my temper. During a five-minute break, I went over and found him staring at the tin ceiling in a semi-stupor.

"I didn't mean to be a prick, Dad."

He shrugged it off. "I ever tell you about the time I hit the first five races in a million-dollar Pick Six at Santa Anita?"

"Not that I remember."

"I had taken this girl to the track—"

"Is this before or after I was born?"

"You were probably five or six."

"What were you doing in L.A.?"

"I had a deal going."

"What kind of deal?"

"One of my deals. What difference does it make? You want to hear this story or not?"

"Yeah, I want to hear it." Did I really, though? Half Dad's stories made me cringe, the other half made me want to go back into therapy.

"So this redhead, Carol," he began, "she'd never been to the track, and just for the hell of it, I figured we'd fill out a couple of Pick Six cards. The carryover was big, so you know, why not?"

"Did Mom know about this?"

"About Carol? What do you think? Look, I'm not saying I was an angel, but your mother was no saint either—"

"Mom played around?"

He whacked the mattress. It made a hollow plasticky sound. "That's not the point of this story! Jesus Christ, let me fucking finish!"

He paused, waiting for what he deemed an appropriate amount of deferential silence before continuing. "Carol thought I was the greatest. I mean, I picked five winners in a row while explaining my thinking to her! She thought I was a fucking genius. So the sixth race, our horse is right there, neck and neck down the stretch. We're both jumping up and down and I get so excited I actually collapse, my legs just give out, and down I go, down like Frazier. When I open my eyes, it's over. The race is over. What happened? Carol tells me our horse lost by a nose at the wire. We were *that close* to a million dollars."

"What did five out of six pay?"

"About six gees. And Carol threw in a blowjob, so all in all…"

"Oh, Dad, please."

He laughed, delighting in my discomfort. "Point is, your life can turn on a dime. I sometimes wonder what would have happened if that horse had won. If I woulda done some of the shit I did after that. You know. The shit that hit the fan."

From across the room, I heard a buzzing sound, the tournament underway again. I hustled back to the couch just as the cards fanned out. Dad continued talking, but without me listening, he gradually wound down. Before long, I could hear him snoring.

By midnight, only a hundred of us were left in the $33 rebuy. We were all in the money. I commanded one of the big stacks and was using it to advantage. The electronic sounds of the game were hypnotic and repetitive, the musical whip-cracks of bets, the sorry *phhts* of folds, the beeping countdown in which a decision had to be made.

I kept thinking about the story my dad told, wondering why, in his inebriated state, he'd felt compelled to tell it—although I actually knew why. It was the holy grail of all gamblers: the money that would have changed my life.

Not that life-changing didn't happen on occasion. Back in the early 2000s, I had played regularly at Foxwoods with the Fossilman, Greg Raymer. When he won the Main Event of the WSOP and $5 million, he quit his job as a patent lawyer at Pfizer and traveled the world playing tournaments on PokerStars' dime.

If Jean-Michel Basquiat was my Horatio Alger of painting, Raymer was it for me in poker. Of the two, his long-shot success story, however unlikely, seemed the more realistically attainable. I could actually imagine it. But then I looked over at my father, asleep on a blow-up mattress on a paint-encrusted floor, in a space not meant for human habitation, and I knew that his whole life had been sustained on such hopeful smoke.

Yet when the magic did find me, it was as if I'd known it would all along. The one time that I won a tournament in Atlantic City for $36,000, I'd had a similar feeling: utter clarity and the odd sense that what was happening had somehow been preordained. I knew that feeling could change with the turn of a card. But it hadn't yet and as players busted out, one after another, it didn't feel like it would.

It was late, well past five a.m. I'd been playing nearly 12 hours, and despite the rush of having made it this far, I could barely keep my eyes open.

The three of us left were playing for a top prize of $28,533. Second and third didn't exactly suck, $18,464 and $12,726, but it wasn't lost on me that first was approximately what my bankroll had been before the robbery and murder.

In the corner of the screen was a chatbox. Half of the people on it were observers—people with so little else going on in their lives that they found it entertaining to watch strangers play an online poker tournament at five in the morning. They seemed to think, for reasons obscure to me, that I deserved to win. One, named Chuckle2, wrote, "My man Artvark is gonna take this down! He's toying with these d-bags!" Another responded, "Def. My money's on Artvark!" I had actual fans! I could only think that they must have been betting on this. What other possible explanation was there?

If only I hadn't been so damn sleepy, maybe I'd have rewarded their faith! A couple of times I actually did nod off, head slumping forward until I got startled out of my stupor by a buzz prompting me to act.

A measure of my fatigue was that even though I had a chip lead of maybe three to two over Raiseworthy and two to one over PluggedIn, I proposed an even three-way chop of the money. Raiseworthy said, "Nah, grrl, let's keep playing."

It was already getting light out. I was tired and pissed and I started playing recklessly, moving my stack in for no good reason. I knew it was stupid, but I wanted it to be over. The money we were playing for had stopped being real. I felt a little insane.

PluggedIn opened a pot. Raiseworthy, true to his name, three-bet him. I instantly moved in with A-Q suited. PluggedIn folded but Raiseworthy, following a long think, called. He had queens. The flop and turn were clean for him. But the miracle ace came on the river and just like that, *Raiseworthy* was out. He stuck around as an observer for a few minutes, mainly to berate me, calling me a luck box and other less flattering things. I responded, "Maybe you should have made a deal when I offered it." To which he replied, "I didn't, because I knew how bad you are."

I held a 5-1 chip lead, and with the end in sight, PluggedIn and I quickly got our money in on a flip. My small pair held up.

"Holy fucking shit!" I bellowed.

"What?… What's going on?" my father grunted. "What time is it? Are you okay?"

I could only shake my head. "Yeah, I'm fine." I started to laugh. "Sorry I woke you up. It's just that I won, Dad. I fucking won."

15

I Know You Want to Talk About Things

I was nearly blinded by the sun angling in steeply through the windows. Shading my eyes, lifting up my head, I looked at the clock on the windowsill. Nearly 4 p.m. My father was gone, the red wool blanket balled up on the air mattress.

Half wondering if I'd dreamed the whole thing, I grabbed my computer from the floor and flipped it open, clicking on the FullTilt icon. There in the upper right-hand corner was my balance—$30,549.

I hadn't made it up. It was real. I breathed in, enveloped by a sense of wellbeing and peace. The question was, how much to take out? I considered for a moment. An even twenty grand would still leave me a nice bankroll to continue playing with. I ran through a series of prompts, typed in a two followed by four zeroes and hit Submit.

Then I called Laura.

* * *

"Daddy, are you going to stay here tonight?" Hannah asked. She was on my knee, facing me as I bounced her up and down.

"Soon," I said. "As soon as I finish this project I'm working on."

"I want you to stay."

"I know, sweetie pie. I want that too."

Laura came out of the kitchen carrying a vase of fresh-cut roses. "These are beautiful. Thank you."

"Glad you like 'em."

"So what was it that couldn't wait, that you just *had* to tell me?" She placed the flowers on the table.

"I didn't say it couldn't wait. It's just something I wanted to share with you."

"Why do I feel like you're up to something?" she said over her shoulder as she walked away.

"I'm not up to anything. I'm celebrating."

I heard her clattering around in the kitchen. When she returned, it was with a plate of buttery pasta. "Hannah, take your seat, please."

Hannah slid off my knee.

Looking at me expectantly, Laura said, "Are you gonna tell me or do I have to guess?"

"I won a little poker tournament online. And as soon as they send me my winnings, I'll be able to give you money for rent and school."

"Uh-huh. I see."

"Don't sound so dubious."

"I just don't want you to think that's what this is all about. That it's going to change anything."

"I don't think it's going to change anything."

"Good. Because it's not."

"I know."

I read to Hannah while she ate her dinner, then walked back to her room with her and helped her change into her pajamas. In the bathroom, she squeezed out a huge glob of Tom's Silly Strawberry toothpaste, most of which ended up in the sink and on her face. She spit out the rest, having brushed for about ten seconds. "Honey, try and spit into the drain next time, okay?"

She stuck out her tongue at me, and I couldn't help laughing.

"One more story," she begged after I'd read her about twenty. "Please!"

"Time to turn out the light, sweetie. It's late."

She injected as much pathos into her expression as she could, trying unsuccessfully to curl her lower lip. "Please, Daddy?"

"Not tonight."

I turned off the light and called out to Laura that we were saying goodnight. She brushed up against me in the dark and together we sang "Twinkle Twinkle, Little Star," and kissed Hannah's warm forehead and told her we loved her.

"I'm going to make my kale and quinoa thing," Laura said after we closed the door to Hannah's room. "There'll probably be enough for the two of us if you want to stay."

"I'd like that."

I followed her into the kitchen. She took a bottle of white wine out of the refrigerator and handed it to me.

"You want to open this?"

It seemed quaint her asking, since it was actually a screw top. But what the hell. It was an approximation of a manly task. I cracked the seal.

"Only half a glass for me," she said, as I start pouring.

"Right."

Perched on the folding footstool, sipping wine, I watched her chop up garlic, scallions, and kale. It all felt so familiar to me, the intimacy of it, and yet awkward, too, because I wasn't sure what she was thinking. It had been eight days since I left.

"How does Hannah seem to you?" I asked.

"I think she's okay."

"Does she ask you questions?"

"Not really."

"She asked me if I was staying tonight."

"And?"

"I told her no."

Laura scraped the stuff she'd chopped into a pan.

"It's just difficult, figuring out how to explain things to her."

"Nathan…"

"I'm not asking for the answer. I'm just trying to get a handle on things."

"You and me both," Laura said.

Seeking a safer topic, I asked how work was going, but instead of talking about her book, which was what I was asking, she told me that she was looking into getting a full-time job.

"Why?" I said. "When you're so close to finishing? I told you I'm giving you some money."

"That's a Band-Aid."

"It's a pretty good Band-Aid."

"Why, how much did you win, exactly?"

When I told her, she was flabbergasted. "It's crazy that you can do that."

"Right?"

"Is it something you think you can, like, keep doing?"

"I don't know. Maybe. It's still poker."

She squinted at me as if trying to measure the worth of what I was saying. "That's not how you felt before."

"Twenty-eight grand may have changed my outlook."

When she turned to the stove again, I found myself checking her out: wide shoulders, narrow waist, nicely rounded ass. Here, in the kitchen of the apartment I no longer inhabited with her, I found myself lusting for my wife's ass. Was it because I was wondering if I still had access to it? Or because I was afraid somebody else might? I'd always known there was a high probability that she'd wise up, get tired of my act. It was a big part of why I'd kept her at arm's length as long as I had. Deep down I think I'd always known she'd break my heart.

It was hard not to ask her if that's what was happening. But I didn't. I doubted she had any answers anyway. She'd invited me to stay for dinner. I wanted to stay focused on positive things like that, not think about things like David the editor or how he fit into the picture, or when and if I'd be allowed to come home. This was Laura's game now, her rules. My only option was to play along and see where things went. "Can I do anything?" I asked.

"Why don't you set the table?"

I got plates out of the cupboard and reached around her to get the silverware out of a drawer, my arm brushing up against her hip. The accidental contact was ridiculously thrilling, an electric jolt.

During dinner, I babbled like an idiot on a first date. I said things like "This is so good," and "What did you put in this?" and finally, Laura looked at me like I was nuts.

"This is what I always make, Nate. I've made it a thousand times. Look, I know you want to talk about things and that's why you're acting weird…"

"Fine. I'll shut up."

"That's not what I'm saying. It's just…I'm not ready."

"I get it. Let's talk about something else."

I could see she was weighing what to say next.

"Tell me about the book," I said helpfully.

She dropped her gaze, letting a shy smile escape. "I'm getting close." I could tell she meant it and was excited about it.

"You've worked really hard," I said.

"Don't jinx me. I'm not there yet." She stood up and began clearing our plates.

"Hey, I'll do it," I said, rising quickly, taking the dishes from her.

While I washed, she wiped down the counter and dried. The radio was on 90.7, playing dance music. During one song, I dipped down low and shimmied. Laura tried not to smile.

I loaded the last glass onto the dish rack, wiped my hands dry on a dishtowel and rolled down and buttoned the cuffs of my shirt.

"I guess I should be heading out."

"I'm glad you stayed."

"I'll stop by in a few days with the..." I rubbed my thumb and forefingers together.

"That would be great."

At the door, I zipped up my parka, and hugged her, stretching out the moment, not wanting to let it go. Stepping into the cool night, for the first time in a while, I allowed myself the smallest bit of hope.

16

Is This Really How You See Me?

L ogging onto FullTilt the next afternoon, this is what I saw:

This domain name has been seized by the F.B.I. pursuant to an Arrest Warrant in Rem obtained by the United States Attorney's Office for the Southern District of New York and issued by the United States District Court for the Southern District of New York.

Conducting, financing, managing, supervising, directing, or owning all or part of an illegal gambling business is a federal crime. (18 U.S.C. § 1955)

For persons engaged in the business of betting or wagering, it is also a federal crime to knowingly accept, in connection with the participation of another person in unlawful Internet gambling, credit, electronic fund transfers, or checks. (31 U.S.C. § § 5363 & 5366)

Violations of these laws carry criminal penalties of up to five years' imprisonment and a fine of up to $250,000.

Properties, including domain names, used in violation of the provisions of 18 U.S.C. § 1955 or involved in money laundering transactions are subject to forfeiture to the United States. (18 U.S.C. § § 981 & 1955(d))

An airless pocket of panic formed in my chest. I shut off my computer, then turned it back on. The same page came up again, offering nothing more in the way of explanation.

Trying to stay calm, I called Florida James. He confirmed what I already suspected: that the Justice Department had shut down both Tilt and Stars. "There's no point in freaking out," he said. "But it's definitely not good."

"They've gotta give us our money, right?"

"Hard to say," James said. "You don't have a lot on the site, do you?"

I told him about the tournament.

"Jesus, that's unlucky. I mean, lucky to win, but fuck. Not that I imagine the Justice Department wants us *not* to get paid. But I kinda doubt our money is a major concern for them at this point."

Over the next few days, a thousand rumors circulated. Finally came an announcement that FullTilt and PokerStars had reached an agreement with the Justice Department to regain use of their dotcom sites in order to begin distributing funds to players in the United States. PokerStars immediately assured U.S. players that their funds were safe.

FullTilt did not.

Instead, they issued an ambiguous statement that read to me like a bunch of ass-covering bullshit. Bottom line: no money was forthcoming.

The worst part of having my funds in limbo was that I couldn't come through with the chunk of money I'd promised Laura. The last thing I wanted to do was explain to her what happened. In her eyes, it'd just be another bad-beat story.

I wasn't alone, of course. Plenty of others were in similar straits. One online wizard, Daniel "Jungleman" Cates, was rumored to have had six million tied up on Tilt. A speculators' market quickly developed, players willing to buy and sell frozen account dollars at a cut-rate.

D.J. being D.J., when I asked him if he could swing a cash loan, with my FullTilt dollars to serve as collateral, it turned into a cutthroat business negotiation. Some friends soft-played one another when they were sitting at the same table. Not D.J.

"So what are you asking for, exactly?"

I could already tell by his inflection that this was not going to be enjoyable.

"Lend me five, and if I default, I'll give you ten thousand in FullTilt dollars."

"Five? I can't do five. I've got bankroll issues myself."

"So what can you do?"

"I don't know. Maybe…two?"

"How about three?"

"Two. And even that's a stretch."

"We're not talking straight loan. I'm putting up FullTilt dollars as collateral."

"Which could be worthless. Probably are worthless."

"You do know there are people paying fifty cents on the dollar for them."

"Why not go to them?"

"I would if I had more time and I knew any of them. But I need cash right away."

"I'll tell you what. I'll give you two against the whole thirty K of your FullTilt money as collateral."

"What!"

"Hey, I don't normally do loans at all. As you know, since you don't either, and we've discussed it."

"You're such a dick."

"That's how you talk to a guy you're trying to borrow money from?"

"I'll give you ten thousand against the two."

"Make it fifteen."

"Bring me the money right now and we have a deal."

"I'm home. Come and get it."

Welcome to friendship in the poker world.

* * *

On my way back from D.J.'s, with a rubber-banded wad of cash filling my pocket for the first time in a long time, I decided I better drop off the money with Laura before some other unforeseen disaster struck.

Outside our front door, I pressed the buzzer, eyeing my reflection in the glass-pane window. Taking a deep breath, I tried to animate and loosen my face, opening my mouth wide and working the muscles in my jaw.

When she didn't answer and it became obvious she wasn't going to, I decided to let myself in with my key. Why not? It was still technically my place, too. Not as if I was trespassing or anything. At least not in a legal sense.

Upstairs, I knocked, just to make sure. I opened the door to the apartment, calling out her name. Milo the cat stretched, casting a wary eye, before slinking out of the bedroom. I bent down and rubbed him behind the ear, his soft orange tiger-striped fur, the bony edge of his skull. I'd always just tolerated him. He was Laura's cat. But I was almost happy to see him. Apparently, the feeling was mutual, although a moment later he scooted away, spooked by something. I headed for the living room area. The floorboards creaked under my feet. The smell of toast hung in the air, probably from hours ago. A shaft of sunlight angled across the dining table.

There was a pile of mail that Laura had obviously set aside to give to me. I started sorting through it. Con Ed bill, Verizon bill, a couple of credit card offers, a solicitation from *The New Yorker*.

I took out the cash I'd brought and looked around for something to write with. Laura hoarded pens in some secret place. I rifled through the drawers in the kitchen, which were stuffed with takeout menus, ribbons, paint samples, receipts, emery boards, nail polish, Post-its. In the back of one, I found the stub of an old pencil under a baggie filled with rubber bands. I used it to write a note for her on the back of a credit card offer.

Here's some $$ for Con Ed, etc., and for school and rent. I think it's probably easiest if you pay the bills for the time being, so I'm leaving them with you.

After carefully arranging the money and the note on the dining table, I walked back toward the bedroom, searching for any clues that would help me decipher her state of mind. From the middle room, I could see the bed, neatly made, which I found reassuring. I noticed her laptop, open on the desk in the middle room, and even as I told myself I shouldn't, I went over to it and fingered the touchpad. The dark screen lit up on a Word file. At the bottom of the document, a toolbar revealed that I was looking at page 1 of 377. The name of the file was "Someone Somewhere." Feeling both a sense of dread and guilt, I started reading.

They met at a bar on the Lower Eastside. Verlaine. His idea. Best to be far away from Brooklyn, in a place it was unlikely for them to be seen. She told Jim she was meeting her friend Cassie. Jim never questioned her about her nights out or got suspicious. It wasn't his nature. Or maybe he just didn't care. Still, she felt she had to tell him something. It was odd, the little thrill all this caused her, feelings she had forgotten existed. Andrew had a high forehead, a scar over his left eye, thick curly hair that felt good when she ran her fingers through it. As he told her about the garden he was growing at his country house in the Berkshires, she thought he was going to ask her to go away with him for the weekend. She would say no of course, but still, she wanted him to ask and was vaguely disappointed when he didn't. Was it vain of her to think he would? And why was she so sure she would have said no?

I tried to keep my cool, think this through logically, but my heart was pounding so hard I almost couldn't keep reading. I reminded myself that this was fiction. A made-up story. It wasn't real. Laura rarely went out at night. I was the one. But Jesus, what if it was not just a case of her letting her fantasies run wild?

Nia looked at her reflection in the store windows as she walked along Seventh Avenue. She kept seeing a woman she didn't recognize, wondering if she really looked this tired. Sometimes she thought it would be easy to leave him, to start over. There was a whole world out there she was missing. Parties she didn't get invited to, people she only read about in magazines and gossip columns, lives that were somehow bigger than hers and more fun.

Maybe the people who lived those lives didn't have time for regret, for shame, for wondering if their choices were irrevocable. Maybe if she was one of them, she wouldn't either. She wouldn't look at her husband and focus on all the small things about him that she suddenly found faintly repulsive. The way he chewed his food. The slow ponderous cadence of his speech. How he continuously nodded his head when she was talking to him. The way he tended to hover when she was engaged in some task, in the kitchen or sitting at her computer, seeming to want something from her but never asking for it. She knew none of this was fair. Chastised herself for feeling these things. But still, they were there.

She remembered how at the beginning she'd been slightly in awe of his confidence, the way he approached making music, as if he were building a house, laying bricks, hammering nails, putting up a structure you could live inside. Inviting her in. Where had that Jim gone?

Or was she the one who had changed?

Whatever guilt I had about reading her novel without her permission was wiped away by the sick feeling in my gut, the certainty that the husband was actually me, and that this was how she really felt. Did she really think that I spoke with a ponderous cadence? And hate the way I chewed my food?

No wonder she'd kept the book away from me.

They never went anywhere anymore. His idea of adventure involved television and Thai food. Sometimes they went out to dinner and a movie. When she began looking into airfares one night, talking about a trip they might take, he got very quiet, then came up with reasons for why they couldn't go.

Had she forgotten about our going to Nantucket? Montauk? L.A.? What about the trip we took to Belize after I won a small tournament in Atlantic City? Did that count as an adventure? Driving around the island in a rented jeep after the power went out? The romantic spookiness of the pitch-black road, and then suddenly coming upon a small blaze of light, a little outdoor restaurant off the side of the road where the staff had set up torches and candles and cooked fresh fish over a wood fire grill…Did that not count as an adventure?

I skimmed a few more pages. Then came to this:

She'd been standing on line, holding a green plastic basket of groceries, when he caught her eye.

"You go running in the park every morning, don't you?"

His name was Andrew and it turned out that he was a runner, too. Funny that she'd never noticed him, although now that she thought about it, he did look familiar. It was the hair. Thick and wavy and glistening. He smiled at her then, and she felt a small jolt in the pit of her stomach…

She wasn't the only one. My knees felt shaky, unsteady. Again I tried to remind myself that it was fiction. Laura made up stories. She had never killed her boss the way the character in that short story of hers had. There might have been an emotional truth there, but the events were invented. In the midst of these reassurances to myself, I suddenly heard voices beyond the apartment door. Her voice. Hannah's voice.

No time to think, sound of the key in the lock, knob turning. Fuck! Reflexively, I shut the lid of her laptop. Rushing forward awkwardly, I said, "Laura?" in a too-loud voice as the door swung open.

Even with the warning, she was still surprised, her mouth falling open. I was still in motion and looked I'm sure as if I'd been caught doing something suspect. Hannah burst past her mother, face alight.

"Daddy!"

She vaulted into my arms. The corners of her mouth and chin were smudged with chocolate. "Mommy look! It's Daddy!"

"I see that," Laura said, her momentary surprise already evaporating into something less generous.

"I came over to drop off some money," I explained, "and then when you weren't here I just figured—"

"You could let yourself in."

"I should have waited."

She crossed her arms, frosty as fuck.

"Anyway, I was on my way out. I left a note for you on the dining table."

"Don't go, Daddy." Hannah put her arms around my leg.

"We'll make a plan, sweetie. I'll see you over the weekend." I hugged her and headed for the door.

"Nate…"

I stopped, resting my hand on the knob hopefully.

"Before you go, there's something I want to discuss with you."

Yeah, well, there's something I want to discuss with you, too.

Laura took Hannah by the hand, saying, "Honey, Daddy and I need to have a little talk, so I'm going to get you a glass of milk and some paper and crayons and have you sit in the dining room while he and I have our discussion. Okay?"

My stomach churned.

"Mommy, can I have a cookie with the milk?"

"You just had that chocolate."

Hannah curled her lower lip, made her eyes go sad.

"Oh all right," Laura gave in. "One cookie. But only one."

She led Hannah down to the other end of the apartment, grabbing the crayons and paper from the middle room on her way. I saw her glance at her computer but I couldn't tell if she noticed anything. Maybe she wouldn't remember she left it open. Hannah took a seat as Laura went into the kitchen. I heard the refrigerator door open, the sound of the cabinet door, a glass being set down.

Coming back, she eyed me suspiciously. "Nate, were you snooping?"

"What?"

"You heard me."

She waited while I formulated my answer. "I mean…I might have read a couple of pages on your computer."

"Seriously?"

"I'm sorry. I just. The computer was open and it was right there on the screen. I didn't go looking for it."

"How much did you read?"

"Just a couple of pages. Hardly anything."

"Which part?"

"I don't know. I think it was the beginning….Is that really how you see me? Like that character?"

"It's *fiction*, Nate."

"And this other guy—that's fiction?"

"Oh my God, I knew you'd react this way."

"I just want to know the truth."

"It's made-up. It's not us. Fuck. This is why I didn't want to show it to you."

"Look, I only read a few pages. I'm sure I'll feel differently after reading the whole thing, but—"

"Well, that's not going to happen. At least not until I finish it."

There was no point in arguing with her. We were both in the wrong. "Look, I apologize. I shouldn't have been poking around."

"No, you shouldn't have."

"Anyway, I left some cash for you on the table. Did you see it?"

"You said it was going to be more than that…"

"It was. It will be. It's just the, uh, check I got has to clear first." Christ, I sounded as bad as Richard.

"Because if you're not going to come through with it—"

"I'm gonna come through with it."

"—I might have to take a full-time job. And if that happens, you and I will have to figure out what it means in terms of childcare."

Was she serious? Who would even hire somebody five months pregnant?

"It's my friend Melissa," she said as if I'd voiced these questions aloud. "Her P.R. company."

"Aren't you going to finish the book first?"

"I can't keep living like this, Nate. I can't. It's too stressful."

"What'll happen when the baby's born if you're working full time?"

"It'll be complicated. For both of us."

"I don't see why you have to commit to this now. Can't you please just wait?"

"That'll depend."

I didn't have to ask her on what. It was clear that if I didn't come through, if I didn't provide her with the promised funds, she'd do what she had to do. It also occurred to me that I might be wrong in thinking that money was the real issue here, the reason I'd been banished. It was certainly the easiest explanation for what had happened. But what if it wasn't the money? What if it was simply me? On the other hand, if the things she had written about in her book were true, why didn't she just tell me?

17

You Will Not Lose, Will You?

W e got off the B train at Brighton Beach. The afternoon air was salty and lush, even under the shadow of the El tracks.

"Which way?" I asked my dad.

"I think it's this way."

We walked a few blocks down the bustling avenue, past a motley assortment of shops with signs mostly in Russian. A group of men walked ahead in three-wide formation, forcing aside old ladies toting heavy packages. Two of them wore thin leather gangster jackets and jeans, and the third, who was older, wore a snap-brim cap and a tight-fitting patterned sweater.

"Is that our advance team?" I said in a low voice.

"I think I might actually know those guys from the joint." My dad laughed.

We passed open-air fruit stands, fish markets, ice cream shops. I heard snatches of conversation, some in Russian, some in dem-dese-and-dose.

"What's the name of the place again?"

"The Tatiana."

We turned right at the next corner and hit the wooden boardwalk a block down. It was easily 80-feet wide, with a commanding view of the ocean past the long expanse of beach. A stiff salty breeze blew onshore, not at all unpleasant.

A quarter-mile down, we found the Tatiana, its large blue-and-white-fringed awning shading a couple of dozen café tables and chairs. Adjacent was another outdoor café, the Volna. Because it was still early spring and on the chilly side, neither was busy.

Dad said, "I don't see him."

A blond waitress approached. "Can I help you?" She had a thick Eastern European accent.

"We're meeting somebody."

"Would you like to sit?"

"Sure," my dad said.

She led us to a table close to the boardwalk. We ordered coffee. I looked at my watch.

"He's a few minutes late," Dad said. "So what?"

"Did I say anything?"

"You getting cold feet?"

"Maybe."

"You couldn't have told me that before we came all the fuck the way out here?"

"I did tell you."

"No, you asked me to make it happen."

"After I initially told you no thanks, it made me nervous."

"But now you think this is how you're going to save your marriage."

"I didn't say that. I said it *might* help."

The waitress reappeared with our coffees. "Would you like to order now, gentlemen?"

"We'll wait," my dad said.

"You have anything besides milk?" I asked, lifting the silver creamer. "Anything nondairy?"

"Are you fucking kidding me?" my father muttered.

"We haf half and half if you don't like regular," the waitress said.

"Nah, I'll stick with this," I said.

"Whaddya think, they got almond milk in Little Odessa?" Dad said as the waitress walked off. "Or soy milk? Maybe you should have asked for breast milk."

"I took a shot."

"You know I didn't push you into this."

"I'm not saying you did. I just don't like making decisions off a run of bad luck or factors unrelated to opportunity."

"Maybe your luck is about to change," said a growl of a voice from behind us.

We turned and were confronted by a large meaty-faced man with a broad wide nose and a shock of white hair.

"Kirill," Dad said, getting to his feet.

I got up too.

"Leo, my friend. How are you?"

"I want you to meet my son."

Kirill stuck out a hand. It was enormous, fat stubby fingers shaped like frankfurters. I felt like Jack shaking the hand of the giant.

"So, you are Nathan, the poker player," Kirill said. He pronounced my name *Natan*. "Please." He gestured for us to sit back down, waiting until we did, then taking a seat himself.

"Are you hungry? You want to get something to eat? If you want real Russian food I can take you another place. It's a little touristy here, but you get the ocean and the coffee's not bad."

197

"This is fine."

"Good. Let's talk."

"Like I told you," Dad interjected, "I thought you and Nathan should meet, see if your interests coincide."

"Nathan," Kirill said, turning to face me, his surprisingly gentle brown eyes contrasting with his thick crude features and pockmarked skin. "Not that I don't trust your father. But I did a little asking around. I find out you're a very good poker player."

"I do okay."

"There's a game goes on out here. Very juicy. I think you find it appealing."

"How big?"

"No limit, ten and a quarter. With no cap."

"Minimum buy-in?"

"Two thousand."

"And the players?"

"Gamblers. Action junkies. Very sick people."

"They're not going to have a problem if someone they don't know shows up?"

"You'll be with me."

"You play in the game too?"

"I observe."

"And what exactly is the arrangement?"

Kirill turned and smiled at my dad. "He don't waste time. I like that. No bullshit." He turned back to me. "You play on my dime. You win, I get sixty percent."

"And if I lose?"

Now I saw something in Kirill's eyes that was not so warm, not so friendly. "You will not lose, will you?"

"I mean…" I was thrown. "It's poker."

Kirill broke into a wide smile. His teeth were yellow and crooked.

"It's a joke, Nathan. I understand there are ups and downs."

I smiled back, though a bit uneasily. "Okay. I just want to be clear. If I lose—"

"Then we do makeup with five percent added to total each week."

"Makeup *plus* vig?"

"That's right. You make up your losses, plus interest."

"Wow. That's a bit stiff."

"I'm businessman. These are my terms."

I looked at Dad, who shrugged. Seeing my discomfort, Kirill said, "You don't look happy, Nathan."

"I'm just thinking about the numbers. What if I want to end the arrangement at any point?"

"You pay me back makeup and interest, and that's that."

"I have to pay it back?" I could feel myself frowning.

"You don't like it, we don't do this. But if you're as good as I hear, there won't be no makeup."

"I just need a few minutes to think about it."

Kirill fanned out his fingers. "I go make phone call." He got up and walked off, studying his cell phone.

I sipped my coffee and stared out at the ocean. My gut was telling me to walk away—as it had been ever since my dad first mentioned hooking me up with this guy. I couldn't get a clear read on him, but the terms alone should have been enough to scare me off, especially the interest and makeup part. Still, it was a staking situation. No outlay of my own cash—unless I was losing and wanted to end the arrangement. What was the real risk? And what other options did I have?

"What do you think, Dad?"

"It doesn't matter what I think. What do you think?"

"The game sounds juicy."

"So?"

"How about we try it one time, see how it goes?" I said to Kirill when he came back.

"Sure," he said. "As long as makeup and vig get paid, okay with me."

"When and where?"

He looked at me, a sly grin forming on his thick rubbery lips. "What time is it now?"

* * *

The club was one flight up, above Wes and Wanda's Hotsy Totsy Lounge on Coney Island Avenue. Dad hopped the subway back home. I was on my own with Kirill. As we climbed the long crooked stairs to the second floor, I was wired, trying not to show my nervousness.

The door at the top of the stairs opened and an extremely pretty girl of about 20 greeted us. She was wearing a top that exposed her toned silky midriff. *"Dobryj dyen'!"* She flashed a dazzling smile at Kirill and then at me, after which she and Kirill exchanged several more words in Russian.

"Nathan, this is Anya," Kirill said.

"Hello," she said, ducking her head sweetly before leading us into a small security anteroom. Her tight skirt accentuated her figure and long legs. We were buzzed through another door, which opened into a dimly lit space with red-velvet walls. At the center of the room, a strip of small overhead spotlights cast focused beams on a poker table. Around the table sat a group of players in a variety of attitudes, stacks of chips in front of them, a messy pile in front of the dealer. One of the players faced away from the action, bent over a TV table, shoveling food into his mouth. Two others straddled turned-around chairs, their heads resting on their forearms, while two Russian girls in a minimum of clothing rubbed their backs.

A heavy-set man got up and man-hugged Kirill. He was bald save for a horseshoe of close-cropped gray hair crowning his head. He

200

had a thin-lipped mouth so small it might have been created with a bottle opener. And icy blue eyes I would not have liked looking into for any length of time. Speaking English, Kirill introduced him to me as Viktor. Kirill and Viktor spoke in Russian for a brief while. Then Kirill said, "Please, Viktor, Nathan is our guest tonight, so maybe we all speak English now."

Viktor relayed the request to the table in Russian. One of the players said, "Sure. Why not?" Then he immediately said something in Russian and the rest of the table laughed.

Viktor hissed "Enough!" in an angry voice, cutting the laughter short.

"It was a joke," Viktor explained to me. "This one," he pointed to the player who spoke to the rest in Russian, "said, 'If the guy's a fish, we'll talk fish.' I apologize for him. He thinks he's funny, but he is an idiot. Right, Gary?"

Gary shrugged, making a *phtt* sound through puckered lips.

"I'll get you chips," Viktor said.

I took one of the two empty seats and looked around the table, nodding guardedly. A few of the players nodded back with equal enthusiasm. It had been a while since I'd sat in a cash game in New York without knowing a single face. After conferring with Kirill, Viktor brought me three thousand in chips.

I unracked, studying faces, forming quick impressions. They looked like players from any other poker game. Tracksuits. Hoodies. Polo shirts. Sunglasses. Expensive chunky rings and watches. Arm and neck tattoos. A couple of them were in their twenties. One or two were near sixty. Most were in between. They looked like wise guys and hoods. But then so did plenty of guys I played with.

Whenever one of them forgot and spoke in Russian, Viktor shot them a look and said, "No Russian! *Ne Russiky!*"

The game was just as Kirill described it. I began cautiously, trying to get a feel for the rhythms. One of the younger guys, wearing sunglasses and the beginnings of a beard, moved in his entire $4000 stack on a board of 4-5-K after a guy opened for $200 and got three callers. To my surprise, the original bettor snapped with K-10, then sucked out when a 10 hit on the river. The young guy slammed down his 4-5 face-up.

"You stink, Gary. You're a lucky son of a bitch like nobody I've ever seen."

"I thought you were on a draw, Alexey," Gary laughed. "If you hadna bet so much, I probably would have folded."

"Oh, I see. It was my mistake, getting you to call with a terrible hand."

Despite my intentions to lay low, sometimes the cards dictated the situation and things took on a life of their own.

In this case, sitting on the button, I called $125 with J-10 suited and three callers in front of me. The flop came a lovely 7-8-9, and to make things even sweeter, there was a bet and a raise before I had a chance to act. My adrenaline surging, I forced myself to slow down before acting.

"How much is it to me?" I asked.

"Twelve hundred."

I counted my chips as if considering.

"A little over two thousand nine hundred," I said at last, pushing my chips forward.

"You're all in?"

"Yeah, he's all in. Do you see any more chips? Are you hiding any in your hand?" Viktor said with a laugh.

"I call," the interrogator said without further thought. He was one of the younger guys, swept-back thick red hair, mirrored sunglasses.

I didn't even bother to ask about doing business. I was playing on somebody else's dime and I had the nuts. Why complicate things?

The dealer put out the turn and the river. A running pair of deuces.

"Full house," the redhead said, turning over pocket sevens.

I barked out a quick laugh, turning up my cards so that Kirill and the others could see my bad luck.

"A game of skill," Alexey said bitterly. "Ask Gary."

I looked to Kirill, who beckoned me over with a barely perceptible tilt of the chin. We took a walk to a corner of the room. One of the Russian beauties asked us if we needed anything. "Not now," Kirill said.

"Well, that was unfortunate," I said.

"So you reload," said Kirill matter-of-factly.

"Another three?"

"Why not do five?"

"You sure?"

Kirill nodded.

And that was that. Viktor brought me three thousand in blacks and two in green. Back into battle.

"We just got a puppy," Gary was saying. "You ever have a puppy? A focking pain in the ass."

"You got a kid, you get a puppy. It's a rule," Viktor said.

"Yesterday, my wife calls me. There's puppy shit all over the house. Okay, so what am I supposed to do about it? Why are you mad at me? Why are you calling me? Maybe you want to put the puppy on the phone? Let me have a word with him?"

Gary continued his running monologue. Only the two players involved in the hand weren't listening or laughing.

"I get home, there's a pile of shit in one corner, another pile on the rug. I say to my wife, Why the fock didn't you clean it up? She says, 'I wanted you to see it.' Really? She thinks I don't know what it looks like? She couldn't have texted me a picture?"

One of the two guys in the hand griped at Gary as the pot was pushed to his opponent, "Gary, you think you could shut the fuck up for once in your life?"

"This is what he does," said Alexey. "First he sucks out on you, then he talks until you lose your mind and all your money."

I had better luck with my second bullet, grinding my way up over $7000. There were only two players I considered "tough"—the aggressive young red-haired guy and Viktor. Mostly, I tried to steer clear of them. But sometimes a confrontation was unavoidable. So when I made it $100 from the button with pocket 10s and the red-haired kid reraised to $400 from the big blind, it wasn't as if I considered folding, it was just a question of whether or not to escalate the situation further. Calling was actually my way of keeping things small. I'd see what the flop brought and go from there. Having position on him was a big advantage.

As it turned out, it wouldn't be necessary for me to outplay him: the K-10-3 rainbow flop gave me middle set. Even better, he led out for $650.

My only thought at that point was how to get all the money in. If he had aces or AK and I raised, it would probably induce a shove. Alternatively, I could call and wait to raise until the turn, but if an ace or a nine hit, it might kill the action or even put me behind. Since I felt almost certain he had aces or AK, I thought it made sense to try and get him to commit right away. I announced a raise to $1400.

Pursing his lips, the kid nodded, made a clucking noise, leaned back, then shrugged and said, "I'm all in."

"Huh," I said because somehow hearing those words was always a slight shock even when that was the objective. I looked at his chips again. He had me covered for the five thousand I had left.

No real decision though. "I call."

"You're behind," he said and turned over pocket kings.

It was like a Sunday punch. I never saw it coming. The table erupted in a cacophony of Russian, this time without Viktor's admonishments.

As the dealer put out the meaningless turn and river (no, I didn't hit the miracle fourth ten) and shoved the massive $14,000 pot in the kid's direction, I just sat there, catatonic, too stunned to do anything but watch him stack chips.

When I was finally able to stand up, get away from the table, and try to process the mindfuck of going from thinking I had the nuts to realizing I had only one out, I came face to face with Kirill.

To my surprise, the hulking Russian wasn't upset. He flipped up a palm as if to say, what can you do?

"You want to keep going?"

I took a deep breath, realizing he was serious.

"I think I'm going to call it a night."

"You sure?"

I didn't know how to respond. I was numb.

Kirill drew in his lips, nodding back approvingly. "I will call you tomorrow."

One of the girls let me out, smiling sympathetically though more likely it was just pity. I walked the couple of blocks to the B train and waited out on the elevated platform in the chilly night air, trying to figure out what the hell had just happened to me and why my luck seemed to be running so bad.

18

Put Your Trust in Leo

I t was still dark out when I woke up. The glow of the streetlight outside illuminated the lumpy silhouette of my dad on the mattress beneath the window. I tried falling back asleep, closing my eyes, trying to keep my mind from replaying the night yet again. Not that it made any difference, but the fact that the red-haired Russian kid bet out after flopping top set kept nagging at me. Why would he do that? Who bet out top set like that on a board like that? It never even occurred to me to think about top set as a possibility given the action. Not that it was likely I'd have been able to get away from my hand anyway. But still. I might have *thought* about it if not for the kid betting out on the flop. How had he not checked? It was like he *knew* I'd flopped a set.

* * *

"You feeling any better?" Dad and I were waiting downstairs on the front walk of what I now thought of as Laura's.

"Should I be?"

"Go back out there, turn it around."

"You make it sound easy."

"You're discouraged."

"Worse."

"How?"

I still wasn't sure how to explain it.

"Daddy!"

Hannah came running down the path.

I caught her and lifted her in my arms. She was wearing a pair of bunny ears leftover from Easter.

"Poppa Leo!" she chirped over my shoulder.

"Hiya sweetheart."

Laura came down the front steps.

"Hi Leo. Wasn't expecting to see you."

"Hey, doll."

She turned in my direction and gave me a quick kiss. "Hi."

"Hey."

We stood there awkwardly. Her eyebrows arched slightly above the translucent frame of her sunglasses.

"You look nice," I said. She was still barely showing in her blousy white shirt and jeans.

"Thanks. Why don't you text me and let me know when you're coming back from the park?"

"Sure."

I really wanted to ask her where *she* was going. But I didn't, and she didn't say.

* * *

Standing outside the wrought-iron fence of the merry-go-round, I continued to ruminate about what happened out in Brighton. Hannah and my Dad were inside the carousel house, sitting atop majestic pole-bound horses, waiting. The distinctive, slightly creepy Wurlitzer music started up, and the carousel began to move, slowly at first, then picking up speed. Hannah's joy was tempered by terror. Dad shrugged and gave me a thumbs up each time they passed. About the third time around, I grew restless and took out my phone.

I hadn't talked to or seen Russian Eddie since the night of the murder, since the interrupted hand that seemed to be the point at which everything in my world had gone wrong. It was hard not to think about how different things might have been if the club hadn't been held up that night, if Max hadn't been shot, if the crackdown never happened.

"Nate, how are you? I'm sitting here playing five-ten at the Borgata. Where are you?"

"I'm with my kid at the park. Listen, I wanted to talk to you about something—"

"That was unlucky, what happened that day," Eddie said. "Very fucking unlucky. Bad for you. Bad for poker. Worse for poor Max."

Dad and Hannah waved at me as the carousel whirled by again. I waved back weakly and turned away.

"Listen, I went out to Brighton Beach the other day."

"No shit. What for?"

"I, uh, I actually played in a game out there."

"Jesus Christ. You played Brighton?"

"I probably should have called you first, huh?"

"I would have told you it was a bad idea. Whose place did you play at?"

"Viktor's?"

"Viktor's, really? Fuck."

"What's wrong with Viktor?"

"What isn't wrong with Viktor?"

"I was brought there by a guy named Kirill. He put me in the game."

"Kirill Koretski?"

"I actually don't know his last name."

"I hope for your sake it's not Koretski."

When I explained the arrangement and described what happened, Eddie said, "I'm not saying this is what they're doing, but right now, you owe money, right? You gotta win eight gees before you get a penny?"

"Right."

"So you go back there, now you're playing for Kirill and Viktor until you make it up."

I was getting a knot in my stomach.

"They need guys like you," Eddie continued, "good players who can win straight up without resorting to cheating. As long as they keep you in makeup, you'll be earning for them. They'll have you play in some other games where you'll be a stake horse but all the money'll go to them because of your red figure. The minute you get back into the black, you may find yourself at the wrong end of another cooler back at their game.

"The thing I'm wondering is why a smart guy like you would get involved with the Russians? You really should have spoken to me first. Who connected you to this Kirill guy anyway?"

I looked up and saw Dad coming toward me from the carousel house. He had Hannah by the hand.

"I'll call you back, Ed," I said, getting to my feet.

"I was starting to get dizzy on that fucking thing," Dad said. "But she's had enough anyway, right sweetheart?"

"Do you have to talk that way in front of her?"

"Oh, come on. She's not growing up in some fairytale. This is

Brooklyn."

"Poppa Leo said I could have ice cream, Daddy."

"Is that right?" I frowned at my father.

"Sure. Why not?"

Hannah looked at me like a puppy in a store window. Impossible to walk it back now. "All right. Fuck it," I said.

"See?" my father said. "Didn't that feel good? Let's get you some ice cream, kid!" He knelt down to high-five his granddaughter.

Later, going home after dropping off Hannah at Laura's, the two of us waited on the elevated subway platform near a homeless guy on a bench. His feet were wrapped in dirty cloth, his face and arms caked in grime.

Dad sat on the far end of the bench, upwind of him. I remained standing.

"Your friend Kirill, Dad…his last name Koretski by any chance?"

"Last I heard."

"I'm such an idiot."

"What are you talking about?"

"It was a setup. You hooked me up with your Russian mob buddy and I got roped in like a sucker."

"What are you talking about? Kirill was backing you. Why would he cheat you?"

"Because now he's got me on a leash."

"That's ridiculous," Dad said. "It makes no sense."

"You're right. It doesn't make any fucking sense. Which is how I know it's true and why I have you to thank for getting me involved in it."

The air on the platform stirred. The rumble of an approaching train.

"I don't know what to say," my father said.

"Don't say anything. It's my own fucking fault."

The train wasn't crowded. We sat down in the scooped-out seats.

I reflexively scanned the ads overhead. "Tell us where it hurts. Your career that is." "Now you can have beautiful clear skin with Dr. Zizmor." I glanced at Dad, imagining what his ad would be: "Put your trust in Leo. Things can't get any worse."

At the far end of the car, a guy was looking in our direction and grinning. I realized I knew him. Buzz-cut hair, hollow cheeks, sunken eyes, toothy grin. He got up and made his way over, all six and a half feet of him, fighting to keep his balance as the train lurched around a curve.

I was trying to remember his name.

"Avner," he said, reading my face.

"I remember bluffing you out of a big pot at the Siena Club about a year ago."

He laughed. "That was a bluff?"

"I thought I could get you to fold."

"Well, it worked," he said. "I'm actually on my way over to the club right now. Is that where you're headed?"

"No." I looked at him quizzically.

"I thought you might have heard. The Count's back in town from Paris. He dropped ninety dimes the past two days."

The Count was Henri-Phillipe de Cardevac, a rich playboy layabout whose poker losses were legendary. Once a fixture on the New York scene, he hadn't been seen in a couple of years. At least until now.

"Playing five-ten?"

"Twenty-five-fifty."

Hearing this was like getting inside information on a stock you didn't have the money to buy.

"Game's been going pretty much round the clock since Monday. I went home and slept for a few hours and now I'm on my way back."

We pulled into the 4th Avenue station. "Come on, Dad. This is our stop. Nice to see you, Avner. Say hello to the gang."

211

It was hard to say what the chances were of Avner and me being in the same subway car at the same time or what might have happened going forward if either one of us had chosen the car ahead or behind—just as it was impossible to know what would have happened if my mother hadn't spilled wine on her blouse and left a party at the exact moment my father was riding down an elevator in the same building. Or what causal relationship there was between that moment and one thirty years later when I would see and follow a pretty girl out of a bookstore because I wanted to extricate myself from a conversation with a bore I'd randomly bumped into. Could my mother and father have met some other way? Would I exist otherwise? Would Hannah? And were these useful questions to ask? How many nights had I tape-looped myself to sleep replaying a hand, wondering how differently things might have gone if I had called instead of raised or if another card in the deck had come out instead of the one that did? How many times had I thought about how one rave Roberta Smith review put Polly on the map? Or wondered why a dumbshit hoodlum's itchy trigger finger had launched a bullet at one particular guy lying on the floor instead of one of the other hundred people, including myself, doing the exact same thing?

So yeah, I was aware of the randomness of running into Avner while he was on his way to the Siena, but that didn't mean I was thinking about where it might lead. I was mainly just irritated; it underlined for me the fact that I was essentially out of action.

That irritation, however, did serve as a catalyst. Because combined with my curiosity to see if what Eddie said was true, when Kirill texted me a few hours later, wanting to know when I was coming back, I replied, "Yes," and the next day embarked on another trip to Brighton.

This time the night went differently. No coolers and no suckouts. The crew was largely the same, with a couple of new faces. Kirill sat at a table in the back, sipping coffee and flirting with the waitresses.

Viktor didn't play this time, just hung around, kibitzing, wearing a burgundy velour tracksuit with white stripes on the shoulders. At one in the morning, ahead $5,600, I cashed out.

Kirill congratulated me, saying, "You're still twenty-four hundred in the hole. That's nothing. You'll make that up next session and start earning."

During the long subway ride back home, I thought about what my play should be going forward. If Eddie was right about Kirill and Viktor, they'd stack the deck against me again and I'd get myself back in the hole. But was that even the issue? I tried to imagine what Laura would think or say if she knew what I was doing. Maybe my best move now was to quit while I was behind. Problem was, I didn't even have the $2,400 I needed to extricate myself from the Russian's clutches.

19

Down for the Count

The shrill ringing of the doorbell, someone pounding their fist heavily on the wooden door. I threw off my blanket and got up from the couch, aggravated and still half-asleep, wearing only a pair of boxer briefs. I staggered forward as the thumping continued.

"Hold it, for Chrissakes."

I turned the knob and pulled back the door. My dad was standing there with a shopping bag.

"Where the fuck are your keys, Dad?"

"In my pocket, where d'ya think? I thought you'd be awake. How you gonna make any dough lyin' in bed?" He brushed past me and beelined for the kitchen area, putting down the shopping bag and plucking a couple of plates out of the dish rack.

I followed, still rubbing sleep out of my eyes.

"What gives?"

"Russ and fucking Daughters is what gives. Lox, cream cheese, bagels. The whole shmear."

"You went all that way for bagels?"

"Not just bagels. While you were jerking off playing poker with those Russian gonifs, Ray lent me fifty bucks and I went to Yonkers." Dad clapped his hands together like cymbals. "Hit the fucking triple. Twelve thousand and change!"

I stood there blinking, nearly unable to take it in.

"You're allowed to look happy," he said. He unloaded the contents of the shopping bag on the counter, which included a fat brick of cash.

"Holy shit!"

"Take it."

"What?"

"Take it. I want you to go play in that game that tall kid on the subway was talking about."

"Are you serious?"

"Dead serious."

"Dad, if you're really feeling generous, I need to give Laura a chunk of that money."

"No." He took a knife to a bagel and sawed it in half. "Laura's gonna have to wait. I want you to put the whole twelve gees in play. No half-measures. No fucking around." He pried the lid off the cream cheese and slathered up a bagel. "By the way, this would be a lot better if you had a fucking toaster in here."

"Dad, Laura's gonna divorce me if I don't get her another five gees by Monday."

"She might divorce you anyway."

"So you're not going to help me?"

"I am helping you." He took a huge bite of the bagel, chewing noisily. "You just have to trust me."

Trust me. The words were as ridiculous as the bagel crumbs spilling

215

out of his mouth. And yet…

There was always the *and yet*.

"You need to do this," he said. "And you can do this. I'm telling you as your father. Don't ask questions. Don't try to think about it logically. Don't worry about consequences. Just play the fucking game."

* * *

The Siena Club looked the same as it always had. The only difference was they'd added a layer of security, built a second doorway a couple of feet past the first one, with a short walled-in passageway. But the moment you got through that, everything else was the same. It felt good to be back, breathing in the familiar aroma of fresh espresso and Umberto's garlicky red sauce mixed with the smell of tobacco fumes leaking out from the glassed-in smoking room.

"Well fock me if it eesn't Nathan Feeshure," said Iggy. "We all thought you retired."

I clapped hands with the towering Siena club padrone. "How could I stay away, Ignominius? I gotta feed my craving for Umberto's pasta."

"Don't keed me, Nathan Feeshure. We all know why you're here. Who's your friend?"

"Fellas, this is my dad, Leo Fischer."

Dad raised his arm like he was going to do a karate chop.

"Bullshit, you can't be Nathan's Dad. You've got hair on your head and you're good-looking."

"Nathan, I thought Doyle Brunson was your dad."

Three tables were crammed into the tight quarters but only one was in use. Being here was like a throwback to the old days, and, especially after my recent experiences, a welcome and comforting change. Here was Syrian Sal, Avner, Louis G, Dave Catskill, Lenny Garfinkle, Drunk Mike, D.J. And of course the star attraction, Henri-

Phillipe de Cardevac, aka the Count.

I didn't know if Henri was actual royalty or not, but I did know his family money came from banking and there was a lot of it.

I also knew that even if I didn't much like Henri, I wasn't allowed to show it. It was bad business and doing so would get you summarily disinvited from the game. All the same, it was annoying to watch everyone suck up to him.

From his Cybex-chiseled torso to his spa-pampered perfectly tanned skin to his biscuit brown Brunello Cucinelli cashmere hoodie, his entitlement wafted off of him in gentle Bulgari For Men-scented waves.

He treated the other players like they were well-paid lab monkeys in a science experiment he was conducting to amuse himself, often posing grammatical riddles to the table (such as "What is the third word in the English language, aside from 'hungry' and 'angry,' that ends in 'gry?'") as if the failure to answer correctly would be proof of inferiority.

I had to admit that some small part of me actually wanted to be liked by this monster of vanity. It was inexplicable—though I suspect that my fellow reprobates felt the same way.

Looking at them, I had a sense of mongrel kinship. We shared the same mission, but also a tacit awareness that the hunters could easily become the hunted.

"Nathan, we only got the one seat. Did your dad want to play?"

"Nah, nah, I'm just here to watch," Dad said.

"So Nathan's Dad, you going to enjoy watching your son give me all his money?"

"I just might."

"Get yourself some chips, Nathan," Iggy said. "I'm stuck balls. I need you in this game."

I walked around the corner into the adjoining little alcove, and there she was, Caitlin, sitting on a stool behind a rolling red cash cart, looking every inch the fresh-faced ingénue from a 1960s' French New-Wave movie. I felt my face go hot. I hadn't expected to see her again after all this time or be undone by the blueness of her eyes.

"I thought you were through with this," I said, stepping closer, hugging her. Her dark hair was tomboy pixie short. She smelled like cigarettes and coffee.

"Just when I thought I was out..."

"They make you an offer you can't refuse."

She pointed her finger at me and smiled. "You okay? D.J. told me things weren't so great."

"Yeah, not so great." I wondered what the deal was with her and D.J. Last I heard, they were done, but knowing D.J. their status could easily have changed again. Was it terrible that I'd thought about what I'd do if I couldn't save my marriage? That those thoughts included her? Maybe it was just because there was no one else to fantasize about. Or because I liked talking to her, felt comfortable, felt like she understood. "What about you?"

"I'm okay," she said. "It's easier being friends." She nodded toward the other room.

I nodded back with understanding and perhaps a little bit more. Reaching into my pocket for my roll, I counted out five thousand. I had another seven behind if I needed it. She handed me a rack with two columns of black chips and two green.

"Do I need to wish you luck?"

"If there's a word for something more powerful, then that."

She placed her hand on my arm and looked at me as if maybe whatever the force was could be transmitted that way.

Carrying my chips to the other room, I tried to regain equilibrium and focus. Guys had been shuttling in and out of this game for days, leaving only when Henri-Phillipe took a break or they ran out of money. Apparently, they'd just reconvened after one such break, so yesterday's money was off the table. It was as if the game was starting anew. Right now, Henri-Phillipe had everyone covered with fifteen thousand.

"Why didn't you call me about this?" I said to D.J. as I took a seat between him and Henri.

"You told me you were done with live poker in the city."

"Apparently I'm not."

Dad pulled up a chair behind me.

I turned. "Listen, Dad, I don't know if you can sit here. Henri, are you okay with my dad sweating me?"

Henri took a look at my father, sizing him up. "I suppose it doesn't matter."

"You don't ask me?" D.J. said.

I ignored him. "You're fine, Dad."

"Leo, just be sure to wink when he's bluffing," Drunk Mike said.

"If I wink every time he bluffs, I'll end up looking like a chippy in a whorehouse."

The guys all laughed. Dad was made for this crowd.

In most games I played, a twelve-grand bankroll would be plenty big enough. Not here, not now. This was a short stake and I badly needed to make some hands early on, something I obviously couldn't control. Being under-bankrolled was a significant handicap. Play too tight, I'd gradually get grinded into oblivion. Fail to pick my spots carefully, I might go bust in twenty minutes.

Dad sat over my shoulder for forty-five minutes as I folded unworkable hand after unworkable hand. Then he ordered a cup of espresso and a plate of Umberto's pasta and headed over to a corner chair with a folding table and a day-old *New York Post*.

"Nathan, even your father's getting bored," Iggy said. "Loosen up."

I forced myself to laugh because I didn't want them to see my frustration. When I finally did play a hand, ace-ten in position, I thought I got lucky on the ten-high flop. Dad stood up to watch as I bet and got called by Drunk Mike. On the turn, a seemingly innocuous deuce, I bet again. But this time Mike raised. A lot. Basically, I had to make a decision for all my chips.

My dad moved closer to get a better view. Mike was a solid player and saw the way I was playing. He was going to put me to the test. But he might also have a hand. Might have flopped a set. Might have called preflop with a pair of jacks. Might have hit two pair.

The longer I thought, the further away I was from knowing. In the end, I realized that I was going to have to fold. My mantra, learned long ago from a nickel-dime maestro named Fat Henry, was *When in doubt, throw it out*. Even so, it sucked not knowing. I should have thought about what I was going to do before I got myself in this position. If I had to fold to a raise, maybe I shouldn't have bet. But what I'd done? Weak, very weak.

And that weakness was driven home when Mike turned over his hand: a complete bluff.

I counted my stack. Twenty-three hundred. I folded the next hand and the hand after that. My father leaned close and whispered in my ear, "Get up."

"No." I pouted, sucking in my lips, just like I used to when I was a kid.

Dad gave me the stare. "Let's go outside."

I felt as though I were being punished. Grumbling, I got up.

Did I hear snickering in my wake? Caitlin unlocked the inner door for us.

"We're coming right back," I told her.

We walked down to the corner. Dad lit a cigarette. Inhaled.

"What the fuck are you doing?" Smoke streamed out of his mouth along with the words.

"Dad, I had to fold there. You don't understand—"

"I'm not talking about that. I'm talking about you sitting there with two thousand dollars in front of you. How are you gonna win that way? I thought we understood each other."

"Dad—"

"I said we're going for it and you said okay."

"I know but—"

"Play the game. Don't play the money. Play the fucking game."

"No, you're right. I just—"

"Just what?"

"You're right."

Back inside, I gave Caitlin the case money, the remaining seven thousand. Predictably, when I carried the chips to the table, the razzing started.

"Now you got enough mazoomah to get blinded off for the rest of the night," Lenny Garfinkle said.

"Suck it, Lenny."

"I plan to."

A hand soon developed between Syrian Sal and Henri. After Henri opened for $125, Sal three-bet to $450 and Henri called.

On the K-10-7 flop, Henri check-called Sal's bet of $550. A five came on the turn and he check-called a bet of $1,250. The river was a three and this time, after Henri checked, Sal bet $3,200.

Almost instantly, Henri check-raised all-in.

Sal reared back, genuinely stunned. The rest of the table silently rejoiced. Everyone liked seeing the shark attacked this way. It was the unlikeliness of it, the minnow ramming its nose into the shark's eye. Then again, Henri loved to move his stack in when it seemingly made no sense. He loved the polarizing bet that meant he either had a monster or nothing.

In this case, the complicating factor was the five on the turn and the three on the river. Everyone knew that 5-3 was Henri's favorite hand. He played 5-3 like it was pocket aces, routinely getting all his money in with it preflop.

In this instance, though, since he hadn't played the hand aggressively, it was hard for Sal to think or worry that he might have five-three.

"You want me to call, Henri?"

"How do I know, Sal?"

"Are you pretending you have three-five?"

Henri shrugged.

In the end, given that he had A-K and had flopped top pair, top kicker, and given that he only had another couple of thousand behind, Sal did what pretty much anyone there would do. He called.

Henri tabled the 5-3.

"No fuckin' way!" Drunk Mike yelled.

"That is craaazy," D.J. said.

Sal just stared at the board, trying to figure out how the hell Henri had *gotten* to the river. You could see him working it through. "I bet the flop and he calls out of position with five high, so he could *what?* Hit a five on the turn? And then a three on the river for a running two pair?" It was nonsensical. Inexplicable. But this was Henri. The reason we were all there.

After reloading for ten grand, Sal opened the very next hand, and I found myself faced with a dilemma of my own. There were two guys in the game that I'd told myself I didn't want to tangle with: D.J. and Sal.

Ace-jack of hearts in position after a raise wasn't a great hand, but certainly playable. Even so, folding wasn't the worst move, given my bankroll limitations, and that was what I might have done if I didn't think Sal was so tilted.

It was one of the few areas where I had an edge on him. Sal was definitely more susceptible to blowing up than I was. I mean, looking at him, I could almost see the steam coming out of his ears. If I didn't try to exploit that then I really didn't belong here. But instead of just calling with my A-J and waiting to see what the flop brought, I followed my dad's advice and forgot about the money, forgot about bankroll. I needed to play like I just didn't give a fuck. Which is why I raised.

"Four fifty," I said, casually tossing out the chips.

If Sal had a big hand, I wanted to find out right away. Aces, kings, queens, ace-king, ace-queen, I was almost a hundred percent sure that Sal, out of position, would play back at me with one of those.

Instead, he merely called. I filed that in the data bank, and we went to the flop.

It came an ace and two littles.

Sal checked. I bet six-fifty. He took his time, then called.

The turn was another little card.

Again, Sal checked. There was $2300 in the pot. I took my time, thinking, as I had failed to do earlier, about what my plan was if I got raised. My gut told me that Sal wasn't very strong, but I also felt certain he was planning to check-raise me. It was just something about the way he checked, a certain tension in his body. I went ahead and bet $1,400.

Sal muttered something, and after a few moments, I realized that Steve Drummer was now looking at me expectantly.

"What did he say?" I asked.

"He said 'all in,'" Drummer said.

I laughed. "Seriously?"

There was thirty-seven hundred in the pot and Sal's reraise was an additional six thousand.

"Jesus, Sal. I know you're steaming but why would you do that?"

The outsized raise was almost exactly what Henri just did to *him*, the polarizing big bet that meant monster or nothing. I'd been planning to move in on Sal if he raised, but now he'd stolen my thunder. My options were binary: call or fold.

I tried to banish the suffocating surge of emotion that was threatening to short-circuit my brain. *You had a read*, I told myself. *Don't let the situation overwhelm you.*

I knew if I called and I was wrong, I'd be broke. That'd be it. Utter devastation and ruination. Any sliver of hope that I could retake control of my life gone. Marriage over. Credibility lost. Transformation into my nightmare version of myself complete. Folding the winner in this spot would be bad, but it would still leave me with six thousand dollars—enough ammo to resurrect myself.

"I don't get it, Sal. Why all in?"

Sal grinned. "I'm doing you a favor, believe me. If you want more specific advice, why don't you tell me what you have and then I'll tell you what to do."

This was Sal's game. The coffeehouse. If you let yourself listen, he'd sell you water during a deluge.

"Give me a minute," I said.

"Take your time," Sal said. "I want you to be sure to make the right decision."

Mike Caro said that a good player figures out what his opponent wants him to do, then disappoints him.

So what was Sal trying to get me to do? Why had he check-called the flop bet? There were no draws out there. Sure, he could have flopped a set or two pair. But it was also possible that he just had a weak ace and put me on a bigger one. He'd seen how tight I was playing. Logic indicated I couldn't take a lot of heat. If Sal really did think he was outkicked, his only path to taking down the pot was to make the move he'd made.

But what if I were wrong? In my mind's eye, I pictured Sal turning over a set or two pair, and the sick feeling I'd get from the punch-in-the-gut news I sort of knew was coming.

Looking for a reaction, I cupped my hands behind my chips as if I were about to push them. Without missing a beat, Sal reached for his cards as if he was about to flip them over. The guy had all the moves. My hands were still on the chips, but I was paralyzed. Everyone was watching, waiting. I looked at my dad. His expression gave me nothing to go on, but I thought again of what he'd said. *Play the game.* And before I even realized I'd made up my mind, my hands were pushing forward, the chips spilling in the direction of the pot.

"*That's* a call," Steve Drummer said—and from Sal's reaction, I knew instantly.

The river card changed nothing. Sal shook his head and turned up ace-four suited. With a surge of triumph, I flipped over my ace-jack.

Raking in the nearly twenty-thousand dollar pot, my hands were trembling, heart pumping.

"Son of a bitch," Sal said. "I didn't think you had the stones."

I looked over at my dad, who pumped his fist. Caitlin had come over to watch, too, and she mouthed the word "Nice."

There was nothing better, maybe nothing in the world, than knowing that you had picked off a killer shark like Syrian Sal with a marginal hand in a difficult spot. Especially in front of an audience. Everyone loved a winner.

As I sat there, basking, the aroma of the garlic wafting out of the kitchen suddenly smelled more delicious than anything I'd ever smelled before. I realized I was starving.

I poked my head into Umberto's lair and asked the red-sauce maestro to make me a plate of pasta. Then I went to take a piss. Even that had a heightened intensity, like the best, most satisfying piss I'd ever taken. I grinned at myself in the mirror. Winning really did change everything. My skin, my shoulders, my whole body felt vibrant and powerful. On my way back to the table, my dad intercepted me.

"That was fucking balls out, kid," he whispered.

"Thanks, Dad."

"How much you up now?"

"I'm sitting on about twenty-two thousand."

"Don't let up."

I could see he was worried I might blow it. But I knew now that I wouldn't. Something had just shifted. I felt like myself again, like I'd gotten back my mojo.

By the time Umberto brought over my bowl of pasta, I'd won a medium-size pot off Iggy and then a big one off Henri when I flopped a set. In under an hour, I went from nine thousand to forty-seven thousand.

"Cheese?" Umberto asked.

"Absolutely."

"Fresh," he said, rubbing a hunk of Parmigiano against a grater.

I handed him a green chip.

"This is the best, isn't it?" D.J. said after Umberto brought him a bowl too.

"Nothing better," I said.

"I'm sure it tastes very good," Henri said, "when you are running lucky. But I would never eat anything from this kitchen." Henri's meal was a raw vegan concoction in a Tupperware container.

"What's wrong with the kitchen?" D.J. asked.

"You've never noticed the mouse turds on the counter?"

D.J. stopped his fork midway to his mouth. I kept right on eating.

"Henri," I said, "I don't mean to alarm you, but the plastic container your food's in? It leaches chemicals into food that act just like estrogen."

"No no, my container is BPA-free."

"BPA-free is bullshit. Everyone knows that."

"*Casse-toi!*"

Several of the guys stifled laughs, trying not to smile.

"Iggy," Henri said peevishly, "I need more chips."

"Sure, Henri. How much?"

"Fifty thousand. I want enough to cover everyone."

Caitlin brought out a rack of pink five-hundred-dollar chips and placed them in front of Henri. It didn't take long for him to put them to use.

Maybe four hands later, Iggy and Avner limped in for fifty, and when I found two eights on the button, I bumped it up to three hundred.

Henri, on the big blind, looked down and slid his rack of pinks into the pot.

"*Wha-aat?*"

The whole table started laughing like it was a joke. A fifty-thousand dollar raise on a three-hundred-dollar bet? Everyone folded back around to me. I was the only one left. I shrugged, turning up my hand for all to see.

"Not exactly worth fifty K."

I was about to toss the two eights into the muck when Henri said, "Wait!" He turned over his cards: an off-suit five and three.

"Are you fucking kidding me?" D.J. said.

Now everyone was talking at once, laughing, holy shitting, creating such a commotion that even Caitlin and Umberto crowded around the table.

I swallowed hard, having no idea what to do. This wasn't poker anymore. This was some weird head game. A mind fuck. The rich guy basically saying fuck you. You want some? Come and get it. Except you can't, can you? It's too much, too big a risk.

He was right. I had over forty-seven thousand dollars. My original twelve, plus thirty-five in profit. Was I willing to gamble it all, even as a heavy favorite, on one run out?

Somebody, maybe it was D.J., said, "You're eighty-three percent."

Eighty-three percent! To double my money. My head spun.

Of course, you have to have a tolerance for risk to sit down at a poker table. It's a given. I didn't crave it the way some guys did. I didn't get off on it. When Phil Laak said, "Poker is pain," he was talking about risk and luck, the inevitability that you were going to get unlucky, you were going to feel pain. Being a pro meant managing risk and money wisely and never putting yourself in a spot where that inevitable pain would be crippling.

"Come on, Nathan. What are you gonna do?" This from Iggy.

"You don't want to play it, I'll buy it from you," Lenny Garfinkle said.

"Really? How much?"

"Let's see. Five to one. I'd need to put up your forty-seven, so that would mean…" He stared at the rack of pinks, doing some quick calculations. "I can pay you twenty."

"Fuck that. I'll give you twenty-three," Dave Catskill said. He was an older guy, in his sixties, who supposedly made a bundle investing in ski condos in the Catskills.

"I'm already stuck my ass. I'll make it twenty-five," Syrian Sal said.

"No deals," Henri said. "He's not allowed to sell the hand. I made this play against him. Not any of you."

"He can sell it if he wants to," Sal said. "Why not?"

"What about it, Iggy?" Dave Catskill said. "This is your club. What's the ruling?"

"What the fuck," Iggy grumbled. "You all gonna whine and complain no matter what I do."

"Don't be a pussy, Iggy. Just make a ruling. Nobody likes you anyway."

"All right. Fine. The ruling is one player to a hand."

"Iggy," I said. "You do know they mean something else by that rule?"

"I don't give a fock what *they* mean. This is what *I* mean. Nobody can buy this hand from you. It's your choice. Call or fold."

My father interrupted at this point. "Do you guys mind if I have a word with my son?"

Henri muttered something I didn't understand under his breath, then shrugged.

Dad put his arm around my neck and walked with me to the far corner of the room.

"This is real money, Dad! Forty-seven thousand."

"Is that money in play?"

"What do you mean?"

"You were sitting there, weren't you? Was that money in play?"

"Yeah, but—"

"So you were willing to gamble it?"

"This is different."

"Is it?"

"I had more control."

"Did you?"

"Anyway, it's not about that. This is a bankroll decision."

"We already made that decision when you bought in."

"But things have changed."

"Hey, you know what? I'm your backer. I get to make this decision."

"Dad…"

"I love you, son. But I know you know that no opportunity comes without risk. That rich motherfucker is practically begging you to take his money. So please, let's go take it."

He kissed my cheek and half-pushed me back toward the table.

I moved back to my seat but didn't sit down. I picked up my cards, shook them angrily in front of me, looking at them like they were about to cause me pain. Then I looked at my dad, who looked back, his gaze unwavering, his mouth set. What he wanted for me, from me, was as confusing as ever. I wasn't sure what I wanted either. Did I hate him or love him? Was he just a bum who craved loss and devastation? Was I letting him pull me into the same dirty garret where he lived? Did he want me to be a loser too? Could he not stand the idea of me winning? Or did he merely want my company, a way to feel less alone? Whatever the truth was, I knew that I still *wanted* to believe in him, believe that he really did want the best for me and always had, as the father in me knew about the father in him—and the only way I could show it was this. I threw the cards down on the felt face up, saying, "I call."

Avner and D.J. had their phones out, taking pictures. "No one's gonna believe this shit."

"I'm here and I don't fucking believe it."

It was doubtful that even in the WSOP Main there'd ever been a hand with as much emotional consequence or as slow and excruciating a denouement. Steve Drummer, after counting out forty-seven thousand from Henri's rack and sliding back the rack with the remaining pinks, gathered all the chips into a huge pile in the center of the table. Then, looking around to make sure everyone was ready, he rapped his knuckles on the felt, burned a card and dealt out three more cards face down.

"Big cards," I pleaded. "Big cards."

Drummer turned them up and spread them.

Pandemonium.

I swung away from the table and closed my eyes, unable to breathe.

I looked back a moment later, just to make sure.

The flop hadn't changed.

Three of spades. Seven of hearts. Five of clubs.

Some of the guys were giddy, laughing at the ridiculousness of it. Henri took it in with a smug supercilious half-grin. He wasn't surprised at all. He was playing his lucky hand after all. And he knew that it was a rule of life: The rich asshole always wins.

Or maybe: the poor schmuck always loses.

Whatever the rule, I was already thinking about what came next. How my life was over. Again. Even if Laura never heard the story of how I lost forty-seven thousand on one hand, if she never heard that I could have walked away being able to pay all our bills for the next year, if she never knew the truth…. Even then I was fucked.

Fucked. That's what came next. I was thinking about how to frame this and that was the frame. With a picture of me inside it.

The room had gone silent except for the ringing noise inside my head. Drummer knuckled the table and dealt the turn card.

A four of hearts.

I wished there was some way to stop time. Turn it back. Or off. Have a do-over.

D.J. put a hand on my shoulder.

My dad came up behind me, whispering in a barely audible voice that he was sorry. From Caitlin, I got a look of pity that cut like a knife.

Drummer dealt the river card.

A six.

For a second, I didn't even realize what it meant.

It wasn't until Henri slammed his fist down on the rail and everyone started screaming that it dawned on me what had just happened.

The six had given me a straight.

I was frozen, too stunned to do anything. The sick feeling I got after seeing the flop hadn't gone away, like the time in the supermarket with Hannah. It went too deep, hurt too much. Even winning wasn't enough to allow me to forget.

"That! Was! Fucking! Epic!" D.J. yelled.

"Holy shit, bro! This is going right up on YouTube!"

Henri stood up, shaking his head, watching as Drummer shoved the massive pot in my direction. Then he began gathering his things. Cellphone. Backpack. Plastic food container.

"That's it, I'm done with this game," he said. *"Poker peut embrasser mon cul."* He headed toward the door. "Somebody let me out, please!"

Iggy unlocked the doors and there went Henri. The Count down for the count.

"Fuckin' guy," Sal said. "He moved in with five-three off for fifty K against an overpair, loses, and now he's done with poker."

Everybody laughed.

Except me. I understood exactly how Henri felt.

20

If I Were a Mosquito

Three days later, I was standing outside the door of the Siena, holding Hannah's hand, knowing one thing for certain: Laura was gonna divorce me if she ever found out about this.

What happened was that Iggy called me to tell me he had my money, and if there was one thing I knew, it was that you never said no to a guy offering to pay you. Especially when it involved these kinds of numbers, and especially in light of my recent misfortunes.

The problem was, my dad was off somewhere and not answering his phone, and Laura had something she was doing. I felt like I had no choice but to bring Hannah with me.

Standing underneath the security camera, I began having second thoughts. Would it be worse to leave her sitting at the bar of the restaurant next door for ten minutes in the care of a waitress?

It was three in the afternoon. Chances were it was only Iggy in the club alone. Better to keep her with me than leave her with strangers.

I bent down, so my face was level with Hannah's. "Under no circumstances," I said, "are you ever to tell Mommy that we've come here. Do you understand?" Hannah's eyes were wide and guileless and they did not blink. "Mommy would not like it if she knew, honey. And we don't want to upset her, so please promise me this is our secret."

"You're silly, Daddy."

"Promise me."

"But Mommy knows you go to the poker house."

"Just promise me, kiddo."

"Okay."

Iggy opened the door for us. Inside, to my surprise, a six-handed game was going full swing, some of the same guys from the other day gambling it up.

"Look at what the cat drug in," Dave Catskill said, seeing Hannah and me. "Getting the whole family involved now, huh?"

"If I had any idea you degens would be here, I would never have come."

"Hi sweetheart," Catskill said. "What's your name?"

"Hannah."

"You're beautiful, Hannah. Has anybody ever told you that?"

Hannah nodded yes.

The guys cracked up.

"Your Daddy is a lucky man," Drunk Mike said. "But I bet you knew that."

"My daddy says poker isn't luck."

This killed them. They laughed so hard that it scared Hannah, who hid behind my legs.

"Come on, Iggy," I said. "Let's take care of this before Child Protective Services comes after me."

Iggy led me into the alcove with the red cash cart. I'd brought an empty backpack, which I unzipped in preparation. Iggy unlocked one of the drawers in the box. Banded five-thousand-dollar packets were arranged neatly inside.

"Fresh from Moneybags' bank," Iggy said. He counted out eighteen of the packets and stuck them on top of the box. Then he pulled out a nineteenth, broke the band and counted out forty bills. There were ten left over, which he pocketed. "You want to count the others?"

"Not necessary," I said. I started loading the packets into my backpack.

"Daddy, is all that money yours?"

"Yes."

"Is it a lot?"

"Kind of a lot."

"They're blaming you for Henri quitting," Iggy said. "Me, personally, nothing could be sweeter—unless it had been me winning his money."

"I bet he comes back."

"I don't know. And I don't care."

"You may not see me for a while, either, Iggy."

"You? Why?"

"I need a break."

"Now you can afford one."

He walked me and Hannah back out to the front room.

"Got a seat with your name on it," Catskill said.

"Not today, fellas."

"Why don't you put some of that glimmer back in play?"

"You don't want my action, believe me."

"Hannah, darling, maybe you want to play with us?"

She shook her head, again hiding behind me.

"It's okay if you don't know how. We'll teach you."

"Come on, Hannah," I said. I took her by the hand. "How would you like a milkshake?"

* * *

In the vestibule at Laura's, I rang the bell. While we waited, I unzipped the backpack and removed two of the five-thousand-dollar packets, sticking them in my pocket.

"Remember," I told Hannah, "don't tell Mommy where we were."

"I won't, Daddy."

Laura was waiting upstairs in the doorway.

"Hey." She kissed me lightly on the lips.

"Hi."

"So what'd you guys wind up doing?"

Hannah shrugged in an exaggerated way that made Laura suspicious.

"What did you do?" Laura said pointedly, looking at her, and then at me.

I decided I better take charge before things got out of control. "Well, it's possible that we got a milkshake," I said.

"Nathan! I thought we talked about that."

"I know. But they're so good. A chocolate cookie dough milkshake? Why didn't they have them when I was a kid?"

"Hannah, your daddy spoils you."

"It's true," I said.

"Don't sound so proud of it."

"Mommy, can I watch?" Hannah asked.

"Maybe after we wash your hair."

"Pleaaase."

"We'll see."

"Plleaaase!"

"I said we'll see."

"Actually," I said to Laura. "You have a few minutes now? Maybe we could let her watch and you and I could talk?"

Deep breath. "All right. But just a few minutes." Laura looked from me to Hannah. "Are we clear on that, Hannah?"

While Hannah stretched out on the rug in front of the TV, we planted ourselves on opposite ends of the stained blue couch by the two big windows at the rear of the apartment. Laura sat crossed-legged like a Buddha, fingers interlaced, hands resting on her swollen belly.

"I'm not trying to pressure you," I said. "But Hannah's confused about things."

"Is that what she's been saying?"

"She wants to know why I don't sleep here anymore."

"And what do you tell her?"

"What I've told her all along. That I'm at my studio trying to finish a big project, that it's easier for me to sleep there while I work on it. At some point, though, that's not going to be enough."

"For her or for you?"

"For everyone."

"Why don't you just ask me what you want to ask me then, instead of putting it on her?"

"Okay."

"Okay, what?"

"I'm asking you."

"What are you asking?"

"Laura, why are you making this so hard? You know what I'm asking."

"Then say it."

"I want to move back in."

She tilted her head to one side then turned and looked out the window at the sky. "Are we being real now?"

"That's all I want. I just want some clarity. I don't like this. I don't like the way things are. I don't like us being apart."

"Really?"

"Really."

"That's interesting because for the past few years I've gotten the feeling that not only do you not mind us being apart, you actually crave it. You need it. You look for any excuse you can to make sure that we're apart."

"That's not true."

"Well, that's how it felt to me. Do you know how many nights I've spent alone since we got married?"

"I've been working!"

"Funny how you call it that."

"It *is* working. It might have been something else once, but now it's work. You think I've wanted to spend all that time out of the house?"

"Sometimes. Sometimes I think you'd rather be hanging out with a bunch of degenerates than with me and your daughter."

"You spend your days in front of a computer screen making up stories. I spend my time at poker tables with cards in my hand, and in front of a canvas with a paintbrush in my hand. That's who we are."

"You mean were. You think I don't know that you haven't been painting? You haven't once asked me to come to your studio. Not in a year."

"And you haven't let me read your book. What does that prove? We both have our reasons."

"Look, I haven't been straight with you," Laura said.

My stomach lurched.

She opened her mouth to speak. I could tell it was bad. There was a whisper of sweat on her upper lip. Tension in her shoulders. Cold fear in her eyes. Fuck. It was the worst thing it could possibly be.

"It's not mine."

When she didn't respond right away, I said, "Is it *his?* Is that why you're not saying anything?"

"That's actually the funny part."

"You mean you *thought* it was."

Her face began to crumple from the strain of holding back tears.

"So you lied to me. It wasn't fiction. The stuff about him."

She was crying now.

"Does *he* know? Whose it is?"

She nodded.

"Well, that's great. That's just fucking wonderful. I guess he wasn't too thrilled."

"I know you won't believe me, but I'm glad it's yours." She kept sobbing.

It was my turn to be quiet.

"Please don't be mad…"

"Ugh." I felt sick. I got to my feet.

"I'm sorry. I'm sorry I've hurt you."

I didn't want to show how much.

"Nathan…"

"I gotta go."

"Please Nate."

I went into the middle room. Hannah was glued to *Yo Gabba Gabba*. "I'm going now, sweetie."

"Bye Daddy." She was stretched out on her stomach, looking at the screen.

I returned to the other room. "I almost forgot," I said. "This is for you." I pulled the two banded five thousands out of my pocket.

"Jesus," Laura said.

"It's ten."

"But three days ago you didn't have anything."

"Things can change in a hurry, can't they?"

"Please don't leave, Nate."

I turned around and walked out.

* * *

Back at the studio, with my father watching, I dumped the remaining rubber-banded green bricks out of my backpack onto the paint-spattered work table.

He nodded approvingly. "Don't let anybody ever tell you that money doesn't fucking matter. It matters."

"Yeah, maybe." I counted out the twelve grand I owed him, then another twelve on top.

"You don't have to do that."

"Just swear to me that you won't do something stupid with it."

"Can I tell you something?"

"What?"

"Promise you won't get mad?"

"Why would I make a promise like that? What are you going to tell me?"

"I didn't exactly hit the triple at Yonkers like I said I did."

"What?"

"I borrowed the money from a shylock. I felt bad about the thing with Kirill. You needed a way out."

"So you doubled down? Are you insane? What the hell would have happened if I'd lost that twelve?"

"Nothing would have happened, not to you."

"I'm talking about you."

"They'd have had to find me."

"All that bullshit about hitting the triple was an act?"

"Convincing, huh?"

"Doesn't say much for my reading ability."

"Think you'd have been able to win if you'd known the truth?"

"I probably wouldn't have been able to get out of bed."

* * *

I made the trek, alone, out to Brighton Beach the next day and paid the Russian the $2,400 plus interest (it came to another $360) I owed him. I shook his hand, thanked him for the opportunity and breathed a huge sigh of relief as I walked away forever.

For his part, Dad did the same, paying back the shylock the twelve grand plus the juice he owed. And just like Ray said, Dad's landlord Mancuso turned out to be a reasonable guy. He and Dad managed to patch things up after Dad paid all the back rent plus the next two months in advance.

The day I helped my father move back, Ray took me aside and said, "I'll make sure I stay on top of him this time. I won't let things get out of hand, you know, where he's falling behind."

"I'll try to do a better job myself," I said. "I'm hoping maybe he learned his lesson, though I doubt it."

With Dad out of the studio, I was surprised to find that I actually missed him, missed his company. I couldn't help thinking about all the righteous anger I'd carried around for so long and how much easier it was to let it go. There was a lesson in there somewhere. Who the hell knew? Maybe everybody just needed to back the fuck off and relax.

The morning after he moved out, I picked up my brushes and began painting again.

It didn't happen right away, but a few days in, I found the flow. I'd spent the previous few days leafing through art books and playing solitaire. It was the cards, actually, that were the spark. All the time I spent looking at cards, seeing them but not *seeing* them. What were they? What did they mean to me? How had I let them become such an integral part of my existence?

The windows were wide open; a soft breeze carried the smell of spring. I had Prince on the iPod. My mind gradually emptied and there was just the canvas in front of me and the brush in my hand.

When daylight began to fade I realized that I'd been going for eight straight hours without a break. By then I was tired in mind and body. A tired that felt good. I poured myself a glass of wine and cooked up some pasta on the hot plate.

And I sat there looking at what I'd done.

It was hard to withhold judgment, to just see the work as someone else might, but that was the goal. It was a big canvas, four by five. Thick with paint now, a torso and a face, distorted, almost like a burn victim, grotesque in a way, slightly menacing. I'd layered the paint inches thick in places, great rippling swatches of color, cadmium reds and yellows, yellow ochre, titanium white, ultramarine blue, oxide black. In the upper left-hand corner, I'd painted the number 6. Same thing in the lower right-hand corner. I had a ways to go, but it felt like it was taking shape.

Poker had gotten me back here somehow. The hand with Henri had shifted something, opened my eyes to the lunacy of how I'd been living. That sick feeling I'd gotten seeing the Count outflop me was now deep in my blood, in the fiber of my being, in every breath I took. I needed some way to let it out and this was it.

* * *

Laura made it clear she wanted me to come home. She knew there was nothing she could say to fix what happened. But she still loved me and hoped that was enough.

All these weeks, I'd wanted to go back home, have her ask me to come home, and now I was the one who wasn't sure.

* * *

"The check clear?" the voice on the end of the line said.

"Yeah. I'm all square with Chrome now. But don't let that give you the idea you're not a fucking prick, Richard."

"Maybe you'll feel more forgiving when I tell you why I really called."

"I'm all ears."

"Your paintings. The ones I took with me to Miami? A woman came into the gallery yesterday, said she'd seen them there."

"Yeah?"

"She bought two of the big ones on the spot."

"Two of them?"

"You don't know anything about it?"

"How would I know anything?"

"I got the feeling from her that she was fronting for a collector. She sort of hinted around but wouldn't tell me who it was. I'm thinking maybe it was Saatchi. But who knows?"

"And she bought those two big ones? Damn!"

"She's coming in today with a cashier's check. I'll see if I can find out more then. Assuming she gives me the check, you'll get your share as soon as it clears my bank. You really sure you don't know anything about this?"

"What the fuck is your problem?"

"Nothing. It just seems odd is all. Anyway, it doesn't matter. But it did get me thinking…I'd like to come by your studio, see what you're up to. There might be a spot open in the schedule this winter."

"What about Finn?"

"Don't worry about Finn. I'll deal with Finn. Just let me know when I can drop by."

* * *

Laura went into labor three days before her due date. She felt it coming on after dinner and called and asked me to come over. We stayed up watching TV for a while, then tried to sleep, side by side in what had been our shared bed. I managed to doze off, but she was up most of the night. In the morning when the contractions and pain began for real, I called a cab and woke up Hannah. The three of us rode across the bridge into Manhattan, to NYU Downtown, the same hospital where Hannah had been born. They gave us a room, but Laura's labor progressed so slowly that at one point, urged by a nurse, Hannah and I went outside to get some air.

Laura actually seemed relieved to be rid of us, and it gave me a chance to explain to Hannah that Poppa Leo would be with her in the waiting room during the delivery and that he might have to take her back home for the night at some point.

With one of her little hands in mine and the other holding Flora the sock monkey, we walked down Gold Street, both of us aware of the big change that was coming, though it was safe to say with different concerns. It was a beautiful day, the narrow downtown streets full of tourists and pinstriped Wall Streeters out on lunch break. In City Hall Park, I bought Hannah a fat doughy pretzel from a vendor under a Sabrett umbrella, rubbing off the salt flecks, which were big enough to melt snow, because I knew she didn't like them. Nearby on a bench, a couple, apparently in the midst of a fight, sat separated by at least several feet of green-painted wood. I knew they were together by their attitudes and postures, her face tight, arms locked across her chest, his face not even visible because his arms were spread across the top of the bench and his head was leaning back so far it was almost as if he were looking at the world behind them upside down.

"Daddy," Hannah said, chewing on her pretzel.

"What, sweet?"

"What if Mommy's having the baby right now?"

"I don't think she is."

"But what if she is?"

"The nurses are there. They'll make sure she's safe."

"I'm afraid, Daddy."

"Don't be afraid, honey. It's going to be fine."

"I want to go back and see Mommy."

"There's really no need to rush."

"I want to go back now!"

"Okay." I laughed. "We can go back now."

Walking out of the park, we passed a cluster of tulips, their red, yellow and purple bulbs nearly incandescent. I pointed them out to Hannah, saying, "They're pretty, aren't they?"

"I want a sister, not a brother."

"I think a brother will be nice too."

"But I don't like boys."

"Really? You don't like boys?"

She shook her head.

"I'm a boy."

"You're my Daddy." She stopped and looked at me. "Are you and Mommy still married?"

"Sure we're still married."

"Then why don't you sleep in her bed anymore?"

I let out an abrupt laugh. "Wow, you're pretty direct, little lady, aren't you?"

"I remember seeing you sleep very nicely together once."

"Yeah, I remember that, too."

Frowning, she dragged Flora along the hood of a parked car.

"Don't do that, sweetie, you'll get her all dirty."

"Can we leave the baby at the hospital after he's born?"

"I don't think that would be a good idea."

"So we have to take him home?"

"Yeah, that's usually the way it works."

She mulled that over for a few moments, then said, "Daddy, do you know what the best part of life is? It's that you don't die right away."

"Yeah, that's definitely one of the best parts."

"Mosquitoes don't live very long. I'm glad I'm not a mosquito."

"I'm glad, too."

"If I was a mosquito, I'd already be dead."

* * *

My father showed up at the hospital mid-afternoon. He opened the delivery-room door and stood there without coming in. Laura was doing squats by the side of the bed, expelling loud breaths. I was on the couch with Hannah, reading her a Curious George story.

"Hey, Dad."

He didn't move from the door frame. "Whole family's here. How about that?"

"You can come in, Leo," Laura said. "No one's going to bite you."

"Yeah?" He didn't move from the door frame or look convinced. "How you feelin'? Everything going okay?"

"I'm uncomfortable but it's not as bad as the last time."

"Maybe I oughta go to the waiting room."

"Sure, Dad, why don't you do that?" I said. "I'll bring Hannah there as things progress."

"Yeah, I think that's…" He didn't finish the thought, just nodded and waved awkwardly and left.

"Ever dependable," Laura said, shaking her head.

"Hey, at least he's here."

"True."

An hour later, as Laura's contractions got closer together and more painful, she said, "Where's the nurse? I can't take this."

"Okay. Hannah, honey," I said, "it's time for me to bring you to Poppa Leo."

"I want to stay."

246

"Sweetie, I wish you could. But you can't."

I took her down the hall, stopping at the nurse's station on the way. "My wife's in Delivery Room three-oh-six. She's in a lot of pain. Can someone check in on her?"

Before going back, I dropped Hannah off with my dad. "Hannah, you hang with Poppa Leo for a while."

"I don't want to!"

"I know. I know you don't," I said. "And I understand. But Mommy needs to focus all her attention on your baby brother right now, and I have to help her. So it's better if you're with Poppa Leo."

I left her screaming, my dad looking at me like I'd handed him a bagful of warm shit.

Laura was all alone when I got back to the room.

"The nurse still hasn't come?"

"No. Where's Dr. Kaplan?"

"They said she's on her way in."

"You're being so great," Laura said.

"What?"

"I'm just…" She looked like she was about to start losing it.

"What is it?"

"No. It's just…" She couldn't say whatever it was. Instead, she gasped for breath and her face contorted with pain. She took another sharp breath, gritting her teeth.

"This is stupid," I said. "I'm going to get the nurse."

I got to my feet just as the nurse came in.

"What seems to be the problem?" She had a long angular face. Hair tied back tight. Little humor or warmth in her eyes.

"The pain."

Without emotion, she presented Laura with her options. She could continue to endure the pain, or she could be administered a narcotic like Demerol or Fentanyl that would maybe even allow her to sleep for a while, or she could go straight to an epidural. Since Laura still wasn't dilated anywhere near the point where childbirth was imminent, pain management seemed to make the most sense. We'd gone through a similar routine with Hannah, Laura's determination not to take drugs eventually wilting. I totally understood. If it were me, I wouldn't have waited as long as she did.

The nurse tried several times to insert an IV drip needle but she kept missing the vein.

"Ouch! What the fuck are you doing?" Laura snapped at her.

"You have really small veins," the nurse said. "I'm sorry."

Laura turned to me, wild-eyed. "Will you please tell her to stop manhandling me?"

"Enough!" I hissed at the nurse.

"Okay, but—"

"Please, just leave."

"All right. But it's not my fault that she has small veins."

She shrunk from my baleful glare, scurrying quickly out of the room.

I marched back to the nurse's station, refusing to leave this time until they sent another nurse back to the room with me. The slender Asian man who eventually accompanied me seemed to have no trouble finding one of Laura's small veins. He quickly set up the patient-controlled IV drug pump, so Laura could administer further doses to herself as needed.

Before the Demerol began doing its job, Laura squeezed my hand. "I know you're still upset with me," she said, choking back a sob. "I really wish you weren't."

I nodded, trying to look sympathetic.

"I wish there were some way I could show you how I feel. And I'm not just saying that because I'm a pathetic mess right now."

"Hey, we'll have plenty of time to talk about this later. Right now, just think about how we're gonna get to meet this incredible new person in a little while."

Her face grew wet with tears. "I just don't want us to keep things from each other anymore."

"I know."

"I want us to be close."

"Yeah."

"Tell each other everything."

"I want that too." But how would it work? There were things I didn't need to hear about or picture more vividly than I already did. Things she didn't need to know either.

"I'm so tired," she said, closing her eyes.

I watched as her breathing leveled off, grew shallower. It was peaceful in a way, sitting there watching her. She looked so serene in sleep, so innocent, her face relaxed, worries gone. I remembered back at the beginning, when we were having sex all the time, how she'd sometimes fall asleep after, right in the middle of me talking to her. I wouldn't even realize at first. I'd just keep talking. Eventually, I'd stop and look at her, the way I was looking at her now, feeling a tenderness beyond words. How simple things seemed then. Or as simple as they ever got for me. The crazy part was, despite everything, they still didn't seem that complicated. I wanted to protect her—even if I also kinda hated her and wanted to kill her.

With a sharp and sudden intake of breath, she opened her eyes. Surprised, she turned and looked at me, and said, "You're still here."

Two hours later, with me stationed over her shoulder shouting encouragement, she gave birth to our second child, a boy we named Reo.

21

My City

On a cold Friday night, three weeks after the country's first black president was sworn in for a second term, I celebrated my own smaller milestone: my first solo show in over two years. It didn't snow this time though the forecast called for a near blizzard. An unexpected wind blew in from the south and the city was spared. Richard didn't leave town. His assistant didn't check into a mental ward. And the Genome got so crowded that for a while it was nearly impossible for anyone to see the paintings.

I stood in a spot near the back of the gallery like a head of state on a receiving line. Charlie Bascombe made an appearance. So did Polly Lymarin. Even my dad showed up, saying, "Look at all these frauds."

When I told Charlie what my dad said, he laughed. "I think the old bastard's pretty proud of you."

"Yeah?"

"At least he's bragging to anyone who'll listen that you're his son."

Richard was in a buoyant mood. He kept bringing over collectors for me to meet. At one point I heard, "Here's the artist, Nate Fischer," and got blinded by the flash of a Camcorder in the hands of Barry Sinclair, the self-professed "subversive, half-assed art reporter."

"Hey," I said, waving stupidly at the camera, holding up my can of Pabst Blue Ribbon.

"Oh, hey, look, here comes Richard Felkiss, the owner of the Genome," Barry narrated as Richard, with his nose for the camera, stepped into the picture. "Richard, you've been showing Nate for some time now..."

"I have," Richard said. "And I'm very excited by this new work..."

I wondered why I still felt so awkward and compromised by all this, the public explaining, the *selling*. Was it really any different than trying to sell a bluff or pretend weakness to get a call? Was it just because it was happening in the hallowed art world as opposed to a poker table?

Laura caught my eye. She had the baby in a sling and held Hannah by the hand. Barry Sinclair still had his camera trained on Richard and didn't notice when I stepped away.

"We're heading out," Laura said in a low voice.

"Already?"

"Yeah. Hannah's had enough. And Reo's hungry."

"Well..." I leaned in and kissed the baby's stocking-capped head.

"Good night, Daddy," Hannah said as I hugged her.

"Good night, sweetie."

"I hope you're enjoying the moment, Nate," Laura said.

"I'm trying."

"Richard told me it's half sold out already."

"That would be nice if it's true." I looked around for him but he and Sinclair were nowhere to be seen.

"Anyway..." Laura wrinkled her nose. "We're gonna go. It's late for the kids."

"I know."

She lingered.

"How about coming over for dinner tomorrow?"

"Can we see how it goes?"

"Sure." Looking melancholy, she turned to go. I watched as she and my children made their way through the bottleneck of people near the door.

I was still standing there when Richard tapped me on the shoulder. "Nate, I want you to meet someone. This is Caitlin Russo."

Turning casually, I said, "Oh hi," as if I had no idea who she was.

"Hi," she said, returning my smile. She was wearing coral-pink lipstick.

"Caitlin's the one who bought a couple of your big pieces a while back in Miami. Remember?"

"Sure, I remember." The way Richard looked from one of us to the other, I knew he still had his suspicions.

"I've been trying to find out more about her but she keeps her cards very close to the vest." His eyes sparkled playfully.

"Oh, there's nothing very interesting about me," Caitlin said. "I just happen to like Nate's work."

"In that case, I should tell you that if you're thinking of adding to your collection, you might want to pick out something tonight. Tomorrow it may be too late."

"I've got my eye on a couple."

"Which ones? Maybe I can help you decide."

"I'd prefer to ask Nate about them." She looked at me meaningfully.

"Of course. I'll leave you two to talk," Richard said, laughing in a charmingly conspiratorial way. "I'm sure you'll share anything you find out, Nate."

I managed an enigmatic smile.

"And naturally," Richard said to Caitlin, "you're invited to the little dinner we're doing after."

"That's so nice of you! I'll try to make it."

When he was safely out of earshot, she whispered, "You think he's onto us?"

"At this point, it doesn't really matter."

"It doesn't?"

"We've already accomplished what we set out to do." I gestured around the gallery.

"I still can't believe it actually worked."

"Are you saying you doubted the plan?"

"I just—"

"You doubted it."

"I doubted it."

"Compared to the art world, the poker world is bathed in sunshine and light."

She smiled, running the fingers of her free hand through her short dark hair. "Do you think I should buy another painting? To really cinch things?"

"I don't think it's necessary, and I'd just as soon not give Richard any more of my money." Or, to be more accurate, though I didn't say this, give him back any more of his own, the $22,500 he paid me for bearding the auction.

"He's not so bad, you know. At least he believes in you."

"As long as it's convenient for him. But yeah, you're right."

"What would he do if he found out the truth about me?"

"Probably laugh, at this point."

"And this after-party? Should I go?"

"I'm hoping you will."

Caitlin fingered the collar of her blouse, clearly uncomfortable.

"I saw the way she looked at you, you know."

"Laura?"

"When she was leaving. I saw."

"How did she look at me?"

"It was the way you looked at her too. Come on, Nate. You must know what I'm talking about."

"I don't know how you can see that."

"The same way you know someone's cards even though they're face down." She touched my cheek. "Work it out with her, Nate."

"I've tried."

"No, I mean it. Work it out. Get past your wounded pride."

"What if I can't? What if I don't want to?"

"Then you won't. But I'm not going to be the reason."

Richard came up to me just as Caitlin disappeared into the crowd.

"What the hell, man? Did you scare her off?"

"I might have."

"Tell me you didn't come on to her. I know she's hot, but—"

"Hey Richard, are we doing okay tonight?"

"That's not the point, Nate. She's a potential buyer. You can't be scaring off potential buyers."

"I hear we've sold out over half the show. Is that true?"

"We've got promises."

"Then let it go, okay?"

"You gotta learn to be politic, Nate. It's not just about you and your carnal urges."

"Thank you, Richard. Your input, as always, is appreciated."

The last stragglers stayed until the beer ran out around ten o'clock. Then a bunch of us cabbed over to the Brass Monkey. Richard had reserved one of the upstairs rooms and we ate and drank until well past two. Near the end, I stumbled up a flight of stairs to the roof deck to get some air. It was deserted, no one out in the frigid night but me. On one side of the deck, the lights of Jersey were visible across the river. On the other, a wooden wall partially blocked the view uptown. I climbed atop a tall slatted table to have a look. Past the winking shadowy buildings of lower Manhattan, the Empire State Building glowed blue and white, the rest of Manhattan gleaming and flickering around it like footlights. For once, it felt like my city, like it finally belonged to me. I wasn't just the invisible king of the underground. Still, it was hard not to wonder where I'd have been at this moment but for that miracle six on the river. Or where my dad would have been. In a hospital? On the lam from Russian leg breakers? Drinking himself into oblivion? Even if by some miracle I'd produced the exact same work that in theory had led to this night, Richard would never have given me a show. Not without the buzz I'd created by getting Caitlin to buy my work with my own money. I was spooked just thinking about these things.

On my way back downstairs, I realized how much I'd had to drink, but I guess I kept going past the point of no return, because next thing I knew, it was morning, the sun on my face making it hard to breathe. I had no memory of getting back to my studio or falling asleep on the couch with all my clothes on.

I lay there for a while, head throbbing. Finally, I summoned the strength to stagger into the bathroom, pee, take a couple of Advil, drink some water and fall back asleep. Mid-afternoon, I woke up again, this time feeling almost human.

Still horizontal on the couch, I looked at the pieces on the wall that hadn't made the show, trying to remember what I could about the previous night. I was pretty sure if Caitlin had let me, I'd have gone home with her.

"I saw the way she looked at you, the way you looked at her."

Did she have a better read on me than I had on myself? Was she protecting me or just protecting herself? I thought about all the decisions I'd made that had led me to the place I was in. Some of those decisions, I knew, were made for me by a force I thought of as luck or fate.

We liked to think we were in control. Certainly, we wanted to be. Sometimes we were. You could look back through your life and replay things a thousand times, trying to figure out what might have happened if you had done one thing differently. Poker players always did that, especially after a loss. It might not change the outcome, but it did provide a way to think about the future, about what you'd do the next time you were in a similar situation. Because inevitably, if you played long enough, something similar would come up and you'd be faced with another opportunity, another chance to get it right.

Would you make a better decision this time? Would you do the right thing?

I dragged myself off the couch, dug my phone out of the pocket of my jeans, and tapped out my password. Then I touched Laura's name and raised the phone to my ear.

Acknowledgments

Thanks are owed to the many people who have supported and encouraged me, both spiritually and practically. First and foremost, my wife Alice O'Neill, who read this book through a number of drafts and was always acute and spot-on in her criticisms, as well as relentless in urging me to dig deeper and go further. Thanks, baby.

I'm very grateful for everyone who supported the crowdfunding campaign for Arbitrary Press, with special thanks owed to Barry Munger and Sarah O'Neill, Andrew and Diane Alson, David Michaelis, Susan Mailer and Marco Colodro, David Alson, Ken Hoberman, Steven Paul Lansky, Sarah Spencer and Sam O'Neill, Peter Hirsch and Cusi Cram, Guy Lancaster and Kate Mailer, Brent Pellegrini, Lucy Winton, E.J. Kahn III and Lesley Silvester, Brenda Potter, Jill Kearney and Stephen McDonnell, and Michael Tedesco.

I'm indebted to Rachel Ake, who designed the amazing cover. And to Deke Castleman whose editorial acumen was helpful and appreciated.

I'd also like to thank, in no particular order, Brian Koppelman, Beverly Donofrio, Matt Klam, Tom Beller, Matt Matros, Nick Dileo, Nick Lawrence, and Tom Teichholz for their help and many favors past and present. Thanks are also owed to my early readers, including Amy Handelsman, Pam Thur and Tonio Scali.

I also want to thank my agents Doug Stewart at Sterling Lord Literistic, and Dillon Asher at Gotham Group.

As always, I want to thank my amazing mom, Barbara Wasserman. And a special shout out to my now 14-year-old daughter Eden River O'Neill Alson, who allowed her novel, *The Novice Twins*, to be the inaugural publication of Arbitrary Press.

About the Author

Peter Alson is the author of the highly acclaimed memoirs *Confessions of an Ivy League Bookie* (Crown, 1996) and *Take Me to the River* (Atria, 2006); and coauthor of *One of a Kind* (Atria, 2005), a biography of poker champion Stuey Ungar, and *Atlas* (Ecco, 2005), the autobiography of boxing trainer and commentator Teddy Atlas. His short fiction has been published in *Manhattan* and the collection *He Played For His Wife* (Simon and Schuster, 2018). He lives in New York with his wife, screen and television writer Alice O'Neill, and their daughter, Eden River.

You can connect with me on:

- 🌐 http://peteralson.com
- 🐦 https://twitter.com/PeterAlson
- 📘 https://www.facebook.com/peter.alson
- 🔗 https://www.instagram.com/peteralson

Also by Peter Alson

Confessions of an Ivy League Bookie: A True Tale of Love and the Vig

One of a Kind: The Rise and Fall of Stuey "The Kid" Ungar, the World's Greatest Poker Player (with Nolan Dalla)

Atlas: From the Streets to the Ring: A Son's Struggle to Become a Man (with Teddy Atlas)

Take Me to the River: A Wayward and Perilous Journey to the World Series of Poker

Highway 61